MW01002572
for
Boys

Queer Stories for Boys

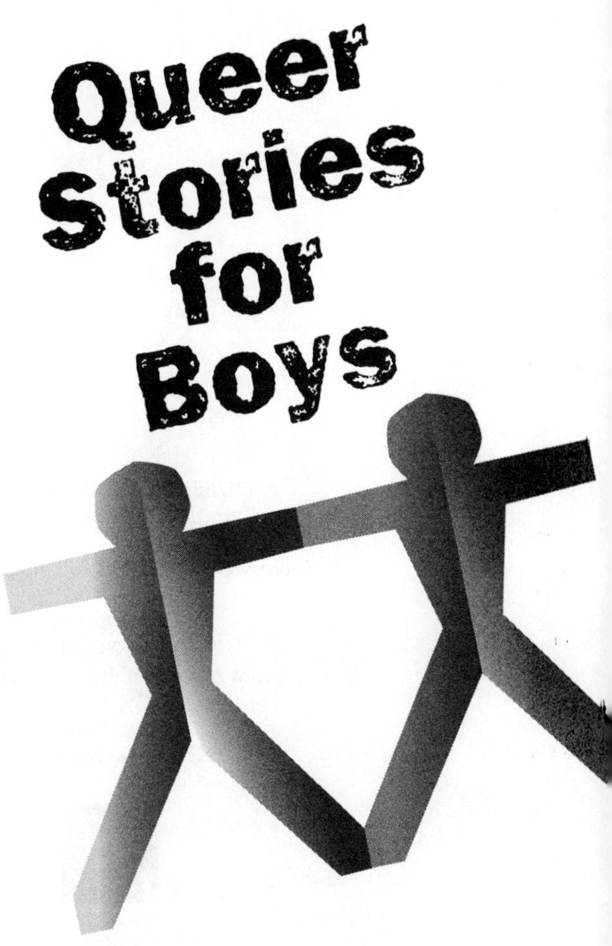

True Stories from the Gay Men's Storytelling Workshop

Edited by
DOUGLAS MCKEOWN

THUNDER'S MOUTH PRESS
NEW YORK

QUEER STORIES FOR BOYS
True Stories from the Gay Men's Storytelling Workshop

Published by
Thunder's Mouth Press
An Imprint of Avalon Publishing Group Incorporated
245 W. 17th St.
11th Floor
New York, NY 10011

Library of Congress Cataloging-in-Publication Data is available.

ISBN: 1-56025-650-8

9 8 7 6 5 4 3 2 1

Designed by Maria Elias
Printed in the United States on recycled paper
Distributed by Publishers Group West

CONTENTS

INTRODUCTION

TRYING NOT TO LIE

One evening in 1995, I sat waiting for an Off-Off-Broadway show called *Queer Stories for Boys* to begin. I was skeptical. It sounded like it would be all about sex. Not that there's anything wrong with that, but a whole evening? Two minutes into the first story, I was hooked. These were regular people, not actors playing parts. The stories they told, if not always specifically "gay," were definitely queer. There was a compelling sort of symbiotic osmosis going on between them and us in the small Dixon Place audience, memories surging in both directions over the footlights. As outrageous as some of the stories were, they rang true. Exactly how true? I think it was David Sedaris who said, when asked that question about his own, brilliant stories, "They're true *enough*."

I joined the Queer Stories for Boys Storytelling Workshop group soon after that night and learned that truthfulness has to be *achieved* through a whole process, of which the retrieval of memories—unedited memories—is only the first crucial step. Tom Ledcke, an actor and writer who ran those early workshops with a fine mix of fearlessness and easy humor, had founded the group in 1992, after being inspired by performance artist Tim Miller. Putting on several public shows a year, Queer Stories for Boys eventually moved into The Lesbian, Gay, Bisexual & Transgender Community Center on Thirteenth Street, where we have been ever since, trying not to lie. All of our stories continue to be at least as true as they are queer.

The challenge of transferring the osmotic experience of

storytelling to print has been daunting. Many of us are not writers in the usual sense—if there is a usual sense—and most of these stories began in the air, meant for the ear and the eye (and not necessarily for the queer eye and the queer ear alone). I am grateful to Ronald Gold, writer-editor par excellence, who has been an indispensable guide and support in preparing them for this collection.

I also want to thank John Oakes and Andrew Merz for their unconditional enthusiasm, and Harry Schulz for introducing me to Queer Stories in the first place. Queer Stories has continued to grow in large measure thanks to the nurturing and generosity of Dixon Place's Ellie Covan; like so many other artists and writers of all stripes, we are indebted to her. Finally, I would like to acknowledge every one of the men who have passed through the Queer Stories workshop over the years, including those who never chose to tell their stories in public, but whose remembered experiences have enriched us all.

Douglas McKeown
September, 2004
www.queerstories.org

FAMILY / CHILDHOOD I

THE GANG

Ronald Gold

RONALD GOLD was born in Brooklyn in 1930, entered Brooklyn College at fifteen, and took twelve years to get a degree. By that time, he'd been a junkie in San Francisco and had his head shrunk in Topeka, Kansas. After a career writing for various publications, including Variety, *he became a full-time gay liberationist at age of forty-one. He was one of the founders of the National Gay and Lesbian Task Force. He is remembered for his role in persuading the American Psychiatric Association to take homosexuality off its sick list. In the early 1980s he quit activism to "learn how not to have to be effective," which he learned so well that he hasn't had a full-time job since. He's had four live-in lovers since 1959 (he prefers to call them "mates"): a Cuban, two Puerto Ricans, and a Bangladeshi. It was while he was living in Bangladesh that he wrote his as-yet-unpublished book,* Polarity: The Psychology of Paul Rosenfels.

When I was eight, we lived for the summer in a house by the beach. I went to the beach every day and played in the water and sat in the sun.

There were other small boys in other houses by the beach and every day they came too, and ran in the sand and splashed each other and played together. They had a "gang," and a leader, and rules. Every day I watched them, and some days I moved closer. But they never spoke to me or splashed me or asked me to join them, and after a while I didn't go to the beach anymore, but sat in the sun on a patch of grass in front of our house, thinking my thoughts and watching the men in their tan and black and blue and white; the women in less tan, but yellow and red and brighter blue, all going down to the beach. And I watched the other small boys on their way to the water.

As I sat on the grass one afternoon, I looked up, in the direction of the beach, and saw the gang of small boys, their leader in front, all coming toward me, down the street together. Quickly, I looked down at the grass again. They could not be coming for me, and there in the grass was a ladybug to think about.

When I looked up again, they were facing me, standing on the sidewalk near my patch of grass with their leader in front of them. They glanced at each other seriously for a moment, then they all looked at their leader. "Come and play with us," he said to me. I said nothing, but got up slowly. They turned around and we all walked back up the street silently, slowly, the leader in front and me following.

There were open spaces between the houses, and behind the houses there was an alley. About halfway up the street, the leader turned into one of these open spaces and we followed him. When we reached the alley, he sat down on a wooden box, and we surrounded him. "We are going to play guard duty," he said.

One by one, he called the names of each of the boys, and assigned them to positions guarding the open spaces between the houses. He took some care in selecting a boy for each position, and when their names were called they moved stiffly and formally. When they reached their places, they stood at attention. Soon, there was a small boy before every open space that led to the street, and only the leader and I were left, he still sitting on his wooden box, and I standing in front of him.

"Try to get away," he said.

THE MAN IN THE STALL

GEORGE PFIFFNER

GEORGE PFIFFNER studied theater at London's Royal Academy of Dramatic Arts and at the Ben Bard Playhouse in Hollywood. He worked in early television with director Sam Peckinpah, as a designer and craftsman, later earning his living variously as a hospital attendant, a health department inspector, a telephone lineman, and an editor at Woman's Day Magazine. *In New York, he is currently an honorary Snark (a women's amateur theater club) and a member of the Instant Shakespeare Company. George is eighty years old.*

The second Saturday in June 1937, the day after the last day of school, was as perfect a day as anyone could remember for the Annual South St. Louis Schools Parade and Picnic.

The long parade started at the farthest of the four grammar schools and passed the three others on its way to Carondolet Park. Because I had graduated earlier that week from the Blow School, I marched with my class wearing our green and white graduate ribbons.

Afterward: "Grandma, I saw you standing by Darmstetter's Bakery. Did you see me?"

"I saw you. You looked very handsome, Georgie, like your father. I didn't see Miz Yockum."

"She was with the Mothers Club Kitchen Band. She was playing the carrot grater with a spoon."

Picnickers fanned out, leaving the area strewn with the colors of the four schools: butcher paper banners, tissue paper shakers, and crepe paper streamers discarded mostly on the ground, and looking nearly as jubilantly festive as the parade itself.

I met my sister Mona, my friend Willy Raymund, and his little sister Janie, near the bandstand as we had agreed. We were on our own, under the care of me, the oldest.

"I want a b'loon," said Janie.

"You got a nickel?" I asked her.

She opened her fist, showing four nickels in her sticky hand.

"Okay, if you want a balloon."

"I wanna blue b'loon," Janie insisted.

"Okay."

She picked out the balloon she wanted. I held it while she gave the man one of her nickels. When she took the thread, she wound it many times around her fist, still holding her other nickels in it.

The gravel and asphalt path changed to a concrete sidewalk as we approached a comfort station. Janie said, "Mona, I got to go."

Mona and Janie disappeared into the women's side, as Willy and I approached the men's. Inside, we were hit by the chill of cold concrete and the smell of stale urine. The urinal was too high for Willie, so we each went into one of the doorless booths. The partitions were covered with scribblings and crude drawings. There were words I was forbidden to use. Near the center of the wall, below my eye level, was a hole. Below it were dried drips and spots.

I thought I saw an eye on the other side looking at me. Stooping a bit, I could tell someone was there. I shouldn't—

shouldn't look. I saw the movement of clothes and bare skin. I looked away, my heart beating wildly. I must have been mistaken. The eye was at the hole again. I buttoned up, but didn't leave. Through the hole I thought I saw a man doing something to himself. I knew I shouldn't put my face closer to the hole to see better. But something had ignited in me that spread a heat and light through my body.

Willy was trying to make the toilet flush by holding the seat down and releasing it, but he wasn't holding it long enough for the overhead reservoir to fill. "Come on, Willy. Leave that alone." Outside, I whispered, "Did you see what that guy was doing in there?"

"No. What guy?"

"Guy sitting in there."

"No, I didn't see. Where?" Now Willy whispered.

"In the other toilet. He was playing with his big pee-pee," I said, using Willy's word. "There's a hole in the wall and I could see him. Come on, I'll show you."

I knew I should not go back in. I should not look at this man again. But I didn't know how to stop myself.

I pointed to the hole. We could see nothing through it at a distance. We stood there for a moment. Then I dashed to the partition, looked around it, and dashed out. Willy did the same thing.

Outside, Willy's face was white.

"Did you see?"

Willy nodded.

"Don't tell. Not your mom, not anyone." Willy nodded again. He didn't ask why.

If my mother knew, she'd give me a good slap. She had lectured me, saying that sex between couples who loved each other was beautiful and sacred, but that men like Arnie Entwerten and Mike Borke, friends of my dad who were forever running after any woman that looked at them, were animals. She said a word, "beastial."

I knew I shouldn't, but I had to go back to the park and see that man who was playing with himself. I went back several times that summer, mostly during the afternoons. The first time, I took a circuitous route (there always seemed to be people around South St. Louis who knew me by sight). I got to the tennis courts, but no one was on them. Good. And I could see the comfort station. A glow, a light, switched on in my body.

Then it occurred to me that if the man was inside, a car would be parked nearby. I couldn't see one. The light subsided. I wished that I might know how to control it, how I could produce it when I wanted, and make it stay as long as possible.

I walked to the path that led to the comfort station. I stopped on the path and watched. Nobody went in or came out. A few cars glided slowly by. A man in one of the cars stared at me.

I was disappointed that there was no parked car, but decided that I had to go in. So I walked in boldly, like it was an okay thing to do. The odors slapped me in the face, but the glow had come back. I looked around, and noticed a high window opposite the doorway. On my toes I could just see the road, as a dark green car slowed to a stop at the curb. I quickly lowered my pants and sat on the stool near the window.

I heard footsteps on the gravel path and then on the concrete. A heavyset man in a business suit walked up to the urinal. He stood there a while and then started looking around. Before he could catch me looking at him, I looked down at his shiny, dark-brown shoes.

"Hot today," he said.

I grunted. I didn't like this man. I wanted him to leave so I could read the walls.

"You live around here?" the man asked.

I squirmed and nodded my head, yeah, and then shook it no, because I didn't think I should tell him the truth. I grabbed some paper, wiped myself, and jumped off my perch. I buttoned and belted my knickers, and hurried out the door—but not before I had a glimpse of his hard thing pointed at me.

I decided to walk home another way. Before I got out of the park, the green car slid slowly past me. When I crossed Beverly Drive, it was waiting for me across the street. I kept my eyes straight ahead.

"Hey kid, wanna go for a ride?"

I kept walking. He drove by me, turned around, and came back. I started running toward the police station half a block away and continued until the park was behind me. Then I looked back. The car was not in sight.

But I went back to the park again and again. One Saturday afternoon in August, I recognized the automobile of the man I'd seen in the stall. Inside, I could see his feet under the partition. I sat in the next booth, leaned over to look through the hole, and saw the eye again. It said, "Hi, you came back. Let me see your peter."

"Hi, it's . . . I . . ."

"Don't worry. Take it out. I'll show you mine again." With more coaxing, I took it out.

"It's not very big," I said.

"It'll grow. Wanna see mine?"

"Yeah."

"You wanna touch it?"

"Mmmm."

"Meet me outside."

The man went out first. He was standing near a tree. "Look, honey," he said, "it's not a good idea to play around much in there. You never know who's going to come pussyfooting in."

He sounded a lot like a woman. "So why don't we just get in my Chevy there, and we'll drive to the other end of the park."

The idea struck me as a bad one. I would feel trapped in a car. I shook my head.

"You can always duck down when somebody drives by."

I shook my head again and walked away, walked home. He did not try to follow me.

It snowed the following November, just before Thanksgiving. I had visited the park many times in between. A few other men tried to pick me up, but I never gave them a chance to try anything so they left me alone. I visited the four other comfort stations in the park and read all of the graffiti. If any guy came in I fled.

The next time I saw the man in the stall, he talked me into getting into his car. When he stopped the car at the other end of the park, he left the engine running, undid his pants and underpants, and lifted out his cock, stroking it. He took my hand and put it under his. "You like that?"

"Mmmm. But—you're wearing silk stockings."

"Sure. They keep me warm."

And I noticed for the first time that he wore cologne, the same scent my Aunt Annie wore. I didn't like these things about him.

The man took my hand from his cock and left it sticking up by itself. It was very pink and had no foreskin. I liked looking at it a lot.

Then he said, "Kiss it." A shocking idea. Why in the world should I want to kiss it?

"Come on. Only a little kiss, kiddo. Come on."

With more coaxing, I found myself bending over it and then kissing it on its mouth. I'd heard the word cocksucker. *Cock-kisser* sounded just as bad. I resisted the pressure of his hand

and slipped my head from under it. No one was going to force me to do something I wasn't sure I wanted to do.

"You said, only a kiss. That's what you said. Just a kiss. You lied. You tried to force me. Drive me back like you said you would. Now!" I'd never dared to speak to an adult so angrily before.

"Okay. Okay." He put himself together, drove to the next circle, turned around, and headed back.

"Lookie here, honey, you have to keep quiet about this or you'll get yourself in trouble."

"And get you into even bigger trouble, huh? Turn left here. Now right. Slow down. Stop!" I got out and thought: *one, well I guess I am a beast now; two, is that the reason I have to get out of this car into a snowdrift? It's humiliating! Three, well, if I am a beast, it just serves my mother right.*

The car drove away, and I walked home with a sick feeling in the pit of my stomach. All the same, I knew I would go back to the park again and again and again, and to other parks in the city, in the world.

MOM

GREG GEVAS

GREG GEVAS joined Queer Stories for Boys in 1995, relieved to find that he was not the only man on earth afflicted with muscialtheater-itis. He is a former actor, currently an IT training consultant, residing in Manhattan with his partner (and fellow theater addict), Mitch Allen. He dedicates his stories here to the memory of master story-teller Constantine Gevas.

"Oh God. Greg, you're not? . . . Oh God, why me, Lord? Why me?"

Every six months, like clockwork, Mom gets hysterical.

I reassure her, "No, Mom. *I'm not gay.*"

She's been on edge since I moved home after college. She senses the change in me: I'm not as uptight . . . I'm quicker to contradict her . . . I never bring girlfriends home.

"Janine, your brother's gay."

"Greg?!? He wants to be an accountant. . . ."

"I don't know, Janine . . . he listens to all that Barbra Streisand. . . . "

My sister Janine was the one to stir things up: she came out at eighteen. She and her girlfriend are together now fifteen years.

Now, I should be grateful Janine's provided some cushioning for *my* coming out. But she's the rebel; I'm the good one. Mom expects me to attain a certain level of status-quo normality. Two in one family just isn't seemly.

Dad, thank God, doesn't require any soul-searching. One day, in the car, he tells me, "Greg, I know what's going on. I don't like it, but you're my son and I want you to be happy. Just be careful.

"Oh, and don't tell your mother."

Mom had had me at forty-one, and she was terrified that I'd be cheated out of a normal childhood because she was too old; or worse, she wouldn't be around to see me grow up. As a result, she overcompensated on the motherly affection.

But wait a minute. Mom's a bohemian type. She prides herself on being a "young sixty." She's an interior designer. She's *surrounded* by men whose normal vocabulary consists of words like "flounce" and "pouf." Once, when I was thirteen, she brought two male friends home to show off her new bed ruffle. She told me they were "cousins." Funny, they didn't look related. One had a shaggy, bleached perm and wore houndstooth-patterned knickers with red knee socks.

I freaked; was this my destiny? Maybe Mom was trying to subliminally warn me.

But, at the same time, Mom never discouraged me from exploring the softer side of Sears, as it were. She wouldn't say anything when I'd dance around the house in a bedsheet to *Can-Can*. No argument when I told her I wanted a Quick Curl Barbie, or a Growing Up Skipper, whose bosom got bigger when you twisted her arm. Christ, she taught me about *furniture*. I was the only kid in kindergarten who could differentiate Louis XV from Louis XVI.

"Remember the fluted leg, Greg."

In exchange, I dragged her and Dad to the theater, museums, on cruises; things they wouldn't think of doing themselves. Dad was ultra low-key; driving to D.C. for cherry blossoms was his idea of globe-trotting. Mom needed to share her sensibilities. Dad was too set in his ways and Janine too strong-minded. Mom helped me cultivate a taste for fabulousness. I was her Roddy McDowall, and she was Auntie Mame. "Life is a banquet, and . . ." Well, you know the rest.

So one day we're driving on the New Jersey Turnpike. IKEA's just opened. Mom and I are going to check out the furniture. Barbra's in the cassette deck. I brought Michael Feinstein for the ride home. Mom loves Michael Feinstein.

"I wish you could play piano like Michael Feinstein. And he's such a natty dresser. Always wears a vest. . . ."

I remember one of her great life lessons: "Layering: the key to dressing for success."

The topic shifts. We discuss Janine. She and her girlfriend are sprucing up the house on Fire Island. Suddenly, Mom starts getting agitated. She clutches her shoulder belt as if to brace herself.

"Oh God. Greg, you're not . . . Oh God, why me, Lord, why me? How did I end up with two?!" She's pouring it on thicker these days; this time I swear she's gonna burst into "Rose's Turn."

I've been dodging this for so long. Five years since I've come out. Ten since I discovered show tunes. Twenty-three since I started gawking at Dad's muscle magazines. Barbra's socking out "Lover, Come Back to Me." The moment seems right.

"I dunno, Ma. Maybe it's genetic." Oh Jesus. Can I take that back? Quick, tell her you were quoting *A Chorus Line*.

"Oh-ho, so you're admitting it!?" The tears well. She feels her forehead with one hand, the other still tugs the seat belt as if for strength. Full Susan Hayward mode.

I'm trembling inside and out, but I manage to spit out, "C'mon, Mom, whaddaya want me to say?"

"Don't you want to spend your life with someone? You

don't want to be alone for the rest of your life? No one to share your life with?"

"Sure, Mom, I wanna be in love someday. . . . "

She looks straight ahead. The silent treatment. Mom's notorious for the silent treatment. When she's really mad, she'll ignore you. Once, she got so mad at Dad, she hid under the bed for hours so he'd think she'd left him.

The steering wheel's all sweaty. I turn on the vent. Barbra's selling "Don't Rain on My Parade," but for once, I don't feel like singing along. IKEA looms in the distance.

Finally, she speaks. "I need a new chest for the upstairs. Maybe something with a pickled finish. . . ."

LIZA WITH A KISS

DOUGLAS MCKEOWN

DOUGLAS MCKEOWN *sold a painting when he was eight, filmed a T-Rex devouring his brother when he was a teenager, and became an influential teacher—several of his students went on to distinguish themselves in television, the movies, and on the Broadway stage—before moving to New York City as an actor-designer-director Off-Off-Broadway. He worked with Tennessee Williams, designing two productions for him, including his last world premiere in New York,* Something Cloudy, Something Clear. *Doug wrote and directed the cult sci-fi horror film,* The Deadly Spawn *(1983), recently restored and slated for release on DVD (2004). He is currently the facilitator of the Queer Stories workshop.*

Back when he was in high school, my brother Scott was crazy about Liza Minnelli. He was a good student. I know because I was a New Jersey schoolteacher then, and Scott was in several of my classes. He was such a good student, in fact, I wanted to reward him with a really good present for his sixteenth birthday. It just so happened that Liza Minnelli was bringing a big, Las Vegas–style show to Broadway. So I sent away for two tickets. Now, this was *not* the sort of thing I would ordinarily go to, not my cup of tea, but Scott, as I say, was crazy about Liza Minnelli. Probably the only straight high school boy in America crazy about Liza Minnelli.

I also sent a letter to Liza Minnelli, care of the Winter Garden Theater, letting her know when we'd be coming to see the show, that we'd like to come backstage, that it was a special occasion, my brother's sixteenth birthday, maybe she could say a few words to him, etc., Very Sincerely Yours. Oddly, I never received a reply.

Well, we arrive at the theater early. Scott's looking all around, slightly in awe. We find our seats, sixth row center on the aisle, not bad. The theater's just beginning to fill up, Scott's craning his neck, he suddenly grabs my arm.

"Look! Doug, look who's sitting back there—it's Florence Henderson!"

I suppress a smile. "Scott, in New York we don't make a lot of, uh, *display* around celebrities, it just isn't done. Especially a minor celebrity like Florence Henderson."

After a minute I look at my watch. We still have some time before the curtain, so I go back out to the lobby for a cigarette. (For me, in those days, smoking cigarettes wasn't only an addiction, it was sophistication. Though I would never have admitted it, I enjoyed standing in theater lobbies, hotel lobbies, anywhere, smoking and gazing at "the scene.")

I come back, stroll down the aisle, the theater is full now, counting up the rows, one, two, three, there's Scott, six—I stop in my tracks. In the seventh row, sitting directly behind Scott, is Jacqueline Kennedy Onassis. On her right, in the aisle seat behind mine, is John Kennedy, Jr., fourteen years old. And on her left is that Princess Lee Radiz—Radza—oh, whatever her name is. I sit down and grab Scott's arm.

"Scott!" I hiss in his ear. "Don't turn around but sitting right behind you, in the seat right behind you, is Jacqueline —"

"I know," says Scott, making a face at me. "I thought you said we shouldn't make a big *display*."

The show starts, and the row behind us fades immediately as Liza Minnelli blazes across the stage. I mean, this was a galvanic performance! Is "performance" even the right word? How was she doing this? She sang full throttle, *and* danced—at the same time—also full-throttle, almost out of the starting gate, and then it went UP from there. What is she on, I wondered? How is this possible? I wasn't even sure what I was watching, never seen anything like it. I mean, was it playback? Was she lip-syncing? Had to be, with all that dancing. So, how'd they do playback with the big live orchestra onstage right in front of us? . . . It wasn't what I'd call great artistry, but it was by no means a train wreck either. Let's just say it had elements of both.

At intermission, the house lights came up on news photographers surrounding us. Somebody had alerted the media during the first act. We stood up and caught a glimpse, a few glimpses, actually, of the row behind us. There they sat, the three of them, staring straight ahead like waxworks, not moving or talking, hardly blinking. I didn't go out for a cigarette, I didn't go to the restroom, I don't think anybody did; the whole theater, the building itself, seemed to be surging forward, leaning in toward the stage, pretending not to be focused on the seventh row. People from the balcony began to materialize along the side walls, inching their way down and trying to look as though that's what they always did during intermissions, hung out against side walls, most natural thing in the world.

Then came the second act, a succession of show biz feats even more improbable than those in the first, and finally, the big finish and many curtain calls and thundering ovations.

Outside it was suddenly pouring rain, and I pulled Scott around back to Seventh Avenue, to the stage entrance. A mob scene. I began plowing us through the umbrellas to get to the door.

"Doug! What are you doing? Doug? We can't go backstage! Come on, we'll miss the train. They're not letting anyone in anyway."

I dragged him up to the metal door and pounded on it till it opened a crack, and the guy said, "Whadaya want?" I told him we were there to see Liza Minnelli. He looked at us like, yeah, you and everybody else. He said, "You'll have to wait outside," and started to close the door.

I said, "Wait a minute, *she's expecting us*!" His face at the crack again. "Can I at least send her a note? Can we at least come in long enough to write her a note?"

And he lets us in. I write a note reminding Liza Minnelli why we've come and asking to see her in her dressing room, and the guy takes it up the stairs at the end of the passageway. We stand and wait. The guy comes back down and stands by the door. Five minutes pass, ten. Twenty minutes. It's not looking good. I glance at Scott. I realize it doesn't matter. He's excited just to be backstage, with real stagehands and real musicians walking past us one by one, out into the rain. Every time the outside door opens, we can see the faces of the crowd striving to look backstage and only catching glimpses of Scott and me. And then I hear a commotion of voices from up the stairs and down comes . . . Florence Henderson. As she passes by us, I think, *hmmm, she was sitting alone in the theater, now she's leaving alone, unescorted; very cool.* Scott looks as though he has just seen the face of God.

Shortly, more movement and down come Jackie, John-John, and the, uh, princess. But they don't come down toward us, they walk right around under the steps and through a door leading to the stage. I say to Scott, "Look at that, they go out the front while the crowd's all waiting around back—their limo pulls up, and they're off, a clean getaway. Pretty neat, huh?"

Scott isn't listening, he's looking at the stairs: coming down quickly is this tiny bundle of electric energy. White fur! Black hair! Long black lashes! On both eyelids! Black eyebrows! Violet, blue, black eyeliner! Red lips! She's moving so fast, in a second she'll be past us and out the door. I rush toward her, leaving Scott behind, and I whisper frantically, "He's—my brother—sixteenth birthday—would—could you—say something—happy birthday—or blow him a kiss or—"

She does not stop, pays no attention to me at all, strides on past me to the door. At the last second she veers to the left, right up to Scott, plants a big kiss on him, turns on her heel, and sweeps out the held-open stage door to the cheers and applause and rain beyond. Scott is bent over from the waist, gesturing palms up and calling after her, "Bless you! Bless you!"

Bless you? Where did that come from?

We just catch the last train back to Metuchen. It's very crowded, so we can't sit together. I see Scott down the other end of the car talking to a total stranger, a lady sitting next to him with big hair and Dame Edna–type eyeglasses. He's very animated, hands gesturing wildly, talking nonstop, his expression going from flushed excitement to serious introspection to sheepish pleasure to wide-eyed amazement, all in rapid succession.

Then I see him stop talking, tilt his face up slightly in her direction and slowly and carefully place a forefinger on a particular spot just above and to the right of his upper lip.

TSETSE FLY

TOM LEDCKE

TOM LEDCKE *is a performer, a writer, and the founder of Queer Stories for Boys. For the past ten years he has been using storytelling in performance as a way to work with at-risk youth, elders, and people with AIDS. Most recently he has been working in the Seattle school district, facilitating performance workshops for students with Asperger's Syndrome. He currently lives in Seattle with his partner of eight years.*

In 1965 I was eight years old and this was the year my mother went to the grocery store and somehow got herself infested with the South American tsetse fly. She said she must have picked it up from the produce section, probably the bananas. According to a magazine article, she didn't say which one, it was common. My sister and I were amazed as Ma described her symptoms, but my father didn't really say much except for, "Oh, Kay." Her name was Kay, short for Kathleen.

The tsetse fly burrowed itself deep into my mother's scalp, causing her head to become incredibly hot and itchy, hot enough to make her dizzy. One minute she'd be in the kitchen fryin' up some kidneys, and all of a sudden she'd drop everything and run to the bathroom to dig out the bugs. Her remedy was to pull out all of the hair from the burning section. Sometimes she'd stay in the bathroom for hours in a pulling frenzy. I can remember the sound of the metal tweezers as they clapped together sounding like some kind of Morse code.

My mother hummed as she pulled, the same two bars of a song like "As Time Goes By" or "I'm in the Mood for Love," accompanied by the frequent "OOOh God, oh Jesus Mary and Joseph son of a bitch." Then she'd continue humming. I just sat outside the door wide-eyed and frozen. It was mesmerizing.

I became obsessed with her private world, sitting for hours listening at the bathroom door, till I heard the medicine cabinet door clap open and shut again. This was her sign of completion. Before the door opened, I'd scurry to the kitchen and wait for her to pass through the hall to her bedroom, both hands to her head, holding her diaper in place. I never understood the diaper choice as a head covering, but that was the least of her concerns. After hearing her bedroom door slam, I'd jump off to examine her tsetse fly battlefield. Hair was everywhere. I guess after a couple of hours of pulling, she just couldn't be bothered cleaning up. My father regularly cleaned out the drain and all he would say was "Christ." My mother quickly followed his disapproval with a feigned exasperation, saying, "Well, tell your daughter to stop cleanin' her damn brushes in the sink. I told her the last time, you know I could talk till I'm blue in the face and she wouldn't listen to a damn word I'm sayin.'"

Moments later Ma returns to her abandoned kidneys boiled down and shriveled. Her diaper is securely in place, fashioned like an Aunt Jemima dust cover. Sometimes the diaper would slip back, exposing her naked scalp. Seeing her scalp took my breath away. With one quick gesture she'd pull her bonnet lower and brush her forehead to make sure no stray hairs were there. This developed into a new unsettling mannerism of brushing her forehead with her outstretched hand and then holding it up to the kitchen's fluorescent light to check for bugs.

She did this constantly after a while, and hummed at the same time "You Belong to Me" or "Who's Yer Little Whositz."

Mother also became obsessed with hair treatments of every kind—oils, creams, and heating caps that looked like football helmets. The theory was that the heat was going to drive the bugs to the surface and they would suffer heat stroke. I'd come home from school to find her in a world of her own as her hands busily scanned her forehead for itchy things. One day she had her heating helmet on while she was watching Mike Douglas; she was also wired to her relaxacizer that supposedly helped her lose weight by sending electric shocks through her muscles, causing the targeted muscles to spasm once a second. It was difficult to hear with her heating cap on and Mike Douglas turned all the way up, so she didn't see me as I entered the room. She was humming "You Belong To Me" over and over again like a scratched record, when off came the heating cap, exposing her completely bald head. Her tortured scalp was red and sore–looking with little scabs dotting her crown. I had never seen my mother bare like this and was vaguely excited as I waited for her to see me, which she did in a short while. Then she screamed, "Sonofabitch sneaking up on me! Are ya satisfied now? Happy?" She snatched her diaper and made a beeline for her bedroom, multicolored wires and pads from the relaxacizer in tow.

My sister Kathy was the only one who talked about Ma's problem. She seemed to understand what was going on because she was sophisticated, smart, and worked at one of the best restaurants downtown, The Blackhawk, where she waited on Chicago's upper crust. She'd entertain us with stories about the fabulous people she waited on, and her dirty louse of a boss who would scream at her for sneakin' food. But Kathy never stayed very long at one place, usually a couple of weeks. She went through every restaurant in Chicago and at twenty-six ended her illustrious career at the White Castle on Western and

Sixty-third. Kathy loved to laugh more than anybody, and at anyone's expense. One time at dinner she swiped Ma's diaper off her head in front of everyone and ran through the house screaming like a banshee. Ma panicked and threw her hands to her head, running to the bathroom squealing hysterically, "Sonofabitch I'll get you I swear I'll flush the damn diet pills down the toilet before you get another one." Ma shared her diet pills with Kathy as sort of an allowance for going to the store or cleaning the house, but Kathy was getting independent because she found her own diet pill doctor, and Dr. Weiss didn't care how many times she got them filled. Kathy became Ma's liaison to the outside world for buying wigs and Rhine wine, because you cannot go out of the house with a diaper on your head, and it's also difficult to try on wigs if you're bald. The wigs were pretty cheap and looked as if they were wrestled off an old mannequin. Ma tried covering her scalp with a nylon stocking, because the inside of the wig was like sandpaper against her tender head. I remember looking up at her in church and seeing sweat pour from her forehead. And her with her eyes closed, trying not to panic, because one doesn't touch their head in church. I learned a lot about discipline from her.

My mother loved to tell stories about when she was a girl, when fellas would stop clear in their tracks when she walked by. One time a fella stopped her on the street to say that she had the most beautiful hair he had ever seen. "It was like Rita Hayworth's," Ma would say. But now she was bald and stayed in most of the time while my father stayed at RJ Liquor up on Pulaski every evening.

This went on for five years until she couldn't get her diet pills anymore. Miraculously the bugs vanished and her hair grew back, but she was lost. About five years later, Kathy got what she called head mites and pulled her hair out too, but that's another story.

MISS BETTY

JAMES CAMPBELL

JAMES CAMPBELL comes from a long line of storytellers. His grandmother was a Pentecostal evangelist, and his father is a Baptist minister. Moving up in the world meant that James was ordained in the United Methodist Church (Baptists who can read). Career dissatisfaction and coming out of the closet resulted in his moving to New York where he coauthored and performed in the comedy Life in Greasy Ridge *followed by* That Greasy Ridge Look, *a satire that* Time Out New York *called "a perfect Spam 'n eggs cure for those big city blues." He also writes poetry, is an avid photographer, and still likes to go to church on Sunday mornings with his boyfriend.*

My grandmother once told me that if she hadn't become a preacher, she would have been a movie star. She certainly had the drive and determination, the glamour and the glitter to have succeeded, if the Lord hadn't called.

When I was in seventh grade, my family and I lived in the little town of Logansport, Indiana. Nothing glamorous ever really happened there, but I was happy nonetheless. In the spring of that year, my grandparents made one of their annual pilgrimages to visit us. At the time, they were driving a convertible, turquoise Cadillac Eldorado. It was a huge, luxurious car with white leather interior and an 8-track tape deck. My grandparents had arrived while I was at school and my grandmother was dispatched, or better said, dispatched herself to pick me up. I waited the long last few minutes of the day, elated when the bell rang. I grabbed my books, threw them in my locker, and ran toward the door. My friends and I spilled out into the warmth of that sunny day. And there she was, in that turquoise jewel of a car. The top was down and her hair was flaming red. She had on these big sunglasses and her hands were covered with rings. She was the most glamorous thing Logansport had ever seen. She saw me just about the same time that I saw her. She blew the horn and shouted "Hey, honey!" Well, that got everyone's attention. One of my friends, obviously blown away by the spectacle of it all, gasped, "Who's that lady?" I smiled. "That's my grandma!"

I was her first grandchild, and she was crazy about me. The feeling was mutual. She was the age I am now—only forty-two—when I was born, so for the first five or six years of my life, I had to refer to her as "Betty" in public. Grandma had a keen sense of justice. Just let her see a child locked in a car in the mall parking lot. My grandmother would write down the license plate number and wait like a spider for the offending parents to return, at which point she would threaten them with social service interventions. My father used to predict that his mother would never make it to old age—"Someone will just shoot you in the head one day, Mom," he used to say. And my grandmother was extravagant with her gifts. She was a fashion plate and I was a young gay boy. Imagine my thrill when she gave me a pink and green psychedelic scarf that fastened around the neck with a ring (it was the '70s!). She gave me money, took me on secret trips to the amusement park, provided funds for me to be an exchange student to Spain, bought my college ring, gave me my second car.

I never told my grandmother, the lady evangelist, that I was gay. I had been duly warned by my father that such a revelation would probably kill her (so much for Catholics and Jews having a corner on guilt). I suppose that I was also afraid of upsetting this wild love affair with the Lucille Ball of Middletown, Ohio. And so I chose silence.

For the previous few years, following my grandfather's death, I had talked to her on the phone from New York almost every day. On a Tuesday this past March, she told me of the horrible night before, when she had been awakened by pains in her chest and a nausea that kept her in the bathroom most of the night. "Grandma, I think you might have had a heart attack." She had had them before. She had survived them before. But this seemed different. "You have to go to the doctor, Grandma." From her doctor's office she was sent directly to the emergency room—and then by ambulance to the regional heart hospital. "Don't you think we should go?" Marcos asked me. Marcos had been to my grandmother's house several times before, and theirs was a mutual admiration society. If she did understand who he is to me, she kept that to herself. "No," I said. "Let's wait to see how this plays out." Grandma was in Ohio, and we were leaving early the next week to visit Marcos's family in Brazil. And my grandma had survived worse than this. Besides, my fundamentalist family would gather there.

"This doesn't look good, Jim," my uncle Herb's voice was coming through my cell phone a few days later. "I think you need to come and see her." And my gut said it was so. Friday night after work, we got in the car and drove to Cleveland. We slept a few hours and then headed down to Dayton. I called my uncle from the hospital parking lot. "I'll come down and meet you in the lobby," he said.

There he was, my Baptist preacher uncle, whom I hadn't seen in years. He was older and gray, but his eyes still sparkled with the mischief of youth. We hugged and then he turned to

Marcos, his arms open wide. We sat down. It was all those things you don't want to hear: her condition is grave; she is slipping; she is confused. Then he looked at my ring and at Marcos's hand and said, "Are you two married?" "Not exactly," I stuttered. He threw back his head and laughed at my groping—a relaxed, happy laugh that spoke a thousand words. And then we all laughed.

"Grandma, I'm here." She didn't move. Her face was gray. The machines beeped and hummed away. "Grandma, I'm here and I love you." Her nurse came in. "Betty, wake up, you have company!" She rubbed my grandma's feet and her eyes fluttered open. "Hi, Grandma." She smiled. She knew. I had beaten the clock.

All day long, the relatives arrived—people I would not have bothered to see except that my grandmother lay in a room, dying. And all day long, my uncle would introduce Marcos and then refer to us in the plural as if it were the most natural thing in the world to do. The relatives would listen, look, comprehend, and in their own way acknowledge.

Hospital rooms suffocate me. I wandered down the hall to the waiting area. My uncle was on the cell with my aunt who was in transit from Michigan. He hung up. "Marcos seems very nice." "He is. I'm lucky." "Well, I want you to know that I have no problems with your being gay. Your father does! But I don't. I'm happy for you."

What in the hell do you do with people who don't respond the way they are supposed to? What do you do with family members who have grown, after you had frozen them in an ugly time and space?

My grandmother had a hard time with her words. They were confused and jumbled. She would reach for names and then lapse into silence. She would doze and then wake halfway and then sleep again. Suddenly she woke with a start. We smiled at each other. She seemed concerned. "What do you need Grandma?" She looked around the room. She groped for words. Finally, she looked at me and said as clear as a bell, "Hey, where's that little fella that was with you?" "Marcos stepped out to get some coffee. He'll be back soon." She smiled, satisfied, and drifted back to sleep.

The day was long, I hadn't eaten, and a migraine had sunk its claws into the left side of my head. Finally, it was time to go. I was ready . . . and so *not* ready. Marcos rose, kissed my grandmother, and said, "Goodbye, Miss Betty." "God bless you, honey," she replied with a smile. I rose and likewise kissed her. One kiss would not do, so I kissed her again with a little desperation. "I'll call you tomorrow Grandma, just like always." I was trying to reassure myself. From the doorway I looked back as one of my cousins was telling her a joke, and there it was, that smile that had charmed me from my earliest memory.

In the lobby my uncle Herb and uncle Greg were talking. The four of us began another long goodbye. Hugs were passed around. "Thank you, Uncle Herb." He ignored my words. "I mean it, thank you."

"You're welcome, Jim."

My grandmother had lavished me with gifts my whole life—wild, crazy, extravagant gifts, but in her dying she had outdone herself. Nothing less than her death would have put me in the room with all those people—and I would have just gone on with my life, assuming that I walked alone.

EMERGENCY CLEANUP

BRAD GRETTER

BRAD GRETTER has been telling his tales ever since he learned to speak. Upon finishing college, he followed his first boyfriend to New York where he ended up with a broken heart and an MBA in marketing. When not balancing budgets in his day job, Brad can be found square dancing, running with his Front Runner buddies in Central Park, and training for the New York City Marathon.

More often than not, I forget that I am what they call legally blind, that I don't see and read the same way most people do. I'm usually reminded of this fact while riding the subway, and I look up from my newspaper to discover someone peering at me with a quizzical look. They're probably wondering why I wrap the newspaper around my head while I read it. Or maybe they're wondering how I got those sooty smudges that vaguely resemble printed headlines on my forehead.

The reason I forget about my visual impairment is because I don't know any better. What I mean is, I have always been legally blind, and my vision has remained that way throughout my life. I was born without irises, a condition known as congenital aniridia. As a result, my eyes cannot focus nor can my eyesight be corrected in any significant way. But from my perspective, everything looks crystal clear. And I cannot comprehend how it is physically possible for someone to read road signs as they go whizzing by them at sixty miles per hour.

Some people consider my visual impairment to be a disability. I, on the other hand, view my vision, or lack thereof, as an integral component of my persona and something that sets me apart. It was in my freshman year of high school, when I was assigned three oversize lockers to house my countless volumes of large print textbooks, that I earned my quasi-celebrity status among my classmates. I can't claim to have ever been popular. But while lumbering down the halls of my high school with two gym bags overflowing with magnifying glasses and large print textbooks, I transformed myself from a mere four-eyed dweeb into the dude with the megabooks. From that point on, my classmates regarded me with a combination of amused fascination and protective reverence.

Even before high school, I could sense the way my vision had distinguished me from my friends and classmates. As a kid, this distinction felt most obvious whenever I visited my optometrist. Every year my mother and I would make a trip down to Yale-New Haven Hospital where I would undergo a comprehensive battery of visual tests. These tests could take up to several hours to complete and could be a bit grueling for a seven-year-old. However, I was unfazed by all of this. I would usually find myself in an examining room surrounded by doctors who were clearly very excited to see me. From behind their high tech equipment I could hear them all talking: "Can you believe this? . . . I have never seen anything quite like it. Truly amazing. I want each of you to get a good look. Complete congenital aniridia. It's extremely rare. There's not even a trace of an iris here."

On one particular visit to Yale, the doctors decided to take photographs of the back of my eyes. This involved them injecting a fluorescent yellow dye into my bloodstream and making me sit very still while they poked and prodded my eyes. They rolled in an enormous camera with long cylindrical lenses that stuck straight out, like rockets waiting to be launched. I watched my mother's calm, stoic expression melt momentarily, into a look that silently screamed, "You're going to use *that* thing on *my* son!?" Realizing that she was being watched, she quickly regained her composure and flashed me a reassuring smile. Then with the aid of some thick K-Y Jelly–like substance, my doctor brought the long protruding lens of the camera into direct contact with each of my eyes, and captured the images he so eagerly sought. There I sat, both eyes numb from the anesthesia, viscous goop dripping down my cheeks, and a bizarre camera on wheels jutting out from my head. This procedure felt as if it to took several hours to complete, rather than the fifteen minutes of torture that I actually had endured.

Finally, we were done. I wiped the goop off my cheeks and Dr. Ortiz shook my hand as I left the examining room. Afterward, the nurses gave me graham crackers and orange juice and instructed me to stay in the waiting room for at least twenty minutes to make sure that I didn't have any adverse reactions. We waited, I snacked on my graham crackers, and after having no reaction to the dye, I left the hospital with my mother.

On our way home, we stopped at the local Safeway to pick up some groceries for dinner. As we wound our way through the store my mother turned to me and said, "Brad, you really handled those tests like a grown-up today. Go and pick out some ice cream for dessert tonight . . . any flavor that you want." Proud as could be, I marched off to the frozen foods section, eager to claim my reward.

The ice cream was laid out in one of those huge open-air deep freezers. In order for me to see the choice of flavors, I had to climb up and stand on the chrome trim piece that ran along the sides of the freezer. There I hovered, precariously balancing myself while I gazed down at a sea of Breyers All Natural ice cream. I still couldn't see well enough to read the cartons, so I leaned even further into the freezer. In fact, I leaned so far in that I was holding on to the edge of the freezer with both hands, my back was arched, and my feet were now sticking straight out into the aisle.

I was about to choose between the double chocolate chunk and the butterscotch swirl, when, without warning, I felt a surging nausea take hold of me. The freezer started to spin. I was completely blinded by snowy white static, and then there was a sudden cold, stinging impact. Everything was black and silent; that is, until some woman turned the corner into the frozen foods aisle and shrieked, "Oh my god! Somebody help! There's a child lying in the freezer." That's when I knew the impact I had felt was really a rock-hard half-gallon of double chocolate chunk Breyers. I tasted the putrid burning acidity of orange juice and graham crackers oozing from my mouth, and realized, not only had I passed out into the freezer, but I had also thrown up all over gallons and gallons of ice cream. The hysterical screaming from the faceless woman got fainter and fainter as I imagined the store manager dragging her off to be soothed and calmed. Suddenly I heard lots of bells and buzzers. A frantic voice announced, "Emergency cleanup on aisle twelve. Emergency cleanup on aisle twelve." From within the freezer, where I lay limp and paralyzed, I could hear people running around, rolling out buckets and mops, then the painful grating sound of a metal folding chair being dragged toward me. Someone hoisted me out of the freezer with a half gallon of double chocolate chunk still stuck to the side of my head, and sat me down in the folding chair. Unable to move, I stared blankly into the frantic chaos. A small group of shocked onlookers stared back in disbelief while the stock clerks bustled around me. The hysteria reached its climax as my mother sprinted down the aisle toward me, clutching a box of Gorton's

Fish Sticks and screaming, "Oh my God, Brad . . . what happened to you? . . . what have they done to you?"

Then everything shifted into fast forward. We were quickly escorted out of the store. I was placed in my mother's shopping cart, pushed through the chest-high delivery doors near the checkout counters, and dumped into the passenger side front seat of my parents' Volvo station wagon. My mother strapped the seat belt around my waist and sped out of the parking lot, heading back to the hospital. Shocked and bewildered, I stared over at a woman I no longer recognized. Adrenaline coursing through her veins had instantly transformed her. She was hunched forward and fixated on the road like a heat-seeking missile locked onto its target. Her jaw clenched, she stared straight ahead, an angry yet frightened expression on her face, gripping the steering wheel so tightly that her knuckles were white. I knew better than to ask her what she was going to do when we got back to the hospital. I already knew the answer to that question. And, oh, how I feared for the safety and well-being of those doctors.

R TROUBLE

DEREK GULLINO

DEREK GULLINO *splits his time between the Lower East Side and the Catskills. He makes a living producing books at one of the few publishing houses left in America. He lives with his boyfriend and two cats. He has currently given up writing in favor of the fiber arts. You can't wear a novel.*

I was reading a book called *Condominium* that I hid in my bottom dresser drawer because it was nasty. I kept it underneath a cheap red safe. I was thirteen. My brother, on the other hand, Douglas, was twelve. He had a speech impediment that made his Rs sound like OZ and a bedroom adjacent to mine. Douglas was into sports. He had all these footballs in his room and cleats and jocks and chinstraps. His room was a mess and it stunk. Even with my door closed I could hear him in there, with his lousy Rs, talking to himself.

He said things like "Oh-ocket. Oh-ope. Oh-abbit." And he p-oh-acticed, p-oh-acticed, p-oh-acticed. Constantly. From upstairs, my mother would hear him and bang on the floor with her shoe and yell, "Douglas, you're driving me c-oh-azy. Do you hear me? C-oh-azy!"

I lay very quiet on my waterbed and read *Condominium*.

Douglas came home from speech therapy one day. He kept

muttering, "Fuck, Fuck, Fuck, Fuck, Fuck." My mother asked him, "What did you say?" Douglas looked her right in the face and said, "Fuck!" "Is that nice?" I said, "Mom, that's the worst word he *could* say. You should hit him." This is my mother: "At least he can say it." "Well, I'm going to tell," I said. "I'm going to tell Dad on him the next time he calls. Dad'll think it's real funny." My mother checked to see if a button on her blouse had come undone during our argument. She said, "Go ahead. Tell him and I'll tell your father on you. I'll tell him about that nasty book you're reading, that book about the little condoms."

I turned my back to her and there was Douglas, muttering, "Oh-Oh-Oh-Oh-Oh."

"Cripple," I called him. "Eh-etahd."

He poked out his lips at me.

"Boys," my mother said, "I can't take this anymore. I just can't. It gets—stop it—it gets right in here," she said, tapping her head with all ten of her fingers. "It gets in here, here, here."

I stormed to my bedroom, kicked shut the door, threw the damn red safe against the wall, and got out *Condominium*. I turned to the nastiest section I could find, and I just read it. I read it just to spite her. I read it to make her hurt and to prove she was unfit as a mother, which she probably already knew.

Douglas knocked at the door. He said, "So-oh-y." He said, "So-oh-y, De-eh-ek." I ignored him. So he began to practice his Rs. My mother banged on the door with her shoe. Douglas stopped. Everything, everything in our house was silent for just a second.

On the floor, where I had thrown it, the red safe hung open like a clam. I saw that the safe wasn't empty as I had thought, not at all. It was full of papers that had been crumpled into tiny balls. They were pictures torn from *Cherry Magazine*, pictures of women playing with themselves. I was horrified.

In the bathroom, I took one of the pictures and ripped it to pieces. I flushed it down the toilet. Fine. So I flushed a couple more and that's when something caught in the toilet's mouth. The pieces floated back into the bowl. The water began to rise and overflow. Quickly, I flushed the toilet again and everything seemed all right, until more pieces came back up from the toilet. And more. They would not flush.

We kept matches in the bathroom, and I lit one of the pictures on fire. I wasn't thinking. I had to get rid of these.

There was Douglas at the door, knocking. He hollered out to my mother, "Mo-oh-om, De-eh-ek's smoking in the bath-oh-oom."

My frenzied mother jimmied the lock with a knife, turned on the shower, and dowsed us all as she extinguished the tiny fire. She snatched the pictures from me. "What are these?" She pointed at the pictures floating in the toilet. "What are those?" Then she saw what they were—those women.

I said, "I found them in Douglas's room. They were in his drawer and they disgusted me."

Douglas tried to defend himself. However, with his speech impediment, he made a lot of noise but absolutely no sense.

I said, "He's a pervert."

My mother saw all the water damage and she'd torn the shower curtain. She was furious and she got down on the floor and she started throwing water at us with both hands, just absolutely shrieking.

Douglas escaped into his bedroom.

He didn't come out until late that night when my mother and I were sleeping. It must have been around two in the morning. This was before my mother began to sleepwalk, and I opened my eyes in alarm when I heard my bedroom door opening and saw a figure move to the foot of the waterbed and pause. Douglas, standing in my bedroom in the middle of the night. He was wearing the oversize jersey that he slept in, and his face was entirely shadowed.

"Oh-ah! Oh-ah! Oh-ah!" Douglas cried, and he cut into my waterbed with a cleat. The waterbed's plastic wave churned beneath me. I was trembling. I tried to rise. My knee sank through the water and it hit the bottom of the bed, and I fell backward into the bedding and the pillows. Everything was soaked. Douglas roared. He continued to cut into my waterbed with his cleat. Everything was ruined. He crawled into the waterbed after me, swinging his cleat, destroying the drenched pillows, destroying the blankets and the sheets. The water destroyed the carpeting. Douglas grabbed at me. My head was underwater, and somehow I had gotten my face wound up in the plastic casing of the waterbed. His hands were on me. I couldn't breathe. And then I felt his arm around my chest and his hand against the back of my head, and instead of killing me he was saving me. He picked me up and stood. He was strong from sports and I was wet and shivering and light as a bone in his arms.

PA-PA AND THE FOOL'S MOON

MITCH ALLEN

MITCH ALLEN *is a singer-actor-writer living in New York City with his partner (and fellow Queer Stories alumnus), Greg Gevas. Mitch has appeared as an entertainer on cruises, at theme parks, and in dinner theaters across the U.S. He has headlined four shows at Don't Tell Mama in New York and has appeared Off- and Off-Off-Broadway. He has appeared numerous times with Queer Stories at Dixon Place and other venues. He grew up in small-town Georgia, but he has now been a New Yorker longer than he was a Georgian.*

Indian summer in Georgia means a return to sweaty days and sweatier nights. That year the full moon fell on All Hallow's Eve, and legend has it that if the full moon falls on Halloween, it is a "Fool's Moon" and fools will rule the night. Ma-Ma, my great-grandmother, had died that spring from the big C. It had been a tough time for the family, but toughest, I guess, on her husband, who we called Pa-Pa. Now, Pa-Pa was a small man who somehow gave issue to six sons over six feet tall; a poor dirt farmer who rarely had two nickels to rub together. He and Ma-Ma had managed to raise eight kids in a two-bedroom house in the days before indoor plumbing. That summer after Ma-Ma died was the first I remember where we didn't all gather for homemade ice cream and watermelon on the front porch at the old homeplace. The house was about a quarter mile between my grandparents' house and my uncle Larry's. Sort of a three-generation sandwich of eldest Hammond sons. In summer you couldn't see from one house to the next, but now it was October, and some of the leaves had fallen so there were glimpses of the other houses when the wind blew just right.

After Ma-Ma died, Joe, their youngest, moved back after getting out of jail. Joe was a heavy drinker. Dwayne, Joe's youngest son, who'd been raised by Ma-Ma and Pa-Pa, lived there too. Dwayne was twelve or thirteen and weighed in at over four hundred pounds. After Ma-Ma died he shaved off his eyebrows. And now after forty years on the wagon, Pa-Pa had started drinking again. And this exacerbated his hardening of the arteries.

When Pa-Pa had a "spell" as we called it, he transformed. It started along about the time of the Fool's Moon. One night Joe woke up and looked out the window. He saw someone out in the field. It was sort of cloudy so it was hard to make out, but he soon realized it was Pa-Pa standing out there, naked, just staring up at the moon, a shotgun by his side. Joe went out to investigate and Pa-Pa took off. Now, Pa-Pa was seventy-five and had trouble even walking, but that night he ran like a young boy. Joe finally found him sitting on the stump of a tree trying to find the moon through the leaves and the clouds, shotgun at his feet. He was talking to the air. When he saw Joe, Pa-Pa said, "I've been talking to the man in the moon. He told me Larry is the devil. He said I gotta shoot him."

Joe touched Pa-Pa on the arm and he came out of his trance. He looked real confused and pale. Joe helped him back into the house and into bed. He found a half bottle of Wild Turkey under his pillow.

They took Pa-Pa to the doctor next day but they couldn't really find anything wrong that hadn't been wrong before. The doctor said that sometimes hardening of the arteries caused ministrokes. A person could become disoriented and even exhibit unusual strength. He said the drinking probably wasn't helping either.

Now, I heard all of this third or fourth hand through the family grapevine. My favorite part was about Uncle Larry being the devil. See, I always knew he probably was. Larry was a mountain. Six five and over 300 pounds. He was the one that every young gay kid has to deal with. The one who taunts him as a "sissy"; who never passes up an opportunity to trip him or throw a ball too hard and give him a bloody nose. I thought Larry *was* the devil, but I didn't know the man in the moon thought so, too.

Why they didn't take the gun out of the house after that night I don't know. But three nights later, Joe woke up to find Pa-Pa gone again. This time he found him standing in the clearing of the woods by Larry's. He had the gun under his left arm and he was looking up at the moon. He was naked again, only this time he had an erection and he was masturbating. When Joe came up on him he could see the waxing moon reflecting in Pa-Pa's eyes. For just a second Joe knew it wasn't his father he was looking at. There was a glee in those eyes that didn't belong to Pa-Pa. "Yes sir, I know. He's the devil. Yes sir, when the moon is fool."

Next morning Pa-Pa was back to normal. But when Larry came over to check on him Pa-Pa wouldn't look at him or speak to him. He went into his room and shut the door. Joe told him about the night before and Larry just laughed—"So I'm the devil now, huh?"

That Saturday night was the night before Halloween, the Fool's Moon of October. Joe got the bright idea to sleep on the sofa in the parlor in case Pa-Pa woke up again. About two o'clock in the morning Joe was startled awake by the front screen door slamming shut. He looked outside and saw a white ghostly figure whoosh by. He rushed to the closet where he'd hidden the shotgun and saw the door open; the brand-new padlock lay broken on the floor. Also missing was a jug of moonshine Joe had bought from some old coot from the county. Joe woke Dwayne up and they went out after Pa-Pa. They couldn't see him anywhere but they heard something howling. It was a lonesome howl, like a wolf, but there weren't any wolves in North Georgia. They kept following the sound and finally found Pa-Pa in the clearing by Larry's house. He was howling at the Fool's Moon, the shotgun raised high in his right hand and the jug of moonshine in his left. Joe and Dwayne hollered and he turned around. His eyes were flashing and his penis was huge. He didn't even look like a seventy-five-year-old man. His white hair was blowing wildly in the wind and his blue eyes were blazing. "Tonight's the Night. The devil's gonna die tonight!" Then he ran across the field toward Uncle Larry's house.

The howling woke Larry's family also. A light came on and Larry came out the front door. Just then there was an explosion. Larry ran toward his truck where he kept his hunting rifle. Joe said Larry looked like he must've shit his pants. Pa-Pa tried to open the truck door but Larry crawled in and locked it. Larry was trying to get his rifle down from the gun rack, but was having trouble. "Time to die, Devil!" Pa-Pa raised the gun, took aim, and pulled the trigger. Nothing happened. He threw the gun at the truck and put his hands under the bumper and lifted the truck off the ground a foot or more. By this time Larry finally had his rifle down, but Pa-Pa lay on the ground balled up like a baby. When Joe and Dwayne reached him they could hear him muttering, "Couldn't kill the devil, couldn't kill the devil."

This time they admitted Pa-Pa into the hospital. He died there a few weeks later from a heart attack brought on by the hardening of the arteries.

But in late October, at the old homeplace, late at night if the moon is just right, you can see a white figure streaking by; and if you listen real close, you can hear him howling at the Fool's Moon.

MEANINGFUL WORK

THE STRONGEST MUSCLE

ROBIN GOLDFIN

ROBIN GOLDFIN *is a writer, performer, and teacher. He holds a Master of Fine Arts Degree in Dramatic Writing from New York University and teaches writing at NYU's General Studies Program. In the summer of 2004, Robin was a guest of The Artists Residence in Herzylia, Israel where he developed a one-man show,* Ten Days To Purim: The Ethics of Rav Hymie Goldfarb. *He is proud to have danced for five years with Laurie DeVitoís's She-Bops and Scats, a concert jazz dance company. Robin has been working with Queer Stories since the late '90s. He is a member of the Dramatists Guild and can be reached at robin.goldfin@nyu.edu*

When I told my mother I was going to spend a week volunteering at a camp for children with HIV/AIDS and their families, she replied, "You must have a strong stomach." Which she knows I don't. To this day—and I'm thirty-five years old—my mother still sends me stomach remedies in the mail. Every piece of spicy food, every hormone and emotion goes straight to my gut. But even my weak stomach was going to play a part in what I learned in my eight days at The Birch Summer Project.

I first saw the ad on the back cover of the *Village Voice*, that bulletin board where you check to see if the person cruising you on the IRT was lonely and spendthrift enough to put a note in a bottle and cast it out to sea. But there among the ads for strangers and strippers, was a call for volunteers to work at a camp for HIV-infected kids. I called the number, they sent me an application, and before I knew it I got a letter informing me of my acceptance, when and where to catch the camp bus, and what to bring, including towels and sheets because they were running short.

But I still had no idea what this place was, where it was, or why they had accepted me so easily. I made repeated calls to try to find out exactly what I would be doing, but I could never get a straight answer. I got cold feet. *I'll tell them I'm sick and can't go,* I thought. *Really, I need to stay home and look for some work. I can't afford to go away.* The truth is I couldn't afford to stay home, either. I was broke, and going away for a week where they fed me was my idea of an all-expense paid vacation. The day before I was scheduled to leave I saw a friend on the street and told him about it. "That's great!" he said and I realized after I opened my mouth that there was no turning back. I went home that night, packed my bags and tried to calm my nervous stomach. I was embarked. But I felt like Dr. Dolittle's Pushme/Pullyou—one head wanted to go forward, the other wanted to go back.

Most of us get on a bus and trust that the driver knows where he's going and how to get there. So why were we riding in circles through Harlem? And once we finally made it into New Jersey, why were we touring downtown Paterson? Then a pit stop at Macy's in Paramus? Thank goodness Lee (later known as "Mr. Lee" after the old '50s song), a head counselor and Birch veteran, had a map, and he gradually helped us wend our way to somewhere in New Jersey and Camp Lou Henry Hoover, home of the Girl Scouts.

This was the fourth year for the Birch Summer Project,

and each summer they were at a different site because they didn't have a home of their own. I later learned that this was the first year Birch was permitted to publicly announce the name of the campsite (previous camps had been AIDS-squeamish). That's one for the Girl Scouts. And this was also the first year the Project members didn't have to eat off of paper plates with plastic utensils. That's two for the Girl Scouts, who gave Birch carte blanche and full use of the their camp (The Boy Scouts of America could take a few lessons here). You can be sure—if I can find a Girl Scout in Manhattan—I'll buy cookies this year.

The first two and a half days were for staff orientation, no kids yet. At the first big meeting we all sat in a circle under a pavilion in the middle of the woods and were asked to speak a bit about why we came.

Came to what? I thought. *I still don't know what I've gotten myself into.*

We all laughed as we found out just how many of us had gotten there through the *Voice* Bulletin Board and *PennySaver*.

The first person to get my attention was Alan. Attractive, thin, HIV positive, and a Birch veteran, he told us why he loves these children, that what he comes back for year after year, is their innocence. Because they remind him of his own innocence, and that everyone who has this virus is innocent. Alan would be running the drama workshop and masterminding the talent show on the last night.

When my turn came I gave a few credentials and told about my work (as director, actor, board member) with the AIDS Theater Project. Afterward, I thought I sounded a bit stuffy, but I'm not one to let my guard down easily.

Finally, a short woman sitting at the head of the circle asked, "It's my turn? How long do I have?"

"One hour," replied a woman sitting on the other end.

"I'll try to make it," Phyllis Susser said, and introduced herself as executive director. Then she launched into her spiel about the history, location, and spirit of the project. She laughed in amusement at how many of us landed there from ads in cockamamie papers. "You're a self-select group," she said, "and all of you have come here for a reason. Not just to give something, but to GET something."

Phyllis—tough, caring, direct, and very smart—psyched us up for the kids and did it in fifty-four minutes.

We watched a video of the previous year's camp where Birch was hosted by Paul Newman's Camp Hole in the Wall. I was not surprised to see someone I knew, my friend Maryann who I had worked with in The AIDS Theater Project and who had died just two weeks before. I also saw her son Jonathan, who from the first time I met him had captured my heart.

It was a few years earlier. Jon, about five years old, came to a rehearsal with his mom. I was directing. He entered the room shyly, but in the course of a few minutes he was sitting on my lap. And then he farted.

"Oops," he giggled, "too much soda."

It doesn't take much to win me over.

When I first applied to Birch, in the middle of the summer, Maryann was in the hospital and I was visiting her. I asked her if she knew about the camp and what kind of place it was. All she said was *go*.

When they passed around the names of the campers who would be coming, I saw Jon's name on the list. Eight years old now and living with HIV. I made sure to get into his group. Jon's dad would be coming with him and staying for a day or two. I was designated their buddy to greet them on the first day.

A big part of the staff orientation was Outward Bound. Birch enlisted their services to help make a group of strangers into a caring, cohesive group in two days. Outward Bound are the people who run those *meshuggeneh* trips into the wilderness where they ask you to explore both inner and outer terrain. One of their biggies is trust. I was afraid it would be too much like gym class. I have "gymophobia," so the first night at Birch I got a stomach ache, and the second day I went to the nurse to get medicine for severe diarrhea. I spent the next afternoon in bed and missed Outward Bound.

I later heard it was okay and not like gym class at all. And even though I missed their games I learned something anyway, maybe something even more important. Being sick and away from the group reminded me just how alienating illness can be.

We had other workshops: Medical Aspects of HIV/AIDS; Universal Precautions; MANAGING KIDS SO THEY DON'T MANAGE YOU (this one in caps and rightly so: sick or well, kids are kids—and we needed a few lessons in crowd control). We were told this is an abstinence camp: for eight days, please refrain from alcohol, drugs, and sex. Smoking was allowed in two designated areas. Coffee, tea, and decaf would be available twenty-four hours a day.

We were introduced to the specialists who'd be leading classes for the children. Hallie in Arts and Crafts; Woody in Woodshop; Alan would be doing Drama; and of course, Ralph the gym teacher. I liked Woody's version of shop: the object is to make sawdust. Whatever comes out of it is a byproduct. And this sums up the general philosophy of the camp: the object is to have fun. Ralph explained his version of an Olympic obstacle course where everyone gets a trophy. At Birch you get an A for just showing up.

The day before the families came we spent time in Arts and Crafts making name tags for ourselves and signs to welcome them. I made a sign with two turtles decorated in fluffy fuzzballs to greet Jon and his father. I found myself taking great care with every choice of material and design, and I realized I could have spent eight days there with no kids at all. I was at camp and having fun.

When the children arrived the next day we were bursting with readiness. Signs waving, smiles blazing, we cheered as two school buses pulled up. Shyness gave way to excitement as strangers got quickly acquainted. The children were separated into four different age groups. The sick and the well slept together. Parents slept away from their children.

Birch treats its mostly volunteer staff very seriously. I have worked at camps before, been hired as a professional, but never have I felt so cared for, so respected, and so trusted. These people—both the camp and the parents—trusted a group of strangers with their children.

For a camp whose philosophy is based on fun, Birch devises a fairly rigorous schedule. Counselors sleep with their campers. There's wake up, breakfast, arts and crafts, boating, drama, lunch, rest time (only the very youngest and their lucky counselors get to nap), gym, swimming, nature walks, flag pole . . . play can be exhausting.

And then there were the special shows. A really good magician played house music and literally made a rabbit appear out of thin air. Forget the cliché, it was *amazing*. We had a puppet show with stories from around the world. Mr. John Strong, a friend of Mr. Slim Goodbody, came with a song and dance to teach the children about their bodies. He wore a leotard with muscles painted on one side and bones on the other. From him we learned that the heart is the strongest muscle in the body, beating some seventy-five times a minute—over 100,000 times a day.

This made me wonder if the boys in the weight room aren't working on the wrong thing. As a dancer I know that real strength comes from the deeper, internal muscles, not from the bumps and bulges—pretty as they may be. The heart is the strongest and most important muscle in the body. Birch is about exercising the heart. It is the essence of the project—they create a space to do it in. So my mother was right about needing strength. She just pointed to the wrong organ.

The days passed. I tend to be a bit of an outsider, keep to myself, and don't blend easily into groups. And all empathy, sympathy, and love aside, the kids were a trial. NO means YES and I'll do what you say only if you can catch me and maybe not even then. Camp counselors are like substitute teachers—anarchy is the order of the day.

For me, camp was about learning to set limits. I threw my neck out on the first day from giving too many shoulder rides. We had nightly meetings where we talked about the children and the day's events. Some of the campers demanded to be carried—refused to walk—and they would work the lot of us until they found a ride. But we decided they were taking advantage, and the next day, after a few minutes of tears and screaming, even the worst little diva walked. Kids adapt.

Nightly meetings. I didn't say much and just wanted to sleep. There was a campwide support group every night at ten, but I never went. One of our bunk meetings turned rather supportive one night, and I sat down in the middle of it. Someone asked, "How about you Robin? Do you feel appreciated? Do you feel complimented enough?"

I paused to consider how honest I might be. "You can't go by me," I said. "If you compliment me, I don't trust it. And if you don't—I'm paranoid."

The group broke up laughing.

I got to be affectionately known as the counselor who hates kids. *Not true.* I was just a bit clearer and louder about setting limits than were some of my coworkers.

One day in arts and crafts, the children made magic wands,

and they were supposed to leave them there for the next day. Somehow, Jon managed to smuggle his out, and after he tired of playing with it he ran over to me.

"Hold this," he said.

"No," I replied. "How did you get this? You were supposed to leave this in A&C."

"HOLD THIS!" he demanded.

"NO!" I repeated. Then he attempted to stick the wand in the space between my pants and my belt bag. I took it out and let it fall to the ground. A piece broke off—he looked wounded. I didn't care and told him he'd have to hold onto it and fix it the next day. He accepted that and carried it off.

Two other counselors standing nearby observed this little test of wills and came over, telling me to calm down. "I am calm, VERY CALM," I assured them, "and I resent your interfering in my child management!"

Belt bags. Distributed freely to the staff to hold our own personal med kits. We each got a Ziploc bag filled with Band-Aids, gauze, iodine wipeys (Jon would get a cut and scream "NO WIPEYS!"), and latex gloves. Just another fact of life.

Gloves. Thin layers to protect. They told us our skin is our best protection against the virus. And isn't that what skin is supposed to do—protect? Except once the virus gets in, we can't get it out again. Not yet. And how it gets into some and not into others. Like a child, I think, *that's not fair*.

One night before going to bed, Jon asked me about his mom. "I miss her," he said. "Why did I have to lose my mom, out of all the thousands and millions of people in the world. Why me? It's not fair."

I couldn't answer.

The adults were worried about Jon. He had no reaction when his mother died. He didn't want to go to the funeral because he feared his "psycho" grandmother (his words) would make trouble. And with all the insight of an eight-year-old, he was right. I was there and Grandma was a nightmare, a regular *dybbuk*.

Jon's dad took him to begin counseling about a month before his mom died. Maryann wasn't able to talk to her son about leaving and by the time that was inevitable, it was too late.

Toward the end of camp, Jon and his buddies were collecting insects. One of the last projects in Arts and Crafts was to make a bug house, a terrarium in a small plastic cylinder. Both the boys and girls relished in this one, but the boys couldn't stop. They invaded the kitchen for even bigger containers and were out for the grand prize: grasshoppers!

Jon caught one, but broke one of its legs in the process. Later that night, as I was putting him to bed, he told me he had let it go.

"Why?" I asked.

"He had a broken leg and I didn't want him to miss his parents. I don't have a broken leg, but I sure do miss my mom."

I knew there was a reason I loved this kid, and I kissed him good night.

Putting the children to bed. Showering little ones is a squealing delight. Then they require a story and a song before relenting to darkness. "Puff, the Magic Dragon" was a bunk favorite, and Jon was usually in the even breath of sleep before we finished the final verse. Sitting atop his bunk, singing, I listened more closely to the words:

A dragon lives forever, but not so little boys.
Painted wings and giant's rings make way for other toys.
One gray night it happened, Jackie Paper came no more.
And Puff that mighty dragon, he ceased his fearless roar.

I always knew it was a sad song, but singing these words to beds filled with HIV-infected little boys filled me with a sadness maybe only song can articulate.

The last night brought the infamous talent show, masterminded by Alan dressed as a wizard. It had campers and counselors reciting poems, singing songs, and performing skits. At Birch, just getting up in front of the group subjects you to thunderous cheers and applause. And like the best theater, it's about giving gifts and making something out of nothing—out of things others might discard.

Our campers performed with their magic wands, but the counselors from our bunk didn't. We were exhausted, five or six counselors managing twice as many five- to eight-year-olds. We couldn't figure out how the other counselors found the time to prepare a performance, let alone the strength.

After the show, my group leader invited me to go skinny-dipping with him and a few others. "The camp really knows we do it," Mr. Lee said, "but they turn a blind eye." So later that night I found myself sliding down a board, naked, into a moonless lake. And now it was my turn to squeal with delight. Screaming and shivering, I was acting very much like my campers did during the day. Something about the cold, cold water and the forbidden nakedness tore right through me, both washed off and washed in the events of the week before. Afterward we went out to a bar and I would have had a beer—been happy to break that rule, too—but I was still on antibiotics from an infected spider bite. Ah, the country.

On the last day we packed the kids off onto their school buses, hugged each other as we waved goodbye, and went to clean up the bunks. Then Birch served us lunch and asked us to talk about our experience. This time I spoke up. I told the group what I had already told Phyllis in private: how well-treated I felt as part of the staff. I told them my antitrust story about compliments and they laughed. I told Phyllis how much it meant to me to spend time with Jon. . . . I had more to say, but there were no words. Then I remembered a line I had been mulling over, looked Phyllis straight in the eye and said, "It's a good thing you don't pay us because you couldn't pay us enough."

The group laughed and Phyllis did, too. Then she turned serious. "We pay you with respect, " she said. And they did.

It rained on the bus ride home, but we didn't mind. The weather had been good for the eight days before. I came back to Manhattan and felt out of place—camp had broken down some of my walls. When I saw children on the street I had this impulse to run up and play with them. The variety of strangers on the street looked suddenly less threatening. I wanted to hug them. I knew that in the city this is not always a good thing. Walls may separate you, but they also protect. Like the skin we live in. And that's my story—in the flesh. Eight days of dragon songs and magic shows, and I was somehow changed. I was able to touch the pain—even make it smile—but not make it go away. That's the magic so many of us are waiting for.

UPDATE 2004

Alan is dead. So are too many others. But Jon and his father are alive and well as of this writing. Jon is a junior in college and will soon turn twenty-one. For me, that's something. The Birch Summer Project—now The Birch Family Camp—no longer has to hide its name or location. *60 Minutes* did a segment. Julia Roberts volunteered one summer. Muhammad Ali became an official spokesman. It's on the map.

Since that first summer in 1992, I have gone back a handful of times, both as visitor and volunteer. On a recent return, now a bit older, showing signs of wear and tear, my dragon songs sung with a bit less pep, I was still humbled by the struggle and strength of the families, the courage and commitment of the volunteers. Or is it the other way around?

HOUSEBOY

ANDY BAKER

ANDY BAKER *is originally from Fort Worth, Texas. He comes from a long line of storytellers. After spending fourteen years in New York City transforming himself into an art therapist, Andy has moved to Amsterdam to follow his bliss and build a new life. Besides writing, his plans include working in the Dutch health-care system. A prolific writer, he most recently published work in* The Diarist's Journal. *He can be contacted at andy.baker@mac.com.*

In 1991, after leaving graduate school, I needed a place to live, and I was presented with the opportunity to be "houseboy" to a gay couple in Brooklyn. In exchange for free rent, I would do one day of housecleaning, all the laundry, which I secretly enjoyed, and a few minor daily chores. Tim was a sixty-three-year-old professor, and Mark was a twenty-six-year-old actor/waiter. A few days after a short interview, I was informed that I had the job if I wanted it. (I later found out I was the only applicant.) I moved in a week later.

On Tuesday morning, I woke up at eight. It was the day I had agreed would be my cleaning day. They would be out of the house, and the agreement was that I would put in "an honest eight hours." I decided I would make coffee and survey the house to decide what room to attack first.

When I opened the door to the landing, I was immediately reminded that there was an enormous amount of laundry. In the chair opposite my door was a ball of laundry that looked like it had been taken out of the dryer and transported to the chair on the landing with the intention of folding it. But the desired items had been extracted, and the pile left to collect dust. It was a completely egalitarian ball of laundry: no preference when choosing colors and fabrics. I wondered about men who didn't get proper laundry training. I thought about my own mother, talking to me about sorting, water temperature, and folding. Maybe she had seen in my thirteen-year-old eyes that I would one day be doing housework for two queens in Brooklyn.

I decided my plan of attack would be to gather all of the laundry from all of the little pockets around the house, take it downstairs, separate it, and wash it. To try to discern which piles were clean and which were dirty would be a waste of time.

At the bottom of the basement stairs, where there should have been a light switch, there was none. Instead, I had to walk into the dark, waving my hand slowly in front of me, until I felt the string hanging from the ceiling. When I pulled it, three weak fluorescent bulbs gave me enough light to walk across the room and turn on the switch for three small lamps and an overhead fixture. It was a complex system. I wondered if Tim thought it was cute to go to all this trouble to turn on the lights.

Beyond the wall with the light switch was the laundry room, equipped with a washer, a dryer, and a very large sink. Both sides of the sink were dirty, but one side was particularly disgusting—encrusted with soap scum and lint. And on the floor beside and between the washer and dryer were piles of lint. I remembered a broom upstairs in the kitchen. "Oh God," I said, "everything is such a fucking process."

Having swept up the lint, I stood in the middle of the room, up to my shins in laundry. I decided to do the dark colors first.

Then I saw two more balls of laundry, one on top of the dryer and one in a chair. "How many clothes do you fuckers have?" I whined.

The laundry started, I walked upstairs and surveyed the first floor. Tim had said that he'd cleaned the whole house just three weeks before, so I thought I would choose a room and "just run the vacuum and do some dusting," as Tim had said. "That should keep you busy for eight hours or so," he'd chuckled.

I chose the "drawing room" (in anyone else's world, it was a living room). Like most of the house, it had been decorated in an earlier decade, with two black leather couches and two wing-back chairs around a low coffee table made of dark wood, like the wood in the rest of the room. There was a large fireplace, a china cabinet, and a long table. Beside the window was the door to the "conservatory."

Mark had shown me the long, thin, L-shaped room, proudly saying the word "conservatory" several times. There were tables on each side, high windows, and part of the ceiling was reinforced glass. There was some ivy, and some seedling flowers, and many, many spider plants. But Mark's pride and joy were his orchids.

He'd instructed me on how to fill the water in the humidifier. He'd explained how the plants were in dirt, but orchids in the wild often grow in trees. He'd turned to an orchid and held it gently in his hand. "Isn't this beautiful?" he'd asked me, as he moved it close to his face. "It's so sensual. It makes me want to put it in my mouth," he'd said with a giggle. I pitied the poor thing. No doubt, he would, eventually, put it in his mouth.

I decided that if I didn't have time, the conservatory would wait. So I gave the drawing room a closer look. There was a lot of dirt and dust on the Persian rugs, and around their edges. Under the furniture, I saw dust bunnies as big as my foot. "You cleaned this room three weeks ago," I said to the air, "blindfolded!" The couch had crumbs in all the nooks and crannies. I would just start, and get as far as I could, doing the laundry intermittently.

During the next eight hours, I took each item from the mantle, the shelves, and the coffee table, and wiped it down. (Several pieces had a mysterious sticky film on them and had to be washed in the kitchen.) I vacuumed the rugs and under the rugs. I vacuumed the couch and the chairs. I moved the tables, and swept and mopped underneath. I even scraped up the muck under the feet of the tables and chairs—muck that came from not having moved them in years. When I moved the couch, I found two uneaten pastries, a cassette tape, eighty-seven cents, and a ticket stub from 1983.

At some point, I realized that most of the dirt had come from the conservatory, and that if I didn't sweep it, Mark would track dirt into the drawing room. I looked at the clock. It was two thirty-five.

The laundry continued. When I brought the first batch upstairs, I looked around for a place to fold. The island in the kitchen was perfect, so I scrubbed it down and used it.

At five thirty, with most of the laundry done, the drawing room clean, and the conservatory swept, I'd done as much as I was going to do for the day. I was exhausted, but very pleased at how clean the drawing room was. What was once a torture chamber for the allergic, was almost sparkling. It smelled clean. It looked inviting.

I showered, put on fresh clothes, and went to the kitchen for a cup of tea. Tim and Mark had come home. "What did you do all day?" Tim asked. His voice had an edge to it. "Didn't you know you were supposed to clean the kitchen? We talked about that, didn't we?"

"Yes, we did," Mark answered for me.

"Yes, we did. In the interview," Tim said. He was pacing a four-foot circle.

"In the interview. We absolutely did talk about it," said Mark.

I said, "I spent five hours cleaning the drawing room."

"What did you have to do? Vacuum? Dust? How does it take five hours to clean one room?" Tim asked, his hands in the air, his voice rising. "If you do one room a week— that is not what we agreed. We agreed you would vacuum and dust the entire house."

"I couldn't just run a vacuum. It was filthy. There was dust and sticky crap on everything. There were balls of cobwebs this big." I held up my hands to show them. "I moved everything and scrubbed it down. Now it's clean!"

"I just cleaned it three weeks ago. It couldn't have been that dirty."

"It really was *dirty,*" I said. "It looks so much different."

Tim walked toward the drawing room. "Let's see it." He opened the door and we walked in.

"Wow, it does look nice," Mark said.

"This took five hours?" Tim asked. "I just don't see how it could take five hours to clean this room. It's not that big."

"There were these gargantuan dust bunnies," I said. "And I moved the couch and found two pastries and this tape."

Mark reached for the tape. "When did we have pastries?" he asked. Then, a second later, "Anne Murray! I thought I lost this."

"One room a week is not going to do it," Tim said. "You have to work faster."

"I don't think it's going to take a whole day to do each room," I said. "Next Tuesday, I'll vacuum and dust the drawing room, and then clean another room. And then, the following Tuesday, I'll move on to another room."

Tim threw his hands in the air. "At this rate, you won't get upstairs until March." He stomped toward the kitchen.

"I'll do your bedroom suite next week," I said.

"I don't know if this is going to work out," Tim said from the kitchen.

Mark and I were on the first-floor landing. "Don't worry about it," he mouthed dramatically, rolling his eyes. "Tim," he said, walking into the kitchen. "He's got a plan. Let's just let him do it like he wants to."

I took a deep breath and walked into the kitchen. "What about the laundry," Tim asked.

"I did seven loads of laundry," I said.

"Well, next week don't do laundry. I think that's what's taking up time. You may have to do laundry on another day."

"No way!" I shook my head. "We agreed on one day."

"Did you do any ironing?" he asked.

"Okay," I said, "What if I spend two hours ironing on another day? There's like thirty shirts down there that need to be ironed. What if I do it on Thursday morning?"

"You work it out," Tim said. "Just do whatever you want. It looks like you're going to anyway."

Mark sighed. "Don't worry. He'll be okay. Just do what you were planning on doing." He smiled a big, silly smile. Then he looked at the table. "Whose is this?"

"Oh, that's the eighty-seven cents I found under the furniture in the drawing room."

"Great," Mark said, sliding it off the table into his hand. "You know what," he said, "you take it." He dropped the money into my hand.

"Thanks," I said, flatly.

"You earned it," he said. "It's like a tip."

"Yeah, like a tip," I said.

DESPAIR IN LADIES' SWIMWEAR

BRAD GRETTER

My idea of Hell starts in an elevator, somewhere between the forty-fifth and fiftieth floors of one of the Rockefeller Center skyscrapers. No fire, no devil, just thick emerald green carpeting, dark cherry paneling, and dimly lit alabaster sconces that cast a warm pink glow bordering on the romantic. A continuous medley of smooth, jazz holiday hits floods my senses, numbing me into submission and reminding me that I should be happy. After all, Christmas is only two weeks away. I'm focusing on the floor indicator lights above the elevator doors, watching as one by one, the little numbers marking each floor light up . . . forty-six, forty-seven, forty-eight. . . . Oh no, forty-eight didn't light up; better mark that down on my notepad, put it in my elevator audit report.

This is my job, at least for this week, the latest in a string of humiliating temping positions. I've been assigned to elevator bank C, floors thirty-six to fifty, and paired up with Angie, an aging Bensonhurst debutante who spends most of her time touching up her makeup and admiring her reflection in the polished brass elevator doors. Our mandate: to ride the newly installed Westinghouse elevators, checking to see that the doors open and close properly, and that all the special features—the bells, buzzers, and digital direction displays—operate on cue.

Angie has turned away from her reflection and is now watching me watch the floor indicator lights. "So, I was tawkin' to Tammy, and she told me the building's management forced Westinghouse to hire us. See, they've been having a rash of minor malfunctions lately." I shudder, picturing Angie and me plunging fifty stories to our deaths in this luxuriously appointed orange juice can, the result of one of these "minor malfunctions" and the climax of my seven-dollar-an-hour workday.

I can feel Angie staring at me as she rambles on, undeterred by my silence. But I don't care. At 9:30 A.M., it's much too early for gossip and bonding with Angie, my new elevator buddy. We're descending now, and I'm trying to focus on the task at hand and block out the sound of Angie's gum snapping . . . forty-eight, forty-seven, forty-six. . . . "Hey! Pay attention to me when I'm tawkin to you . . . who do you think you are anyway?" Angie snaps at me. "Don't go thinkin' you're better than me, 'cause you ain't . . . Ya know, I don't need this job for the money. . . . That's right, I got plenty of that." I roll my eyes and note that this is the third time she's made this claim since I met her thirty minutes ago. Jabbing her index finger in my face, she continues, "No, I'm here to prove a point to my husband, that bastard! . . . Doesn't believe I can hold a job. . . . Well, I'll show him." She stamps her foot and glares at me indignantly. I nod my head and say, "Look, Angie, don't pay attention to me. I'm not in the mood to talk right now. I'd rather we just take notes and fill out these ridiculous audit reports." With her nose in the air, Angie spins around to face her reflection and declares, "Fine. Suit yourself, sourpuss."

By one o'clock, Angie has insulted four office workers, picked a fight with Tammy, our supervisor, and launched into an impassioned monologue detailing her marital woes, divulging the juiciest parts when the elevator is packed with a lunch-hour crowd. At five o'clock I flee Rockefeller Center, taking a brisk walk to clear my head and prepare for my evening temping assignment, straightening up clothing display cases at Saks Fifth Avenue.

How did I get here? It wasn't supposed to be like this. The plan was to move to New York and finish business school with "marketable skills." At least, that's what the career counselors called them. They made it sound so simple, as if employers were going to line up and beg me to take highly paid jobs managing corporate training programs or analyzing investment portfolios. Where was the competitive thrill they promised, the ruthless glamour of it all?

That file of rejection letters—the letters that characterize my education and work history as "distinctive and impressive, yet not fully aligned with our current employment needs"—was not supposed to be a part of my life. Neither was the even fatter file of letters claiming that "we are unable to consider your candidacy for this position due to the volatile political and economic climate resulting from the Persian Gulf War." How could a war, fought halfway around the world for only six weeks, bring the New York job market to a screeching halt? And what about the recruiters, and the job placement specialists: "Oh, you can *only* type twenty words per minute, and you have experience in what? Not-for-profit grants management? Well, I guess that leaves you out of the running for any of our good word processing jobs."

So once again, after a rewarding day of riding elevators, I'm back at Saks, spry and cheery, ready to straighten up countless racks of clothing that have been pawed over by insatiable holiday shoppers. In teams of two or three, we start on the top floor of the store and work our way down, one department at a time. Since our shift starts before closing time, we do one full sweep of the store while customers are milling about, and a second round of straightening after closing. The first cleaning is always the hardest. That's when we encounter endless trails of rejects: crumpled up red snakeskin pants, discarded Wonderbras, and plastic-bejeweled patent leather shoes, all strewn carelessly across the floor. Once cleaned up, it's only a matter of minutes before a flock of Upper East Side matrons descends upon the department, obliterating it with the same ferocity with which they devour cheese tables at art exhibit openings.

The store is now closed, and I'm standing alone in ladies' finer swimwear. The rest of the crew has moved on to other departments leaving me to do a final check of the floor for the evening. The room is silent, except for the persistent buzzing of the halogen lamps that spotlight a dozen mannequins decked out in red and white Santa hats and the season's hottest swimwear. Suddenly reality sets in and hits me. All of it: the dismal never-ending job search; the insane temping assignments riding elevators with Angie; the small barren room that I call home, the same room where tonight I will sit alone, and eat yet another thirty-five-cent package of instant ramen noodles. My head throbs and I feel my jaw tighten, and my ears begin to burn bright red. I berate myself, trying to understand what has happened to my life. Six months ago I was studying international trade policy and cross-cultural marketing in a global economy. Now my life has been reduced to a pile of spandex and designer labels.

That's when it happened. Right in the middle of ladies' finer swimwear. One moment I'm standing there, calm and collected, the next moment tears are streaming down my cheeks. I search the room, checking to see that I'm definitely alone, that nobody is present to witness my impending meltdown. Unable to hold out any longer, I clench my fists tight and sink onto my knees. Looming above me with arms outstretched like the Virgin Mary, a large cream-colored mannequin in a two-piece Calvin Klein suit smiles down at me. I search her sleek fiberglass face for a message, a kind reassuring word, or some glimmer of comfort and hope. I receive nothing in return. Soon my silent sobs give way to loud moans and wailing. At first I feel nothing but shame. Shame for failing to secure a decent job despite my hard work and fancy graduate degree. Shame for feeling so sorry for myself. And shame for what I must look like, crawling around the floor of a department store, hurling my body upon the feet of bikini-clad mannequins, and blubbering like an idiot. And not just any ordinary kind of blubbering. No, I'm talking about hysterical crying that starts out quietly then quickly builds to a crescendo. The kind of crying where your eyes sting so badly you can't see through the tears, your nose runs profusely, and you begin to heave and gasp for air. Well, it was at this moment of peak hysteria and grief that something just snapped inside me, and suddenly, it started to feel good. Real good. So good in fact, I couldn't wail hard enough or loud enough. I was shaking so violently and with such glee, I didn't know what to do with myself. So, I did the only thing that made sense: I shoved my head into the rack of swimsuits in front of me and howled like a banshee. Even with my head buried and my cries muffled, I felt exhilarated and fearless. I remember frantically clutching those swimsuits, grinding them into my face, and luxuriating in the satiny silkiness of the Lycra. I wiped my eyes and nose with gusto, smearing snot and tears over every inch of fabric I could cover. I left nothing unscathed. It just felt so good. Soon exhausted, my crying died down and my breathing returned to normal.

Feeling spent, yet light and calm, I withdrew from the rack of bathing suits, and struggled to my feet. In a state of shock, I leaned against the rack as my euphoria slipped away. It only took a few minutes to clean up my mess; smoothing out and tucking in the damp tear-splotched swimsuits so they hung perfectly aligned. Taking a few steps back, I stood and admired my work, pleased there was no visible trace of the personal drama that had just unfolded. Then, with my head held high and a composed smile, I scanned the department one last time before silently descending the escalator to rejoin the rest of the crew.

Three years later, I'm standing in a crowded East Village bar when from behind, I hear a familiar voice shout: "No drinking on the job, Brad! Don't you have a few racks of clothing to straighten up?" I turn around and come face-to-face with Tom, the supervisor on that job at Saks. He grabs hold of my arm and steers me to a corner to talk. We're probably on our third round of drinks, when Tom suddenly slaps me on the back and exclaims, "Remember that night of the swimsuits?" My hair stands on end and blood rushes to my face at the mere sound of the word swimsuits. "Uh . . . what swimsuits, what are you talking about?" I stammer.

"Don't play dumb with me," he counters. "You know what I'm talking about." Then with a playful shove he adds, "You were so down at the time, I couldn't bring myself to tell you that the entire security team and I watched you on the surveillance monitors that night you lost it in ladies' swimwear. It was quite a performance. All the guards stopped what they were doing, and we all gathered around the screen, just gaping at you."

Leaning in closer, he wraps an arm around my shoulder and coos, "But hey, don't worry about it. There's nothing to be ashamed of. We all have moments of despair now and then." With a firm squeeze of my shoulder he pulls me in even closer and concludes, "And for whatever it's worth, I just want you to know, the guys were really touched. They felt your pain, man, they felt your pain."

ACTIVISM

THREE STORIES OF GAY LIBERATION

RONALD GOLD

I. PSYCHIATRY

When I was thirteen I told my sister I thought I really liked boys, and it was right after that I saw my first psychiatrist. He shot me full of sodium pentothal, and all I really remember about him are his big, round, thick glasses on his big, white, moon face, very, very close to my face. I was scared out of my wits.

The next one was when I was fifteen. I'd just entered college, and I wanted to move out of my parents' apartment—which they thought required medical attention. This pleasantly rumpled psychiatrist gave me his diagnosis: homosexuality. He told me I should get away from my mother. I was grateful for *that*, and three years later I got him to write a note for me to the draft board.

The draft board psychiatrist asked me, "Where do you cruise?" I told him, but he still didn't seem convinced I wasn't putting on an act, until he saw the book I was carrying. "T. S. Eliot!" he said, and checked off the fag box on his form.

At nineteen I went to school in Berkeley, California and soon I was having a thing with an ex-convict named Frank and Eddie (he told some people his name was Frank and some people his name was Eddie). Anyway, it wasn't going very well, so I went to the university counseling department and got this psychiatrist who didn't seem much older than I was. He kept his watch on his desk facing *him*, and once I asked him what time it was. He wouldn't tell me. He wanted to know the *real* reason I'd asked the time.

So I quit him, quit Frank and Eddie, quit school, moved to San Francisco, and became a junkie. After I got busted, I moved back to New York, lived with my parents, worked for my father, and spent my entire paycheck every week on junk. Except one week, age twenty-four, I decided to do what my friend Carl Solomon had done: pound on the door of the Psychiatric Institute, demanding instant entry. Except they didn't take junkies. And I had missed my weekly connection and was getting sick. So I gave all my money to somebody I didn't know—who never showed up with the dope—and I *walked* from the Bronx to midtown for a matinee of *Wonderful Town*.

I was really sick by intermission, so my sister took me to a doctor—and *another* psychiatrist, who shipped me off to the Menninger Clinic. So I was in Topeka, Kansas for five years, and I can actually say I got something out of it. I had a nice place to be locked up in for a while (so I couldn't get to the junk); I finished college; went to work; joined the Topeka Civic Theater; learned to play bridge—and learned that there were plenty of people, including psychiatrists, who were just as crazy as I was, and doing more or less okay.

And, when I got back to New York, at age twenty-nine, I found it wasn't true that I hadn't solved my biggest psychological problem. I found a lover; and right away I began to see that *my homosexuality wasn't a problem*. That homosexuality isn't a problem. So ten years later I was ready for Stonewall. And my next encounter with psychiatry, at forty-one, was as the leader of a zap by the Gay Activists Alliance, at the behaviorists convention. You remember the behaviorists: They're the ones who show you pictures of gorgeous naked men (or women, if you're a lesbian) and then they give you an electric shock.

So we took over one of their sessions and there I met Dr. Robert Spitzer, who turned out to be a member of the American Psychiatric Association committee that could take us off the sick list. Well, I never let go of Dr. Spitzer. He got us a meeting with his committee (news of which I leaked to the *New York Times*), and he got us a major panel discussion at the 1972 APA convention in Hawaii.

There were five psychiatrists on the panel, including Drs. Bieber and Socarides, the preeminent sickness theorists of the day. And me. My speech was called "Stop It, You're Making Me Sick!" I told them that their sickness label provided the biggest rationale for our oppressors, and was the *cause* of our self-hate. I got a standing ovation—from 3,000 psychiatrists.

But that wasn't the best part. The best part was that night. I'd wound up my speech with a plea for the gay psychiatrists present to come out of the closet en masse. But of course they didn't. Instead, something popularly known as "the Gay P.A." was having a bash at a local gay bar (something it seems it did at every convention on the night of the annual ball). I'd got invited, and I invited Dr. Spitzer, since he'd said he didn't know there *were* gay psychiatrists.

I had told him to keep his mouth shut, but when he saw all those heads of prestigious psychiatry departments and the head of the Transactional Analysis Association and the man who gave out all the training money in the United States, he couldn't stop blubbering questions to everyone in sight. The grand dragons of the Gay P.A. were incensed. "Get him out of here," one of them said. And I said "Fuck you, he's here to *help* us, which *you* sure as hell . . . "

Just then an attractive young man in full army uniform walked into the bar, took one look at me, threw himself into my arms, and wept. He was an army psychiatrist from Georgia who'd been at our panel and, after my speech, had vowed to go to a gay bar for the first time in his life. And now here he was, with me and all those gay psychiatrists. He was awash in tears. And Dr. Spitzer was moved to action. That night, he and I drafted the resolution that, a year later, officially took homosexuality off the sick list. The world was round.

Oh well, I don't want to leave out my most recent psychiatric experience. This was some years ago, when I was sixty-two, and my lover Luis, who died at the end of that year, was seeing a shrink. This *openly gay* psychiatrist wrote me a note to say he wanted to talk to me about Luis. I called and asked if I'd be charged for that, and he said not to worry, we'd talk about that when I saw him. Well, he never brought it up, even when our session went on for two hours. So I thought this is a very nice psychiatrist, and I hoped, as I left, to see him again under better circumstances. He sent me a bill for $200.

II. POLITICS

Early in 1972, before I quit my job at *Variety* to work full-time for nothing as media director of the Gay Activists Alliance, I had a chance to combine the two jobs by accepting an invitation from one of the movie companies to go on a Florida junket. The movie was *The Candidate*, about an aspirant to the presidency, and the junket was to spend a couple of days on a train with the actors, et al., who were simulating a whistle-stop campaign trip, timed to arrive in Miami for the start of the '72 Democratic Convention.

In my GAA persona, Miami was exactly where I wanted to be. So I said yes to United Artists, which seemed to make them ecstatically happy (*Variety* reporters made a point of never going on junkets or writing the puff pieces they were designed to produce). So I was flown down to Florida on a tiny, luxurious plane with only one other passenger, the candidate himself, Robert Redford.

Seated in our comfy chairs on either side of an elegant polished-wood desk, we got along fine. Redford told me how much his ranch in Montana had stimulated the ecological and environmental concerns that provided his political focus, and I told him about my intention to lobby, at the convention, for the first-ever gay-rights platform plank. As we got off the plane, headed for our separate cars on the train, we applauded each other's political goals and wished each other well.

My train mates—reporters for other trade papers, local dailies, and regional weeklies—were in full party mode when I arrived, sloshing down the free booze and smoking up a storm. I guess I must have interviewed a couple of people and witnessed enough of the whistle-stop bit to write my puff piece when I got back to New York, but all I really remember from the train trip is a pleasantly woozy haze.

In Miami I joined about a dozen others from GAA, all of us crammed into a single hotel room (these were the poverty-stricken days of gay liberation), where we divided up the tasks for the days ahead. Each of us was scheduled to appear before several state caucuses, where we'd tell the delegates why it would be good for the party and the country to extend civil rights protections to millions of gay taxpayers and potential voters.

The reception I got at some of the caucuses was decidedly chilly, with questions ranging from frozen polite to downright offensive. But Louisiana was a highlight, with Governor Edwards, the chairman of the delegation, positively oozing Southern courtesy and charm. He treated me, I thought, the way he might have treated Indira Gandhi, as something a bit exotic perhaps, but with all the deference due a lady of consequence. Still, I wasn't much encouraged about inclusion of a gay-rights plank.

The others from GAA had similar discouraging reports, but we were counting on a boost from George McGovern, who'd pledged his support and seemed like the likely nominee. So I was especially looking forward to my appearance before the last of my assigned caucuses, McGovern's home state of South Dakota. I got to the caucus room early, but another presentation seemed to be taking place, so I waited outside till that was over and was just about to enter when I was lifted off my feet by two burly middle-aged men, who carried me, as fast as they could, their hands on my shoulders and under my elbows, screaming and kicking through the hotel hallways to the stairwell off the lobby, where they held me, still screeching bloody murder, for what seemed like half an hour.

Maybe because my assailants were wearing convention badges and looked like cops, nobody inquired what was going on as I hurtled through the halls, but even when the three of us were at the bottom of the stairwell and I was making all that noise, nobody stopped for more than a couple of seconds—until one woman looked down, recognized me and said, "What are you doing down there?" It was Shirley MacLaine, whom I'd recently interviewed for *Variety.*

MacLaine, who was emerging as a power at the convention, knew the men for the upper-echelon McGovern lieutenants they were, and she motioned them off as I explained my predicament. Then she pieced the thing together. Just before I was about to make my caucus presentation, McGovern had won something called "The Texas Challenge," which meant that he was a shoo-in as the Democratic presidential candidate, and the press was expected to descend on the South Dakota delegation en masse, to hear the homefolks' reaction. And a gay activist's presentation was the last thing the McGovern boys wanted to be happening at the time.

Maybe something was still going on. We made a mad dash for the caucus room. Not a soul in sight. I made a fruitless effort to tell my story to the press. Have you heard about people "listening with their eyes crossed?" Now I know what that means. Not a word, as far as I know, ever appeared in print. And soon thereafter, McGovern put out the word to his delegates: Vote against the gay-rights plank.

So, escorted by one movie star, saved by another, that ought to be the end of the story. But, for me, it wasn't. A week later I went to Milwaukee to cover the annual convention of IATSE, the International Alliance of Theatrical Stage Employees.

IATSE is the union of blue-collar workers in the film and theater industries: Stagehands, carpenters, grips—even movie-theater projectionists—and its leadership, in 1972, was an ossified bunch not in the least noted for a liberal political stance. So the keynote speaker for the opening session was made to order—Al Barkan, political director of the AFL-CIO. He was there to tell the members that the interests of working stiffs were in defeating George McGovern and reelecting Richard Nixon as president.

"McGovern," Barkan said about halfway through, "cares more about *FAGS* than honest working people." And he was greeted by appreciative hoots and cackles from a good part of his audience. At this point I cast journalistic objectivity to the winds and, seated right up front at the press table, I emitted a series of spontaneous boos and hisses.

Some stares, but generally an amazed silence. And the only public mention of the incident came during a discussion period that afternoon, when a young woman rose to complain (looking straight at me) about Barkan's bigoted remarks, and, not incidentally, to note that even though IATSE's membership included a significant number of women, not one of them was represented on the union's staff or board. Hoots and guffaws from the same people who'd found Barkan's line about fags so entertaining. It was then that I first realized that the men who spew hatred and violence against gays are the same men who *hate women!* From their faces and voices it was clear to me that, to these men, the brave young woman who spoke was like an escapee from the zoo. The amazing and hilarious thing about her was that she could stand up on her hind legs and talk at all.

That night, fairly early, there was a knock on my hotel-room door. It was a poster boy for blue-collar unionism. A T-shirt and jeans. All muscles and electric glow. Could he come in a minute? Gulp, I said. So he sat down on the edge of the bed and thanked me for booing and hissing. He wished he'd had the nerve, he said. So I told him a bit about GAA. We talked a while. He stayed the night.

The next night, and the next, and every night that week, there were knocks at the door, gorgeous hunks who wanted to thank me for being brave. Some nights there was more than one knock, and as one man entered, another, who'd been chatting, got up to leave. But there wasn't a night where somebody didn't stay until morning. It was one of the happiest weeks of my life.

You know, of course, that Nixon won the election. I'd sworn I wouldn't, but I voted for McGovern.

III. HONORARY LESBIAN

Back in the '70s (a time before recorded history to some of you, I know) I was a prominent gay activist, and my name shows up in lots of gay-history books. I don't look at most of them, but I was interviewed extensively for a book called *Out for Good* which got a good review in the *Times.* So I snuck into St. Mark's

Bookshop, and looked myself up in the index. There I was for pages and pages.

So I read them quite gleefully, sitting on a barstool (I guess St. Mark's can't afford lounge chairs) since, much to my amazement, the facts were straight—excuse the expression—and I wasn't misquoted once. Then I got to the last entry, in a chapter on the relations between gay men and lesbians. And I discovered that my old boss Jean O'Leary had told her interviewer that I, Ronald Gold, was "the most sexist man" she'd ever met.

Wee-ll! While Jean was at the National Gay Task Force, I wrote every word of every article and every word of every letter she signed her name to. Most especially, I wrote *all* the stuff about how lesbianism is a feminist issue, the stuff that gained Jean her reputation as a prominent "feminist theorist."

The only time I refused to be Jean's ghostwriter was when she asked me to write her piece for the first-ever coffee-table–size lesbian sourcebook. Seems the book had a section for articles by "friends" of lesbians and I had volunteered. But no men were allowed! So I was damned if I'd masquerade as Jean O'Leary.

Oh, and recently, *after* the interview where she nailed me for posterity, she went right on with her time-honored practice of calling me from time to time—friendly as a fuzzy bear—for advice and recollections about this and that.

I've never confessed this before, but I was *in love* with Jean O'Leary. And why not? She was fresh-faced and electric: a born leader. Just the type I like. Under the circumstances, I didn't make carnal advances, but I certainly understand how an amazing string of famous and infamous lesbians were sucked into her orbit, so to speak. I even had the honor of providing a shoulder to cry on for a couple of those she dumped (including an aide to Jimmy Carter who Jean used to get a White House meeting, then left out to dry in the political shithouse).

Do you think it's odd that gay old me should confess to passion for a (gasp) *lesbian*? Let me tell you a little story.

I was walking along lower Third Avenue a couple of years back, and in front of me was Ms. Sexy Broad. In jeans and a T-shirt. Long hair down to her waist. And a very nice ass (not one of those big, pear-shaped contraptions most women seem to have; but a nice, tight little ass). And behind me, close to the sidewalk, was Mr. Macho Youth, on a bicycle. Whistling. Smacking his lips, and calling out endearments to Ms. Sexy. Well, Mr. Macho and I arrived at the same moment in line with Ms. Sexy, and both of us were amazed to discover she had a moustache and a beard. (No, not a bearded lady. An actual man.) Well, young Macho sped off in a panic, and I was left to think, *the reason they give men and women different clothes and hair styles is to discourage homosexuality.* So we can all be fruitful and multiply.

But what gets me is that *gay people* use these arbitrary gender assignments to discourage heterosexuality. ("Whoa, there's this adorable boy; whoops, it's a woman.") Why do we do that? Because we're hung up in the homophobic notion that we're gay because we can't help it. After all, who'd be gay if they could help it? Well I would! I choose to be gay because it's a lot better and easier to relate to people based on who I am as an individual, not on the roles assigned to men and women. But I also choose to acknowledge that when I see a woman on the street who gives me that sexual frisson I usually reserve for men, it's not just because I mistook her for a man; there's something about *her* I like. That glow. That electric spark. All that stuff I saw in Jean O'Leary.

Maybe she thought I was sexist because I thought she was sexy. You'll have to ask her. I don't think I'm talking to her. Oh, and I guess I'll show up at this year's Gay Pride March as usual, wearing my "honorary lesbian" button.

EPIPHANIES

BRENT NICHOLSON EARLE

BRENT NICHOLSON EARLE *has been a contributing member of the artistic community in New York City for over thirty-five years, as an actor, writer, stage manager, lecturer, photographer, optical designer, and art gallery administrator. He is better known, however, as an athlete and activist. From his ultramarathons to his many arrests with ACT UP, he has been on the front lines of the battle against AIDS since the early '80s. He was also a charter director for thirteen years, and is now an honorary life member, of the Federation of Gay Games.*

Stonewall thirty-five . . . what a milestone. For me, Stonewall not only represents the birth of the gay liberation movement. It has always been a personal marker for the beginning of my life in New York. I moved to the city in 1969—one week out of high school and two weeks before the Stonewall uprising.

The first gay bar I ever stepped foot in was the Stonewall—Easter break my junior year in 1968. I met my first love there that night, Paul Deibert—trim build, gray eyes, preppy but really cute—leaning against an incongruous wishing well in that grungy rear anteroom. Of course, in '69 I thought preppy was pretty hot. I'd never seen any of the Colt men before or the erotic art of Tom of Finland . . . mmmm-mmm . . . thirty-five years since Stonewall . . . helluva lot of memories. I remember the fall of 1984 I had an epiphany—not my first but a really big one. It was a burning bush moment for me, completely changing the course of my life.

Although I'd arrived in New York on the crest of the first wave of gay liberation, I wasn't involved in social causes. I was pursuing my dream of having a career in the theater. At an audition in 1971, I met Broadway dancer Allan Sobek—Nordic, fair-haired, classic profile, and a lithe dancer's body. After a year of heated pursuit on my part, we fell in love and ended up living together for over twelve years. The hedonism of the '70s and early '80s was of mythic proportions, but with my share of experiences at The Anvil and the Continental Baths, I took the sexually free atmosphere of that time pretty much for granted. When I look back now, what I remember most is the excitement of working in the New York theater, the bonding and home life with Al, and the wonderful fellowship we shared with our family of friends.

In spite of the fact that Al was a dancer, partying didn't play an important role in our lifestyle. Oh, once or twice in the summer we'd go out dancing, to 12 West mostly, but all of that changed with the advent of The Saint. Throughout the fall of 1980 and the winter of 1981, I'd been hearing about this spectacular private gay dance club on the Lower East Side, but nothing could have prepared me for what I saw upon entering the transformed old theater on Second Avenue that had once been the famed Filmore East. The Saint was the ultimate fantasy dance palace with state-of-the-art surround sound and a planetarium dome of stars and galaxies overhead. The moment I first ascended one of the spiral staircases, walked onto that suspended circular dance floor, and saw the heavens open and the world's biggest mirror ball spinning above an awesome sea of male flesh, I thought my dreams had finally come true. I eventually became a member of The Saint and, within that dazzling environment, I was welcomed into a tribe of the most beautiful men I have ever seen. Weekend after weekend, we soared to the heights together. There was freedom and connection and music and passion—energy, ecstasy, and light! Talk about your epiphanies—it was almost as if they were nightly occurrences at The Saint.

And then, darkness descended. AIDS cast its deadly shadow over the celebration.

Like so many gay men in the early days of the crisis, I wasn't conscious of how paralyzed I'd become by fear and denial. Although this was definitely not the best time to be getting out of a relationship (*Will I ever have sex again?!*), I severed my emotional and physical ties to Allan. There were a lot of reasons for our splitting up—codependency issues, too much acting out on both our parts—but I also had the feeling that there was something waiting to emerge in me, something that couldn't come forth within the safety and comfort of my life with Al. I can remember thinking this all must have something to do with the play I was consumed with writing about the life and works of Edgar Allan Poe. (*I have to do this for my art!*) So in the late spring of 1984, I shook things up in my life. I moved out of the apartment on the Upper West Side that I had shared with Al.

My friend and mentor, Mel Cheren, owned an old building in Chelsea on West Twenty-second Street, which he'd turned over primarily to the Gay Men's Health Crisis for the first two years of their existence. He offered me a temporary room in the building with the promise of a permanent apartment rent-free in exchange for my taking over the responsibilities of superintendent. In doing so, I also took on the job of overseeing GMHC's move from Twenty-second Street to larger quarters three blocks south.

That year my eldest nephew and godson, Kerry Fly, was one of the fastest high school runners in New York State. Watching him compete, I got inspired and decided to run my first race, the third Gay Pride Run, sponsored by the city's young gay and lesbian running club, Front Runners New York. The night before the race, I remember writing on my race number the names of five friends I'd lost to AIDS. Running around Central Park the next day, I experienced so many conflicting feelings: sadness, exhilaration, dread . . . and, ultimately, gratitude . . . to be alive, to be able to breathe deeply and take in all of the sensations and beautiful sights around me.

Holed up in my one little room on Twenty-second Street that sweltering summer, crammed in with all of my boxes, I became obsessed with watching the Los Angeles Olympic Games on a tiny two-inch TV set. With dreams of athletic glory in my head, I decided to join Front Runners and started running with the club. The first mailing I received from them included an announcement of their second Benefit Run to support GMHC, and I suddenly realized that there was something I could do about AIDS. I didn't have to be frozen with fear anymore. I would face down my demons and ask my friends to support me in the first steps I was to take in making a difference in the fight against AIDS. So on the chilly morning of October 13, 1984, I ran the furthest distance I had ever run, twelve miles—twice around Central Park. During my second lap around, as my muscles tightened and fatigue overwhelmed me, my will to keep going began to leave me. Just then a strong gust of wind blew fallen leaves across my path, reminding me of the lives already lost to AIDS, and of all those that might yet be lost, and I pressed on.

I was completely exhausted by the end, but elated when I tallied my pledge sheet and realized that through my effort and with the help of my friends I had raised over $400 for GMHC.

Limping home to my newly completed top floor apartment on Twenty-second Street, I discovered that I had built upon sand. Mel informed me that he'd decided to turn the place into a gay guesthouse. After investing all that time and money and work, my new home was going to be temporary at best. Al and I had been working to salvage our friendship and I'd invited him over that night to see my new place and then go out dancing at The Saint. Well, it didn't turn out to be the night of celebration I had envisioned. The anxiety over my precarious living situation, along with the muscle pain from my twelve miles around the Park, sent me home far ahead of my usual Sunday morning revelry in wonderland.

Just before dawn, alone in my beautiful new apartment that was not to be, I felt like I had reached the most confused and desperate point in my life—a classic dark night of the soul. I broke down and, through my tears, I found myself talking to my father, who had died from cancer four years earlier. I was asking him for a sign, some kind of guidance, reaching out to him in a way I'd never been able to when he was alive.

I got an answer. I didn't hear it or see it, but I got it just the same. And the message was quite specific: "Follow in Terry Fox's footsteps." Well . . . that sure wasn't what I was expecting and I didn't like the sound of it one bit. I knew of Terry Fox, the young Canadian runner who'd lost his leg to cancer and attempted a run across Canada to raise funds to fight the disease. I also knew that his cancer had returned, he had to abandon his quest, and that he'd died six months later.

Having just completed my first run for AIDS the day before, I figured I shouldn't be taking the message too literally. Maybe it means I should run across America for AIDS. Yeah, from New York to San Francisco—no . . . that would reinforce the idea that AIDS is only a gay urban problem confined to the coasts. And it's not going to be enough to just have yet another run across

America that happens to be for AIDS. That won't grab the needed attention. It needs to be the furthest distance ever ventured and all the way around the country to get the point across that AIDS could end up coming to every part of America and that all Americans should be concerned.

At first I thought I might give up this crazy notion . . . what was I smokin' that night? But it wouldn't go away. I remember calling up my mother, a retired schoolteacher still living in Lockport, New York, our hometown up near Buffalo and Niagara Falls. "Well, Mom, you're never gonna believe what I'm up to this time—I'm going to run all the way around America for AIDS awareness." Without missing a beat, she responded, "I guess I'll have to go with ya." "What?!" "Well, who else is going to look after you on this adventure, do your laundry, make sure you eat?" As usual, I knew immediately that she was right.

The story of how my spunky, seventy-year-old mother did indeed follow me in her old Buick every step of the way as I ran more than 9,000 miles around the perimeter of the U.S.A. from March 1, 1986 to October 31, 1987, is for another time. This has been a story about how one extraordinary moment can create a major shift in your life and place you on a totally new path. I have to admit that I have been both blessed and challenged by such epiphanies. After all is said and done though, I'd like to think that I'm ready for another one.

BILLY'S BACK

ALLEN SCHELER

***ALLEN SCHELER** is a native of Louisville, Kentucky, who moved to New York City in 1989 as a counter manager for Aramis Fragrances. No, Really. Currently, he is a training manager at a law firm and just turned the big 4-0.*

I remember the day had a little nip in the air. I had been unemployed for several months, after losing my job as training director for a software company. I was walking in a fog in the West Forties—Hell's Kitchen, where I live. Another day in New York City without working. What in hell was I going to do today?

My fog lifted suddenly. I looked up and there he was. *BILLY!*

He looked like he did in the pictures, but taller than I thought. Yes, he really did have blond highlights. So I did what I hope any gay man would do when they saw him. I turned around and followed him. He walked a block, me closely on his tail, and he went into Peepworld. I can still see the Video Arcade neon lights, and the gay porno blinking in the light.

I was on a mission. I followed him up two flights of steps and to the back where the booths were, and I can still hear the attendants saying, "Drop some quarters." Bastards. Billy turns and smiles at me and walks to the other end. That's when I said, not to Billy but to the attendant, "Can you make him leave? He's a gay basher. His pictures are all over Chelsea and every gay rag in town. He's dangerous."

With a blank look in his eyes, the attendant said, "Drop some quarters." Another guy approached me and said, "Isn't that Billy?" and I told him yes. By this time Billy thought I was cruising him, so he smiled at me again. I suddenly realized there were cops across the street on Eighth Avenue. I ran down the stairs and across the street. With emotion rising in my voice, I said, "There is a guy in Peepworld who is a known gay basher. His picture has been all over the village and every bar downtown! Can we do anything about this before someone gets hurt?" Another blank stare, and I thought, *if you tell me to drop some quarters I'm going knock you into next week*. Instead, with the typical attitude you expect when talking about gay bashing to cops, Kojak responds, "No, not if he's not wanted for any crime."

I looked over at Peepworld, and Billy was walking out the door with someone, deep in conversation. My emotions were all over the place. I was angry and scared, and then I started to channel Angie Dickinson in *Policewoman.* I pulled out my cell phone and began following Billy and his Next Possible Victim. I dialed 212-555-1212 as I walked.

"Directory Assistance. Can I help you?" *Yes you can, this is Pepper and I need the number of the Anti-Violence Project. Please hurry!* I had followed the two of them for about two blocks, to the corner of Forty-second and Eighth Avenue.

"Yes, AVP? I'm several feet away from Billy—yes, that's right, *Billy.* You know, the gay basher with the bad highlights. He's left with someone from Peepworld, and I need to do something to stop him. Is he wanted for anything that you know of?"

"No, he's not. Where are you?"

I tell him. I feel helpless. *What can we do so the guy he is with doesn't get hurt*? The AVP man is saying, "There's not much you can do, and be careful," when the Next Possible Victim looks at me. Making eye contact, I slowly shake my head, "No." He is looking at me like I'm on crack, and I come up and stand next to him. He looks away. There on the corner of Forty-second and Eighth, it's me, Billy's NPV, and Billy, standing in a line. Just like Gladys Knight's Pips. And I say to the guy, sotto voce, "Don't leave with him."

"What?"

"I said don't leave with him, he's a gay basher."

And Billy heard me. "Hey man, what did you say?"

"I said he should not go home with you because you are a known gay basher, and you're known to be violent. Your picture's all over the Village, and the Anti-Violence Project knows all about you." I hold up my cell. "They just told me."

I think, *what in the fuck am I doing?* Now Billy is only inches away from my face. And I think, *yikes! He needs an exfoliation, not to mention a moisturizer. His skin looks like a handbag, and not an expensive one.*

"Better get out of here, man." His low tone is a threat.

And I think: *Watch his hands. Watch his body.* "I'm gonna get a cop," I say. "Just a block away."

And then he says it. "Go to the gym, you fat ass!"

Go to the gym you fat ass! Now I'm really pissed. He is now every bully that made fun of me in grade school. He is all those guys in my neighborhood back in Louisville who used to chase me home. I think: *Make noise. Bring lots of attention to this conversation. More than likely the Next Victim will leave. And Billy wouldn't dare to pummel me.* I start ranting, not even sure what I'm saying. I don't stop even when I hear my strained voice going on and on. I'm not sure of the points I'm making, or if I'm even making points.

"Man, you are on crystal," Billy says.

I turn to Billy's NPV. "Don't leave with him," I say. "The Anti-Violence Project is all over him. I just got off the phone with them. This guy is bad news." The guy looks at Billy, his new friend, and tilts his head in my direction. Something unspoken passes between them. And then, without a word to me, they move away. In a matter of seconds, Billy has grabbed a cab. In they get, and off they go.

I stand there. *Oh my god, he left with him. What if he hurts him? Will he be OK*? But then I have a moment of pure gay pride, knowing I did all that I could to help a stranger—a moment of "all right for me!" for standing up to Billy face-to-face. Well, maybe it was face-to-pec. He is taller than I am.

MY COMMUNITY

METROCUB

NEIL JAMES

NEIL JAMES *lives in Jersey City, utterly alone. He's a contributing essayist for* David Magazine, *and the* New York Blade, *and is co-founder of Fink Tank 3000 (finktank3000.com), the web's angriest liberal parody site. A true Southern boy, Neil enjoys bingo and scouring Manhattan for the perfect biscuit. Fuck bagels.*

I never actively pursued the title of Mr. MetroCub. Sure a little bit, but it more pursued me. I always thought sash queens were silly folk. Sash queens are a rare breed of gay man addicted to gay beauty contests, paradoxical galas combining faux macho with prom queen girly.

For a sash queen the title is usually irrelevant: Mr. Leather Daddy 1985. Mr. New Jersey 1994. Mr. Cute Buns 2003. Announce your contest and a dozen guys will line up, Vaseline smiles and polished boots, for the chance to be named The Best.

For an entire year, this gay man represents the highest pinnacle of what his gay subculture holds worthy. But all good things come with a price. Egoism is a dangerous drug. As easily as it elevates to euphoric heights, it quickly destroys, leaving the potential sash seeker a broken husk. This is my confession.

I've always been a big guy. At six foot even and a little over 200 pounds I've never been considered obese. But as a child, I wasn't spared the shame of shopping in the "husky" section at Goody's.

Husky, with a little acne and deeply gay, I found no success dating girls in high school. The hot desire I felt for the boys on the football team was buried beneath layers of Southern guilt.

I had a flare for the dramatic, and learned early on that intimate love from one special person couldn't compare to the fawning adoration of the masses. Who needed a girlfriend, or a boyfriend, when a simple, ironic quip got so many laughs? Even the teachers found me amusing!

In 1993, class superlatives were to be voted for at the annual Cedartown High School Senior Banquet. It was a *fancy* affair at the Rome Bypass Holiday Inn. We could choose steak *or* chicken. And the salad was served *separately.*

I was in the running for Most Funny. Normally it would have been a no-brainer. But Jonathan shared the ballot. He had large eyes and an open, pale face that gave him a perpetually surprised appearance. He excelled at fart jokes, crass urinal poetry, and physical stunts. He was the comic of the vocational students.

Our funny-feud had started in fourth grade during auditions for *The Christmas Angel* in Mr. Linderman's English class. Mr. Linderman was a tall, elegant man. He spoke in a soft voice and allowed us to think creatively. *The Christmas Angel* was about an angel statue which comes to life and grants Christian wishes when a little poor girl weeps on Christmas Eve.

I was auditioning for the role of the town crier, but I secretly wanted to play the Christmas angel. For all his fabulousness, however, Mr. Linderman couldn't get away with non-gender-specific casting in the fourth grade. So that role belonged to Kristin Carter, the most popular girl at Cherokee Elementary.

We read for our parts in front of the class. I rolled the lines of the town crier from my tongue with a classic Dickensian dialect. "Hear ye! Hear ye! The village angel is alive! Hear ye!"

The class was wowed by my British accent. I had spent a week watching *Upstairs, Downstairs,* perfecting it.

Then, Jonathan stepped up for his audition. He threw himself to the floor screaming, "HEAR YE! HEAR YE!" He convulsed on the carpet, bellowing his lines. And the class lapped it up like dogs. Chuckling, Mr. Linderman awarded Jonathan the role. I seethed, but Mr. Linderman took me aside to offer me a part in the Christmas chorus. I bit my lip and looked him in the eyes. "No, thank you. I'll be a villager." I cast myself among the rejects who couldn't handle a speaking part.

The show opened with the town villagers: myself, Cindy—severely retarded and sitting on the floor—and Bugsy, who had a behavior disorder. We simply stood onstage for the entire play, shuffling from left to right as the actors entered and exited. I kept my cool when Jonathan took to the stage and I quietly mouthed the town crier's lines as he spoke. The students and faculty laughed at his portrayal, and at ten years old I swore my revenge.

So, eight years later, I was determined not to lose to him again. At our senior banquet, upon my introduction as a Most Funny nominee, I stood and offered a Fresca toast to Jonathan. I floated to his table, knelt before him and sang "Wind Beneath My Wings" from the hit movie *Beaches.* I didn't admit it then, but hands down I was indeed a gay teenager. My lyrical ambush worked! The class cheered my song. Cindy roared, mangling her steak with both hands. Jonathan, unprepared, had nothing to respond with. Class President Kristin Carter called for a vote and I was named Most Funny 1993! For the very first time, I tasted the sweet nectar of popularity. Oh, I was hooked.

The Mr. MetroCub/Mr. MetroBear contest caught my interest the moment I joined the premier club for husky gay men, the MetroBears. The annual pageant featured two separate contests, one for older, gruffer Bears, and one for younger, cuter Cubs. Several of the club's organizers told me about the contest and suggested I run.

The pageant is the MetroBears' largest yearly fund-raiser. Who can resist grown men prancing and preening in jockstraps and buttless chaps? It's not all sex, mind you. Contestants are expected to be up-to-the-minute on current topics. They're quizzed on such subjects as favorite personal lubricant and most comfortable sexual position. The entire affair proves that gay or straight, men are all pigs, and I quietly wanted to be a part of the action. My bewildered skepticism and "Oh, I don't know" naiveté masked a feral animal.

Months before participants were allowed to formally submit their bid, I began notifying fellow club members of my intent to run. I called myself the "Howard Dean of the MetroCubs." What a pity. This was before Dean's tragic "Yeeeeaaargh!" destroyed his campaign. My name recognition was up, and I hadn't found anyone who'd be a threat to my imminent title.

Then I met Manny. He was a good-looking man, vaguely ethnic. Hispanic? Italian? He had an exotic sexuality. His goatee was meticulously trimmed and his eyebrows obviously plucked. He had dark eyes that betrayed something sinister, something dangerous. He often cajoled me into brief make-out sessions toward the rear of the bar. The more he tricked me into kissing him, the more I began to panic. Perhaps Manny was a threat to my title? How could he have flown beneath my radar for so long? Although my bewitching blues had charmed plenty, word spread that Manny's smoldering browns were catching up in the polls.

What to wear for the contest? I had an ace in the hole with my friends Tim and Doug, a hunky bear couple of many years. They squealed at the opportunity to deck me out in their long-ignored leather wear. Calling me their "dress-up-cub," they loaned me a leather harness, a leatherman's hat, a leather vest, matching bicep cuffs, a collar, and various other straps and gadgets guaranteed to elicit a gasp from any audience. Above all, they let me borrow the costume that would define my "erotic wear," a pair of faded overall cutoffs and a weathered straw hat. I was to be a raunchy ranch hand.

On the eve of the gala I dreamed of floating in the ocean. At first, I swam back and forth in the warm waters, unperturbed by the nagging insecurities embedded decades ago by *A Christmas Angel.* Then the water turned cold and I washed ashore on a soggy beach. Shivering and groggy, I opened my eyes. The clock read four A.M. and my mattress was soaking wet.

I'd peed my bed. *I'd never peed my bed!*

I awoke my spend-the-night company, Greg, and we relocated to the living-room futon. "Was it the MetroCub contest?" he asked. I lied, "No. I think I drank too much. Are you weirded out that I peed the bed on our second date?" He lied, "No, not at all."

The night of the contest brought out a who's who of bear glitterati. Mr. International Grizzly 2004 was in attendance, and hosting the event was the illustrious drag queen, Ms. Tra-La-Trash. Rumor was that Michael Musto from the *Village Voice* had replied yes to his invitation. All that along with a porn star sighting. It had become a star-studded gala.

I tried to make myself dirty yet pretty. As other contestants entered the makeshift green room, I sized up my competition. Apart from Manny, the next contestant who posed a threat to my MetroCub dominance was Joe, a brick shithouse of a man, as wide as he was tall, built with impossibly gigantic muscles covering his frame. His pectorals seemed ready to burst through his skin, and his thighs, with their bulging veins, were nearly as big around as my waist.

He pulled from his bag a strange metal box with a dial mechanism and he taped an electrode to his left bicep. A wire led from the electrode to the box, and he slowly maneuvered the dial. Suddenly his bicep jerked and quivered. He was shocking himself! It was fascinating and repulsive.

Grown men with goatees and sideburns, broad shoulders

and Village People regalia, pushed and elbowed for a place in the mirror. We were ballerinas trapped in the bodies of bikers. We received word that the show was underway and we were to be in our first outfits, "bear wear." I pulled on a pair of worn blue jeans and my leather harness. I completed a set of push-ups, and sipped red wine through a straw so as not to stain my teeth.

I could hear the audience laughing at a drag duo performing a musical tribute to Sonny and Cher. Applause soon followed, and my mouth went dry as our hostess introduced the first of the MetroCub nominees for his Q&A session. One by one the contestants went to the stage.

Manny preceded me. I didn't pay attention to his appearance onstage. Instead, my heartbeat counted down the seconds until Ms. Tra-La-Trash's high-pitched twang announced, "Let's hear it for Manny. Now, let's welcome our next contestant . . ."

I don't know what came over me. I exploded onto the stage screaming, "MetroBears give me some noise!" Like a drunken frat boy, I threw myself into the contest.

For so long I'd kept a façade, eager, yet staying slightly aloof. (*Oh, the social irony of masculine men competing for a gaudy crown. How silly! Oh, who wants to be in a Christmas pageant? I'll be a villager, thank you very much Mr. Linderman!*) In fifteen seconds, I stripped away years of pretension. No more detached amusement, no more pussyfooting around. I wanted that goddamned tiara!

When Ms. Tra-La-Trash announced my liberal political standing, I screamed a resounding, "FUCK BUSH!!" pumping my fist in the air. The audience erupted in cheers and foot stomping. When Ms. Tra-La-Trash commented on my leather harness, I tweaked my nipples and woofed at the judges. I remember bounding off the stage with everyone cheering, some on their feet. I slapped high fives on my way back to the green room. In the darkened theater I could see a pair of big-boned women bowing to me, and my friends Doug and Tim signaled me thumbs up. Burly men patted me on the behind.

I changed into my raunchy ranch-hand costume, but then Manny strode into the green room in a black leather Roman emperor's outfit with a matching black crown of leaves; it was historical *and* really sexy. My high came down a bit.

But, in the mirror, I regarded my skimpy overalls, unbuttoned down the sides, one strap slung low with my dusty ranch boots and a worn straw hat. I sprayed water across my hairy chest and patted down the fur. "Whew, it's sure a hot day on the ranch." I lingered over each word. I played them across my tongue like an ice cube on a hot Oklahoma day. I winked and blew myself a kiss. Manny didn't stand a fucking chance!

The other erotic offerings were mediocre. Joe, with the radioactive arms, dressed as a baseball player, and then he stripped. A muscle man in a jockstrap, holding a baseball bat. Timeless, but so cliché.

Manny followed. I watched from the corner of my eye. He engaged Ms. Trash and interacted with the audience. They laughed loudly at his dirty talk and applauded when he lifted his toga to moon everyone, eventually stripping into a black jockstrap. He left the stage followed by reverberating applause.

Again I rushed onto the stage. And I delivered what felt like a thirty-six-minute soliloquy about blow jobs—on the ranch. Tra-La-Trash grabbed the microphone and demanded I perform a sexy pose. I turned, squatting toward the audience, effectively showing plumber's crack and all the plumbing, as my rancher's overalls fell to my knees. The audience gasped. In retrospect, perhaps I should have accessorized with a plunger, not a rake. My part done, I left the stage and collapsed in the green room, thankful the gala was almost over, and giddy that I stood a chance of taking the crown.

Arrogance, anticipation, vanity, pride, ego, they all came to a peak as the contestants stood side by side, facing an ocean of darkened silhouettes. I was again swimming in that dreamy ocean. I was floating, an ephemeral, weightless sensation, as Ms. Tra-La-Trash slowly announced the winner of the Mr. MetroCub 2004 contest.

"Manny! Manny wins!" Joyous, exuberant, golden and shining, he accepted the sash and his wonderfully gaudy tiara. And suddenly, shamefully, I became that sullen, petulant ten-year-old, pouting because he didn't win the part.

Me and fourth-grade me avoided club functions for the next few months. We sat together on the futon. As I flipped channels, he'd remind me how lame the contest was and what a dork I'd made of myself. It took some time, but eventually I couldn't handle his wounded company anymore. I stuffed the little brat back in his box and told him he couldn't come out until he behaved like a real little boy.

I rejoined the bar scene. The first few weeks I'd watch Manny working the crowd. Everyone was still congratulating him. I hadn't yet. I also never commended Jonathan on his heavy-handed, but admittedly funny, portrayal of the town crier. I refused to commit the same error twice.

So one night, both of us a little tipsy, I cornered Manny and hugged him. I congratulated him on his splendid victory. And I was going to wish him good luck on his national bid, but he cut me off. Smirking, he regarded me with those dangerous brown eyes. "That's so kind of you sweetie. I didn't really think you were a threat, but I *was* a little nervous for a teensy second!" He gave me breezy air kisses and minced away.

I turned to the ten-year-old me sitting on the barstool next to mine, contentedly drinking chocolate milk. We secretly began to plot Mr. MetroCub's demise. Revenge is a dish best served cold and with a smile.

BIRDS

RONALD GOLD

Waltzing about the floor were a bevy of dykes: Swedish dykes, black dykes from uptown, even a few Native American dykes for body in the blend. Anyhow, jigging about and draped across things, were a bevy of dykes.

"A covey," said Sylvia.

"Brace!"

"Nonsense! I bet you don't even know what quail come in."

"Splits!"

"Geese?"

Alice giggled.

"Fucks. A fuck of geese."

"Eagles?"

"A possel of eagles."

"Archaeopteryxes?"

"Opteri!"

"Opteroids."

"Look it up! Look it up in the dictionary."

"A-r-c-h-e . . ."

". . . c-h-a-e . . ."

"Archae . . . *A genus of fossil reptilian birds, first found in the lithographic quarries at Solenhofen, in Bavaria. It combines reptilian* . . . It doesn't say what the plural is."

"Call up the library. Call up the public library."

"Hello? General information, please. . . . General information? Can you tell me what the plural of archaeopteryx . . ."

"While you're at it, ask them what they come in."

"I yam sorry, but we do not give gram-MAT-ical informa-MAY-see-un."

"Wait a minute! Can you tell me what they come in? You know, like coveys or bevies?"

"That would be our NAY-tyoor department. I will switch you-oo."

"She's switching me. . . . Hello, can you tell me what archaeopteryxes . . ."

"Opteri."

". . . come in?"

"Beg yer pah-din."

"You know, like bevies or coveys."

"Justa minit."

A couple of the dykes had now begun to take off their jeans. In an instant they were prancing about with only their shirttails covering their jockey shorts. Alice giggled.

"That's a research question. Call back in an hour."

As for the weaker sex, the boys were skipping and whirling with monumental abandon. In various stages of proto-erection and dishabille were yellow-haired cretins, no-haired intellectuals, wavy-haired adolescents, and fuzzy-haired spades. These darker brothers were represented with great profusion and considerable elegance. Belle of the ball was an ebony beauty named O'Toole. Dressed in white from nut-brown neck to sable toe, he was followed about both literally and figuratively by half the twirling fruits, including all the intellectuals. Also Alice.

"Viva Zapata!"

Blaring mambo seemed to bring out the urge for individual expression. Ardent pairs, both mobile and recumbent, broke away from each other and swung and swayed in egocentric circles. Fixed faces, heels to floor, noses craning left, shoulders right. I sat in a corner, glasses glaring. A stick of pot. Here comes Reggie.

"Viva Zapata!" The second time around, some of the pairs rejoined with pelvic vigor. Off came T-shirts, blue jeans, cravats. Out came hairpins, a couple of pricks. Some of the participants went down but not out.

Suddenly there came a rapping.

"Come in."

Bursting the frame of the doorway was the lady from upstairs. Housecoat pink and flaring.

"Niggers!" she shrieked. Across the sprawling multitude, she picked out Betty with her hyperthyroid eyes. "Niggers! The landlord will know. The landlord will be TOLD."

Through the tag-end mambo and screen of laughter, the housecoat disappeared.

Alice, on the sofa, whined. "Whaat shall I dooo?"

"Why don't you go inside and shove some peanut brittle up your ass."

"Let's eat," said Sylvia.

Under the crackers was found a note from Betty's cousin from the Bronx: *I'm leaving. That Jew and that nigger kissing was just too much. I feel sick to my stomach. I'll call you tomorrow, Bill.*

I was shocked once again by being a Jew. Reggie, once a sociology major at the University of Chicago, determined to fight.

"Invite him over tomorrow," he said to Betty. "I'll wait right here. I'll knock the shit out of him." Poodle eyes ablaze. Big red beautiful cartoon lips drawn tight.

I raised my Roman nose to speak. Reached in my pocket for the roach.

"Hello, Nature Department? I called before about the archaeopteri? Have you found out what they come in?"

"They don't come in anything. They're extinct."

BEST FOOT FORWARD

BRAD GRETTER

Despite my reputation, I am by no means a narcissist. It is true that on occasion, with the right lighting, I have unwittingly cruised myself in more than a few barroom mirrors. After years of experience, I've become an expert at gracefully recovering from these public faux pas, pretending to primp and preen like the best of the pretty muscle boys. I'm what you would call cruising impaired. That is, I am legally blind. I can't tell whether the cute stocky guy in the corner is smiling at me or sneering at me. Perhaps I'm looking at the back of his head. Or better yet, maybe he's not an actual living person, but rather, a bronzed shirtless hunk in a life-size Budweiser advertisement. It happens more frequently than I care to admit. Truthfully speaking though, I'd rather be caught cruising myself, than to quietly fade into the shadows and not cruise or be cruised at all.

Fortunately, I discovered theme party nights in gay bars. I'm not referring to your basic Sunday night beer blasts at Splash or Halloween costume disco at the Monster. No, I'm talking about bars like the Eagle or the Spike—those notorious leather bars that once a month, play host to different groups such as the boys from Spank-Me-Hard or the Gay Oil Wrestling Alliance. I firmly believe it is always easier meeting other guys when there are common interests or group activities to participate in together.

My most memorable theme party experience was an evening

at the Lure hosted by Foot Friends, a club for guys into feet, boots, and footwear of all kinds. I found Foot Friends, or Foot Friends found me, the morning before I was to run my first New York City Marathon. Talk about brilliant marketing. Foot Friends deployed their cutest and sexiest men, to a pre-race pancake breakfast hosted by Front Runners, the local lesbian and gay running team. Foot Friends arrived on the scene, armed with flyers promising free foot massages to anyone who finished the marathon.

So, after a celebratory post-race dinner, I ventured over to the Lure. I arrived around 10 P.M., flashing my finisher's medal at the bouncer, who checked me out from head to toe. A leering smile spread across his face, as he opened the door and watched me enter. Once inside, I stood for a moment, letting my eyes adjust to the deep red light that flooded the front bar. With the best tough guy look I could muster, I sauntered across the bar, through the faux back alley lined with fierce-looking leather daddies, and past the artfully lit cellblocks with their mounted ankle and wrist restraints. I finally found my way to the back of the bar where a row of large steel drums formed a small lounging area for the foot massage.

Taking shelter behind the steel drums, several men lay sprawled out on gym mats, while other men knelt before them, intently massaging their feet. I watched the masseurs slowly, lovingly work the feet of the men in front of them. Taking me by the hand, Sebastian, my assigned foot friend, led me to a mat in the corner. In a peaceful whisper, Sebastian urged me to "lie back, relax, and let go . . . enjoy this gift that I'm about to give you." Out of habit I struggled to make small talk. "Shhhh," said Sebastian, "there's no talking allowed." Then with a smile and a wink he added, "But you may moan if you please." So, I lay down, closed my eyes and let Sebastian caress and knead my sore, swollen feet.

I remember the smell of peppermint, eucalyptus, and juniper wafting in the air, as he applied lotion after lotion, working it between my toes and smoothing it into my soles.

Using both hands, he carefully stretched each foot, loosening and releasing the tension that had built up during the marathon. Soon his hands slowed down as he finished the massage. I thanked him, as he helped me up. "The pleasure was all mine," he said. "It's not often I get to work on someone who surrenders so completely." Looking around the bar, he continued, "You should stick around, hang out for a while. It's a friendly crowd tonight. I'm sure you'll have a good time."

Taking his advice, I got myself a beer and took a leisurely tour of the bar. As I expected, there was a great deal of cruising going on. However, that night, I was not at a disadvantage. In place of the usual exchange of subtle lustful glances from across the room, everyone seemed to be walking around with their eyes focused squarely on the floor, or on the playground of feet around them. Some of the guys were quite forward and didn't hesitate to lean over to get a good look. For me, this was a cruising dream come true. No need to be shy, and no need to worry about scaring anyone away by staring too closely.

In the center of the room, a portly gentleman wearing nothing more than a jock strap and a satisfied smile lounged in an Adirondack chair atop a raised wooden platform. Half a dozen men circled the platform, taking turns manhandling his big feet and meaty calves. In the far corner, a smooth, beefy guy in tight red running shorts squatted at the feet of his dark, swarthy master, consumed by the task of vigorously polishing his master's black boots. I found myself mesmerized by the foot porn being displayed on the video monitors that hung from the ceiling. There were no butts, no pecs, not even a set of rippling abs in sight. No, this was about feet—about perfectly formed toes, smooth supple soles, and the most graceful curvaceous arches I've ever laid eyes on.

Then, out of nowhere, a compact little bodybuilder sidled up to me. His opening line: "So, tell me, what size do you wear?" *A size queen of a different breed,* I thought to myself. In a cool tone, I replied, "ten-and-a-half." Then, pausing long enough to see him raise an eyebrow, I added, "triple-E." He closed his eyes and shuddered. Looking me straight in the eye, he licked his lips and said, "I think it's time I inspect those big sexy feet of yours, young man." With a smile and a nod, I replied, "Sure, anything you want."

We wound our way through the crowd, toward a chest-high ledge running the length of the bar. Without any effort, my iron-pumping admirer hoisted me up onto the ledge. Taking hold of my left foot, he teasingly removed my running shoe and sock, and began working my foot in small circular motions with his thumbs. Suddenly I spied a burly bearded bear of a man, decked out in faded jeans and a leather vest lumbering toward us. Before I could say a word, he grabbed hold of my other foot and pulled my running shoe off with a quick, easy stroke. He didn't ask my permission but simply made his intentions known to me with a deep grunt.

I felt like the flavor of the day: sitting on the ledge, my legs spread wide apart, my feet pointing out into the crowd, while two men, one tiny, one massive, stood shoulder to shoulder, laying claim to each foot. They didn't speak to each other, nor did they acknowledge the other's presence. I carried on two separate conversations, pivoting my head from side to side as I alternately addressed each of them. The little bodybuilder quickly lost interest in speaking to me, opting to squat down on the floor where he meticulously and methodically sucked my toes. The bearded bear let go of my other foot long enough to shake my hand and introduce himself. His name was Chuck.

Chuck was by far the more inventive and passionate of the two. He varied his routine, starting off by rubbing his bristly beard in gentle strokes from my toes to my shins. From here, he moved on to circling the balls of my feet with his tongue and licking long trails along my arches. I'd never felt anything quite like it. Chuck was on a roll, and there was no stopping him.

Finally, sweating and panting, he came up for air. "Do you mind if I ask a personal question?" I shrugged my shoulders. "You don't happen to be Irish, do you?" he inquired.

"Yeah," I replied. "On my mother's side of the family." In a startling burst of energy, Chuck flung my leg down, knocking over the bodybuilder who was still quietly sucking my toes. I flinched, worried that perhaps he was about to take out some personal grudge against the Irish on me. "I knew it," he shouted. "I knew it the moment I grabbed hold of your feet. Damn, I'm getting better at it every day," he beamed. Confused, I stared back at him. In an almost exasperated tone he bellowed, "Your feet man, they are SO IRISH! Big. Rugged. Beautiful. Totally, Irish! You know, I can tell a lot about a guy from the look of his feet." Relieved and amused, I looked down at the dazed little bodybuilder sprawled out on the floor and then back at Chuck. "Well, in that case," I said, "by all means, please tell me more."

Two hours and a revealing sole-reading later, I sat alone on that ledge, tucked the slip of paper Chuck gave me with his phone number into my front pocket, and gazed down at my big Irish feet. To the uninitiated, my feet with their rough calluses, hairy toes and occasional bouts of athlete's foot, are at best unappealing, and at worst, downright revolting. But, now, having been introduced to the sacred ways of Foot Friends, I have a whole new appreciation for my feet. For starters, they take me everywhere I need to go in this city. Being legally blind and unable to drive a car, my feet are my ticket to independence. At night, when I'm stressed out and unable to sleep, it's my feet that rub together in a rapid meditative race under the sheets, lulling me into peaceful dreams. After months of grueling training, these feet faithfully carried me through five boroughs and over twenty-six miles to finish the New York City Marathon. And every year on the last Sunday in June, it's on these feet that I march and dance my way down Fifth Avenue reveling in, and celebrating, gay pride.

ATHLETICS

SPEEDO CAMP

HARRY SCHULZ

HARRY SCHULZ *was born and raised in a suburb of New York City in the 1960s or 1970s, depending upon his screen name. His first bicycle was a red Schwinn with a banana seat named "Victoria." He starred in high school musicals. He earned a B.A. in philosophy from Swarthmore College with a focus on Wittgenstein and Aesthetics. He enrolled at HB Studios and studied acting for several years. He became a cater-waiter, and his life became a series of 12-step programs, diets, gyms, and roommates. Harry began studying jazz singing in 1987, and joined the independent record label New Artists Records, where he produced his own vocal CD,* Havin' a Ball. *He finally found that elusive boyfriend, a full-time job with health benefits, and a decent apartment. In July of 2004, he chucked it all to start over in Asheville, North Carolina.*

Deep breath . . .

. . . I remember . . . hating water—being *afraid* of water. I don't mean afraid like a cat of getting sprayed by a lawn sprinkler, or even afraid of the crowded over-chlorinated public pool in town where you could bleach your hair, skin, and bathing suit all in one afternoon. I mean afraid of deep water, water you can't see into, dark, murky water. The kind that has unknown things moving unseen just below the surface. The kind you find in a lake or a bay, the kind a boat moves over.

Now I had never confessed this fear to anyone. Though from the number of times I spent plastered to the bottom of a boat, panting with my eyes closed while it moved across the glassy calm surface of a lake on a windless day, you'd think somebody would have figured it out.

In spite of this somehow, I don't exactly know how, in the summer of 1971 I ended up at a sailing camp on Cape Cod.

I think I was sold on the camp by my mother and her friend Mrs. Pankovic who had sent her son the pyromaniac (according to legend) some six or seven years before. My parents had just divorced and Mrs. Pankovic thought my mother needed a break. I suppose they filled my head with ideas of adventure. I'm sure I had grand and glamorous ideas about what sailing camp would be and my place in it. I don't doubt that in my Million Dollar Movie–soaked nine-year-old mind, the place had some sort of sepia-tinged *Call of the Wild* thing going on with it, and I, à la Walter Mitty, magically would have no fear, but take to the water like Horatio Hornblower, and. . . . Really, come to think of it, there was also the status thing of being the only kid in my neighborhood to be sent away.

It wasn't until I got there—I think it was actually driving up the dirt road and into the camp—that I thought something like, *Shit, what have I gotten myself into?* I really knew I was in trouble the first morning I had to go for swimming instruction down at Pilgrim Lake because, well, did I mention that I hate water?

I had to get up at 6 A.M. They made us go out on an aluminum-covered floating dock. It was so cold under my bare feet because it was covered with early morning dew. How I hated that early morning dew. And I hated that lake. It was cold, and green, and I couldn't see a foot through the water.

. . . I remember . . . Speedo bathing suits. Ill-fitting, navy blue, camp regulation, Speedo bathing suits. I think we were all in them, except maybe the really fat (for want of a better word) kid, who always had an enormous pair of boxer swim trunks that hung down to his knees and were all loose with his butt crack showing. I always wanted to pull up that suit and tie the drawstrings tighter, but it wasn't my style to do things like that.

I shouldn't say "fat kid," but really, it was like our camp had been populated by casting for the *Our Gang* serials—I can just imagine the owners meeting in the spring. "Who's left? We've got a pimply kid, an exhibitionist kid, a foreign exchange kid, a silent loner, they're all covered." " How about an obvious little queer boy—think that Schulz kid will do?" "Oh definitely."

. . . I remember the showers. Big communal ones, and everyone from the smallest boys up to the counselors all showered in them. I remember seeing pubic hair for the first time. I didn't really know what I was seeing. I was very, very modest and shy. I was not going to take off my clothes in front of all those guys and shower with them. I think I tried one time showering in my bathing suit, but that drew more attention to me than showering naked. So somehow, I'm not exactly sure how, I managed to never shower for the entire rest of my stay at camp.

So, swimming lessons.

I remember a particular counselor who taught swimming standing there in his red Speedo—lean, tan, blond-haired, handsome, but sort of mean-looking and scary. I wanted to please him somehow even though I didn't like him. Actually, I hated him. But that Speedo and the blond hair on his legs. . . . That bastard made us jump in that water. Shouted us into the water. Intimidated us into the water. I hesitated, ran, and then stopped at the edge, stepped back, ran, and stopped, teetering on the edge. I remember the dread in that second in midair before plunging in. Like plunging into an ice bath. A dirty green ice bath. Only the fat kid never seemed to mind.

And then the snapping turtle stories. Why is it that camps always have a legendary monster? At least one. This camp's was the gigantic snapping turtle that would bite off a kid's toe, or his pecker. Was that the word they used? Maybe they said "dick." Probably didn't use a word, just a pregnant pause and a subtle glance down. Now I ask you, where was the motivation for me to jump in that water? Only the fear of the mean counselor, of humiliation, of not being "man enough" at nine years old.

So they had this swim meet at the end of my stay there. There was always some competition or another. Sailing regattas, tennis tournaments, relay races, baseball games. They divided the boys up into age groups, and I was at the bottom of the heap. There was only one other kid younger than me. Doug something. He was half my size, the littlest kid at the camp, and he had played the girl in the camp play, but HE could swim. I never seemed to be able to opt out of these kind of things. I always felt that I *had to* do them. I had to do it or else . . . I wouldn't be a boy . . . I would be a . . . well, something less than the kid who plays the girl in the camp play.

We had three competitions. The first, I remember, was the Australian crawl. From one end of the C-shaped floating dock to the other and back.

How I hated the Australian crawl. I had to look up every few strokes because I was afraid I would hit my head on the dock (far away as I was from it). And I never could get a decent breath with my head sideways in the water. And I never could go straight. . . . Little Doug, of course, beat me.

The next was the backstroke. Now this I was *sure* I could do. I thought I could beat him if I put my all into it. And at least I had my face out of the water. But to my surprise and horror, Doug beat me by an even greater length than in the Australian crawl. I was on the verge of being the losingest, the slowest, the *lowest*—worse than the littlest kid in the entire camp.

One competition remained. This was . . . *holding our breath under water.* I was determined that I would win this one, or die trying. I remember a host of Speedo-clad counselors standing on that dock, one with a stopwatch and a starting pistol, while I stood up to my shoulders in the water. Three, two, one—bang!

It was a quiet world under there. I couldn't hear anyone up above. The crowd of boys watching me humiliate myself, they were gone, I was alone, and I held on. I began to think I wouldn't mind a breath of air. I tried to count to myself, fifty-nine one thousand, sixty one thousand, one one thousand. Another minute. I thought, maybe if I open my eyes I can see if Doug goes up for air. I could hardly see in that murk—it was like an underwater scene from *Creature from the Black Lagoon.* I couldn't see Doug at all. Still I waited. I think it was something like two minutes and forty seconds—was that it? I decided at last that I didn't want to drown myself, and I went up for air.

They were just jumping in to pull me out. I suppose they had a time limit they would wait before jumping in to pull a kid out from underwater. I guess it *was* two minutes and forty seconds. Little Doug had come up about a minute before me. A cheer went up—I had won one! Were they cheering because I'd won one, or because I hadn't drowned? Anyway, I had found something I could do better than anyone. Hold my breath.

There is a strange figurative parallel to this in the rest of my life. There are a lot of other things I can hold onto without coming up for air for a long, long time. You think I mean something dirty, but really I mean something more like holding onto crummy rat-infested apartments, dysfunctional relationships, nowhere jobs—that sort of thing.

I remember the final event of the meet was a contest between two teams of the boys to wrestle a gigantic floating watermelon away from the other team, a watermelon that had been coated with Crisco. I'm not lying, this really happened.

Picture it: two dozen boys in their Speedos fighting, in a great, writhing clump, to hold onto a huge, lard-covered watermelon, until, wet and covered with grease, one team maneuvers it to their end of the water, finally emerging from the lake oiled, wet, breathless—and in skimpy bathing suits. Who the hell thought up this game?

I remember . . . a lot of the counselors at that camp were seminary students.

ME AND SPORTS

HARRY SCHULZ

One summer evening my father tried teaching me "catch." This only happened once. We took my brother's worn old baseball mitt and we stood in the front yard. He threw the ball to me and I missed it and missed it and missed it. He tried to tell me how to catch it, but I didn't want to hear how—I just wanted to catch it. My father didn't try that again, although I think I tried to persuade him to. As much as I hated dropping that ball, I thought that "catch" was something I ought to be doing with my father. I thought somehow this was a skill I needed as a boy.

In eighth grade I went out for soccer because my best friend Ted did. I had to do everything Ted did and have everything Ted had. When he got a new bicycle, I had to get one just like it; when he decided to learn golf, I took golf lessons; and when he decided to join the soccer team, I joined the soccer team. Little me, who liked to sew and cook and garden—on the soccer team. I particularly remember a game we played on a cold November day. It began to drizzle, then sleet, then snow. Our nylon shorts and jerseys had come out of an old cardboard box from a storage shed and had been softened by years of sweat and mildew. Now they were splattered with icy mud. My hands were raw, red, and stiff with the cold. I was secretly hoping I would get pneumonia, so that I wouldn't have to play for the rest of the year. I wondered what had made me join this team.

The next year, freshman year of high school, I went out for soccer again—junior varsity. Well *Ted* did it, and I was afraid of how it would look if I didn't, what people would think of me. It would have made me a, well, one of the guys who . . . didn't go out for sports. So what if I was the worst on the team, or maybe the second worst, so what? The coach knew that I was, and he had me sit on the sidelines the whole time during games and occasionally threw me in the last two minutes when he knew for sure that we were going to win (I couldn't then lose it for us) or that we were going to lose (I certainly couldn't win it for us).

I went out for junior varsity soccer again my sophomore year. That year we had a substitute coach from another school who had this crazy idea that in high school sports everyone was to be given a chance to play. He made us all work out equally hard (no giving up on the slow guys like me), and I remember him giving me advice on how not to run (I was always rather dramatically sliding down the field in the opposite direction of the action). I also remember he asked us all if we had jock straps and "cups." We had a whole lecture on how important they were. I can remember the knowing laughs from the other guys, elbowing each other in the ribs and smiling. I nodded my head, yes I had one, though that was a lie. I couldn't ask my parents to buy one for me. Neither did I have the courage to sneak down to the drugstore, because I just couldn't bring myself to take that package labeled "athletic supporter" with the drawing or picture of it on the cover, or the one labeled "cup"—which came in *sizes* for god's sake—up to the gray-haired lady behind the pharmacy counter. I was just very lucky that I was never slammed in the groin with a soccer ball, just in the head a few times.

One of the last games that season I was put in the forward

position and nearly scored a goal that would have won us the game at the last minute. I had brief fantasies of my life turning around and my becoming a hero soccer player. But the coach of the varsity soccer team was a real smug little jock, and I knew I would have had no chance with him the next year. He'd put me back in my old place real fast. So . . . the next year I went out for—well, I should say *Ted* went out for, and then you'd know: Ted went out for cross country.

This is a grueling sport, long distance running. We began training a month before school started. I had never done anything like this. The coach was a real motivator. He would drive alongside us as we ran down the country roads; while we wheezed and dragged our feet, he would exhort us to keep going, scolding us if we stopped. It is an endurance sport, and you'd think that I would know something about endurance, being a little gay boy.

But this was beyond all my experience. By the time we got to our first trial meet in mid-September, I was in pain.

I don't know to this day whether it was real or psychosomatic, but I ended up in a doctor's office getting x-rayed. I tried to be slightly dramatic about it all, affected a slight limp but kept a stiff upper lip, put a brave face on it. I was desperate for someone to tell me to quit, to stop running, but no one did, and rather than face the embarrassment of quitting, of being one of the guys who . . . *you* know—I rejoined the team halfway through the season and began running races.

Three and a half miles. I remember that number. My first race I pushed myself to make it all the way—couldn't bear the thought of dropping out. I came in last. But as I made it to the finish line, I remember my history teacher, Dr. Farrell, cheering me on from the sidelines, and I have to say it felt good. I had really pushed myself and I had accomplished something.

I kept running in races after that, and at each one I did a

little better. Third from last, fifth from last, ahead of the last twelve people. I was getting better. This was something new to me. I sensed that I had the potential to actually be good at a sport. But the season was drawing to a close.

It was the last race, one of those clear, crisp autumn days. Teams from every school in the county seemed to be there. We started out in the usual pack, the starting pistol snapped, everyone was jockeying for position and I was trying to pace myself so I wouldn't wear out. It was a windy, hilly, wooded track, sometimes slippery, sometimes rocky. About halfway through, I got my second wind and started sailing. I was passing guys left and right. Me!

And that's when I caught up to Ted.

Now Ted, my longtime best friend, was known for being one of the fastest guys in the school, but he had developed a cramp, and it was slowing him down as he tried to work it out, and he asked me to stay with him. He asked me not to run past him. I have since wondered why, wondered if he just would have felt embarrassed to be passed by me, the guy who had always been last on the team, the guy who wasn't a jock, who was one of the guys who. . . . But I don't really know to this day. I do know that I stayed with him and that we crossed the finish line together. There was some joking about that later, about how queer it was.

Nineteen years later, I found myself living around the corner from Ted in Greenwich Village. We became best friends again, saw each other every day. We talked about old times, our parents, the boys we had crushes on in high school. He was gay, too. An old friend of mine from college, whom I had talked to about Ted, though he had never met him, said to me recently, "Oh, you were always in love with Ted." But now that I think of this story of the cross country race, it seems to me that *that* was not my . . . motivation. Oh, maybe I was in love with Ted then. And it's true, I'm willing to hold myself back when I'm in love. But *I* think it was something about my being gay that made me stay back in the race, just as I think it was something about *his* being gay that made him ask me to.

Twenty-one years ago I could have sailed past him and done my best time, but at that moment I knew already that I didn't have to do it, and I guess I didn't think that I had anything to prove to anyone else. And you see, I would have sailed ahead alone, and I don't want to be alone. I'm afraid of being alone even though it seems to me—living in the isolation that so many of us gay children experience—that really I have been alone most of my life. Maybe that's it. Or maybe I was somehow invested in being second-to-last. After all, it's not a very *visible* position.

THERE WAS THIS GUY

MAYBE THEN

TOM LEDCKE

I'm always looking out the windows. I have plenty of time while Ma sleeps off just another little glass of Rhine wine. I flit from window to window checking out the world, afraid of missing some cute boy pass by or the greasers kissing and almost fucking in the park next to our house.

At sixteen I only fantasize about sex. I collect underwear ads from the JC Penney catalog, and jerk off countless times a day to James Brolin from *Marcus Welby, M.D.* or a tattered Mark Spitz poster I found in the trash. One time Burt Reynolds was on *Dick Cavett* showing his *Cosmopolitan* centerfold, and *TV Guide* promised they would show everything. I was so nervous and jittery while watching the show that I kept one hand on the dial the whole time, ready to change it, just in case Ma came stumbling in. When they actually gave a little glimpse of the centerfold I nearly fainted.

We live on the South Side of Chicago in a two-story square box with two additions tacked onto the back. Our house has two bathrooms, two bedrooms, and two kitchens. We have two kitchens because Ma decided that she was tired of walking upstairs, so instead of moving her bed downstairs, she added another kitchen upstairs next to her room. I sleep in the TV room, lulled to sleep by Merv Griffin and Jack Paar.

The good thing about the house is that every room supplies a different vantage point for my spying. The window in the family room lets me spy on the greasers, and the windows on the other side of the house look over the Kaczmareks's backyard. Soon after moving in, our new neighbors leveled all the trees, tulip beds, and grass for a wasteland of cement to park their boat, cars, and pool. They also put this big boulder in the front lawn. My mother says, "They got a lot of taste, too bad it's all in their mouth." One time the Kaczmareks went on vacation and had their gorgeous cousin take care of the house and clean the pool. He was older, maybe twenty-one. This guy's real big and tall, with the widest shoulders I've ever seen. He has short, dark blond hair. I think he has blue eyes, but I can't see that far. He's always caressing his tight stomach, like he just can't believe how good it feels. That makes me nuts. He does his chores and lifts weights in a little red bathing suit. I watch his every move as I dance from window to window like a trapped bird; he waters the cement, and lays in the sun, occasionally brushing that big bulge—sometimes he squeezes it. This usually forces a squeal out of me, then Ma calls out from her room.

MA: Tom . . . Tom . . . what are ya doing?

TOM: Nothing . . .

MA: You can't be doing nothin'.

TOM: Watching TV . . .

MA: What are ya doing in the house on a beautiful day like this for? You should be out playin'. . . .

TOM: Playin' what?

MA: How the hell am I suppose to know. Plantin' somethin' or cuttin' the grass, doin' somethin' outside.

TOM: I don't want to do anything outside.

MA: Hell with you then. (The snoring continues. . . .)

TOM: *Hey . . . she's sleeping, let's go to the window. . . . There he is, oh god look at that big perfect Polack ass of his. Bend over for me. . . . I want to touch you all over, and have you lay on top of me. I can feel that hairy belly brush up against my face . . .*

MA: Tom . . . Tom . . .

TOM: WHAT!! *Go to sleep goddamn you.* (The snoring continues.)

My arm gets numb holding the curtain for so long. Ma sleeps most of the time, wrestling with every breath. (Snoring sounds.)

You are the most beautiful man I've ever seen. My heart is beating so fast I'm dizzy. I want to be with you forever. My god he's getting up. . . . Yeah, he's rubbing his chest like he really likes himself. I run to the kitchen window to see the front of him. *I think he's going inside. Now I'll creep past Ma.* (Snoring) *I've got to be really quiet . . . I'm at her bedroom window. He's opening the door and going in the house . . . he's gone. There he is, right across the way. Now he's going in the bathroom just looking in the mirror, rubbing that flat belly.* My body is vibrating so bad, I gotta hold my head against the windowsill so I can see. *Oh my god . . . oh my god, he's taking his bathing suit down, past that beautiful butt, those big thighs, I'd do anything for you, thank you God, thank you God, please make him turn around, please! I'll do anything, go to church every morning if you do. He's starting to turn.* (Loud snoring.)

MA: TOM!!!

I'm silent, frozen (snoring). I glance back at his window, he's gone. Ma starts muttering.

MA: What the hell are ya doin'?

I think fast.

TOM: Hey, you know what the Kaczmareks did? They planted weeds next to that big boulder they put in their front lawn. They're nuts, huh?

MA: Oh, nothin' they do would surprise me. They ruined that damn house.

TOM: Yeah.

Later that night as we ate our TV dinners—

MA: Sorry I was so sleepy today, I just couldn't get up. I had the nuttiest dream though. All I can remember is you were little again. Marge was living here. I guess before she married Don. Daddy was in the backyard with Jimmy and Dave. Kathy was looking at a leaf, like it was the greatest thing. Betsy was holdin' you, and I was just lookin' out the downstairs kitchen window. I'm callin' and callin', but nobody turns around. Do you have your homework done?

I remind her, it's July.

MA: Oh. Maybe when we get back from lookin' at rugs we could watch Merv, 'cause I think Totie Fields is on. She's good for a laugh, huh?

I don't answer, I just think about tomorrow. When maybe then—he'll turn around.

CIGARETTE BUTTS & CHEAP COLOGNE

DAVID FERGUSON

DAVID FERGUSON, *as a member of Queer Stories for Boys, has presented his work at Dixon Place, Solo Arts, HERE Theater, and the Lesbian and Gay Community Center. For his day job, he is a psychotherapist and founder and coordinator of a GLBT therapy unit at a Manhattan mental health clinic. He lives in New York City.*

When other kids asked me what my father did for a living, I'd tell them he was in the television industry. Actually, he installed TV antennas. He'd climb the roofs of apartment buildings, two-family houses, split-levels, and colonials, and bring the perfect pre-cable picture to families in Queens and the Five Towns. His ulcers would constantly flare up as he spent hours with housewives who "got ghosts on *The Guiding Light.*" My father needed company on those long, lonely trips. Neil started working as his assistant and, in a very short time, threw our little family into turmoil.

Neil was about twenty-five, six foot three, lanky, and slightly cross-eyed in a little boy kind of way. He wore green Wranglers that fit just right on his butt, a tool belt strapped across his waist, and, like my father, he had the rough hands and dirty fingernails of men who worked out of doors. He wore cheap cologne, chain-smoked, and drank too much beer. Every day after work, Neil would come home with my father and plop his skinny ass on the couch, stretch out his long legs, and drink and smoke. At first, he'd stay only a half hour and complain that he had to get back to "the old lady," otherwise known as Judy, his wife. Judy was overweight, with a butch DA haircut which was a little outré back then on Long Island. She also chain-smoked and kept her cigarettes rolled up in her sleeve. Housekeeping was an art that eluded her, and their apartment looked like the aftermath of an all-night poker game. She spent her days listening to baseball on a transistor radio or lying on her bed with the blinds closed, warding off the ever-approaching migraine headache. They had three kids, ages two to five, who expressed their creativity by making food designs on the wall. Their daughter, Bonnie Sue Parker, was named after the gun moll in *Bonnie and Clyde.*

So, Neil was never too eager to get home, and that half-hour eventually stretched into half the evening. My mother was not too keen on Neil. She didn't like the dirty clothes and cigarettes, and took great exception to his nightly visits. He'd be in the living room on his fifth beer, while we ate in the dining room. My mother quietly smoldered. On occasion I would hear strangled conversations coming from the kitchen.

"Bill, how long is he going to sit in there, he's got a wife and kids to go home to."

"I'm not going to kick him out of my house, he's a guest."

"He's taking advantage of you."

"That's your problem, Shirley, you can't get along with people."

"You're never on my side. You never stand up for me!"

I, on the other hand, couldn't have been happier with Neil's extended stays. I never got tired of looking at his legs seductively stretched out, as I angled for the best view of his crotch or waited for his frequent forays to the bathroom, so that I could hear the sound of his pissing, hoping that somehow he might forget to close the door. As soon as my father's truck pulled up into the driveway, I would run downstairs and try to look nonchalant as I waited for Neil to come into the living room. I would listen with rapt attention to Neil's story about how some woman in Queens got all snooty just because he had tracked mud on her stupid white shag carpet. The content of some of these stories eluded me, as I tried to get as close to Neil as possible without seeming too obvious. I got all heated up, dizzily inhaling the cigarette smoke and beer on his breath. I always thought that my father got a little suspicious of my intense focus on Neil's stories. He started getting competitive. He dragged out his old tales recounting the shenanigans of fellow merchant marines, Bingly Bob and Dutch, or characters on his old crew in Levittown, like his foreman Carmine DiRossi who, in spite of having only one arm, could saw two-by-fours like a bitch in heat.

As Neil and my father vied for my attention, I was Scarlett O'Hara on the porch of Tara with the Tarleton twins. I laughed coquettishly in all the right places, which only egged them on. My little brother would get into the act by hauling out his baseball card collection, trying to entice us into a trading match. While the men yucked it up in the living room, my mother banged the pots and pans around in the kitchen. I often wondered if she subliminally sensed my infatuation, and this only fueled her fury. She and Neil were locked in a pitched battle for the affections of the Ferguson men and the score was Neil 3, Shirley 0.

One had to give my mother credit—she never gave up. She developed brilliant strategies to express her disapproval of Neil. She took to nighttime vacuuming, which of course drowned out any conversation. She'd vacuum around his legs, never asking him to move them and he never volunteering. She'd vigorously spray the room with air freshener or turn the television on full volume. Neil's greatest triumph was that he never took a hint. He behaved with my mother as if she were as gracious as Dinah Shore, completely oblivious to her icy, open hostility. My mother's greatest triumph was that after a while she managed never to speak to Neil, and during the entire time he worked for my father, she never invited him for dinner. We ate while he sat in the dark.

I mooned over Neil during the school day. I loped through the school corridors wishing to be invisible. If I were invisible, my thinking went, I could cozy up to Neil at night and kiss him on the lips, or I could actually get behind that closed door when he went for his piss. Instead I had to content myself with the little bits and pieces I could get. One day after school, I found Neil's beat-up Plymouth parked in front of the house, unlocked. I got into it and almost swooned as I was overcome with his odors, the stale cigarette smoke and cheap cologne. In the ashtray, I found the butts of his cigarettes and put one to my mouth. I felt weak with desire. I had transgressed a boundary and was in intimate contact with him. I found a new high and would rush home from school in order to get my fix. One night, after Neil had left, with my mother in the kitchen and my father taking a bath, I found a cigarette in the ashtray that Neil had just smoked. When I put it to my lips, it was still wet with his saliva. I almost came in my pants. I began saving his butts in my drawer, for those times when his car was gone and the butts in the ashtray had been thrown away.

In spite of my intense aversion to sports, I once persuaded Neil to play one-on-one basketball in the backyard. It was hot and he took his shirt off, exposing his sleek, hairy chest. It was the first and last basketball game I ever enjoyed. I grabbed for the ball through his spread legs, I jumped his bare back to keep him from making a basket, and passionately embraced him when I made one. My mother looked out the window and gaped in shock and wonder: her sissy son was playing ball!

As the months passed, my mother changed her strategy. She'd bribe my brother with baseball cards if he'd just stop asking Neil all those sports questions. Night after night she'd cry to me how she felt that her home was no longer hers and how inconsiderate and messy that man was. My mother had undue influence on me, in spite of all my efforts to resist her, and I was a sucker for her tears. She eventually won the war. Before I knew it, I'd decided Neil's cologne was overpowering, his breath stale from cigarette smoke, and those Wrangler jeans badly in need of a washing. I dumped the butts from my drawer and gave it a good scrubbing.

Neil and his family eventually moved to Orange County, California. My father went back to working by himself and never had another partner. His ulcers got worse. Dinnertime went back to normal, my father sniping at my mother and telling how her cooking was making him sick, while my brother and I sank into our chairs trying to disappear. The living room was too empty without the haze of smoke and the smell of that wonderful cheap cologne.

CON

RICH KIAMCO

RICH KIAMCO was featured on Queer Eye For The Straight Guy *teaching a straight guy Thai massage. He won the Overall Excellence Award at the 2004 New York International Fringe Festival for his solo show,* UNACCESSORIZED. *Rich has performed with comedian Judy Tenuta in Las Vegas, on* The Howard Stern Show, *and nationwide as her love slave/go-go dancer/drag sidekick. He has also performed and facilitated workshops with Peeling, an Asian American performance collective based in New York City. An excerpt of his writing can be found in* Take Out: Queer Writing From Asian Pacific America, *Temple University Press. Go to: www.richkiamco.com*

It was spring 1982, when Spandau Ballet's "True" and Human League's "Don't You Want Me" were on the radio, and Tim O'Connor was on my mind. He was my classmate in gym and science at Blackhawk Junior High School where the cheerleaders had become the butt of jokes from their new "B-J-H-S you RAH! RAH! RAH!" cheer. BJHS—Blow Job High School, I wish. Tim was a muscular dirty blond man/boy. The first I saw with pubic hair! Then again, this was his third year of eighth grade.

We were all required by state law to take showers at least two times a week or we would fail gym class. I was a super-mega overachiever with a menacing GPA, and the thought of getting less than beyond perfect, med school–caliber grades was slightly scarier than being naked in front of a bunch of other boys.

I was always more than willing to help in the towel booth. It strategically overlooked the group shower, like a trailer hotdog vendor stand with counter bar and flip-top side entrance. Tim would usually be the one to go in and hit the showers first. I was terrified, but at least if I had a helper role with towels I could cloak my pubescent homoerotic curiosity with a task.

"CON!" Coach Theole called. Our gym teacher wore white Adidas gym shoes and black Sansabelt slacks with a white polo. The fabric clung to his torso and pledged his allegiance to the abs. He was like a playful sergeant with clipboard and whistle calling out our names over the din—last names only—in manly nicknames. O'Connor became *Con,* Jackobowski became *Jako,* and my name, Kiamco, became *Kamoke.* He'd call out and check off after each boy called back to confirm that he indeed had taken a shower.

"Showering, sir!" Tim yelled back as I tossed a towel to him.

Tim's pubes were a bit darker than his "outdoor" dirty blonde. He'd smile at me after taking the towel and drying himself. He'd look back and laugh, and I'd choke, lose my breath, and get dizzy as I walked past to take my shower. He was a wrestler with smooth, milky musculature, and a bit taller and much beefier than I was—the Filipino A++ in all academics and sewing class. There was a silent scream of delight and terror in my penile espionage. I had certainly masturbated to mental images of Tim, but the real deal in front of me was just blinding. I was paranoid about being discovered, and would force myself through an ocular labyrinth; looking only at the towel, the floor, the wall, the locker, the dial, the underwear, the socks, the jeans, the shirt, the buttons, the belt. All the while taking lightning-flash glances around on a homoerotic reconnaissance mission, gathering stolen locker room mental snapshots to be reassembled into a map of pubescent penises back in my bedroom headquarters.

I'd roll up my gym shorts and shirt into a tube, like a nice cotton jersey uncut phallus. Then plop the flaccid shaft on my science book wrapped in a Marshall Field's shopping bag and my Trapper Keeper, and sling them all on my right hip. I'd then check my hair in the mirror, and see that the cuffs of my jeans were casually breaking over my white canvas Nikes with their powder blue swoosh.

Tim's looks were inversely proportionate to his intelligence and, well, the brains didn't matter, as I was the super-mega overachiever and the sole reason Tim was passing science class. I was wise enough to allow him to copy only a few multiple-choice answers, so he would pass but not get 100 plus the extra credit questions. That would be too obvious, as perhaps was my crush. As the bell sounded, he exited the locker room wearing the BJHS gym shirt that was reversible, with pine on the outside and dirty yellow inside.

A lip of the dirty yellow peeked from under the hem, kissing the rear pockets of Tim's tight, cream painter's pants. The contrast stitching at the crotch made a nice curve as he lumbered along the hall. I walked alongside in my powder blue cowboy shirt that matched the stitching on my designer jeans. Fierce style, but tragically, the jeans were too long in the rise for my four-foot, eight-inch, twelve-year-old frame. The waistband would have tied at my rib cage if not for the powder blue web belt sealing it along the edge of my pelvis, forming a slightly deflated bubble-butt. I would practice postures in the mirror at home when no one was around, imitating the Brook Shields "Nothing comes between me and my Calvin's" pose. I'd bend over with hand on my hip, twisting and straining in contortion to push my right butt cheek out till it pressed against the longhorn embroidery on the pocket. I looked like a pole holding up a circus tent. Jeans: Sergio Valente; Pose: Barnum & Bailey.

The period bell rings, and Tim and I take our assigned seats: a shared black lab desk four rows back, far left. The room is buzzing with the basics: laughing, screaming, spitballs, and combs feathering hair. As a few notes are being tossed across the room, an abnormal amount of rowdiness swells, and Mr. Gau, our science teacher, enters with his slow, giraffe-like amble, befuddled by the chaos. A burgundy necktie gags his white dress shirt. Its clip only reaches half of its width, while his houndstooth poly slacks reach back to 1967. His lips move, but not a sound can be heard over the din. Tim twists his torso to face me, the pouch of his pants still plump with his boy/manhood etched in the microfiche of my mind. Mr. Gau hollers with cupped hands over his mouth, "THE NEXT PERSON TO SPEAK GETS A DETENTION!" as Tim simultaneously says to me, "You wanna suck me?"

The tsunami of teens is silenced by Gau's caveat, as, for the first time, I stare into another boy's eyes. His soft blue irises have the weight of a much darker secret. My lungs freeze and I can't speak. I want to scream, yelp, or cheer, "B-J-H-S you RAH! RAH! RAH!" At this point, I don't even know what a blow job is, but I am willing to do all the homework to find out. Yet all that emerges is a creak in my throat, lust squelched by potential detention hall.

Einstein postulated that on the edge of a black hole, time stands still and the path of light bends. "Kamoke's theory" states that at this edge, all of life's lost moments replay in syndicated repeat. Mr. Gau begins teaching a new lesson, his words blur as I swim through my mental microfiche: aerial shot of Tim's zipper with contours that my hands itched to trace.

The school bell rings and I am numb—in a traffic jam of desires. My heart is revving. My lips are bumper to bumper. My groin is gridlock. Tim disappears into the blur of escaping students: letterman jackets, upturned polo collars, and miniskirts with coordinating leg warmers. I'm left tailgating Sheila Shea, with her brunette feathered hair teased out over the puffy sleeves of her teal/purple horizontal stripe boat neck with inverted rear box pleat. Not a word of the "wanna suck me?" incident was ever exchanged with Tim. Maybe I created the entire scenario in my mind. Maybe my International Male catalog dream sequences had impaired my perceptions of reality.

Maybe I was just horny.

Somewhere between a week and eternity later, Tim asked me, "Wanna come over to my house and play?"

"YES!" I blurt, leaping up and down inside in a Publishers Clearing House frenzy. I manage to get my mom to call his mom for permission and all the "who is gonna pick me up and where" details. Tim and I lived in different worlds: he was a "walker" and I was a "busser." The border between Bensenville and Wood Dale was Route 83/Kingery Highway/Busse Road depending on what part of Illinois you were in. This asphalt canyon split the original township, where the grade school was called Tioga after the Indians. There is something eerie about naming a school after the Indian tribe that was slaughtered there. I technically lived closer to school than Tim, but the highway made busing a necessity.

The last school bell rings, and my anticipation gallops out of the school gates. I scan his V-shaped torso, braced in a cream long-sleeve thermal T-shirt, as the shirt tied around his waist inflates into a flannel hang glider in the breeze. He jumps to touch a branch, and I am blinded by the sunbeams stabbing between the leaves. Walnut Street is lined with towering trees and rows of modest homes drifting by his pushed-up sleeves and downy forearm hairs. His neighborhood streets were all grids while mine were cul-de-sacs and curves. He had pubes and I had hunger.

"Which number is your house?" I asked, as if waiting to rip open the invisible ribbon wrapped around this moment.

"Number 165," he says as his golden locks float above his soft irises. I note that the mailbox with the separate *Chicago Tribune* plastic box underneath has number 157 on it, and the next one has number 161. I deduce that this block has intervals of four and that the next box would be—SLAM! A sharp bite of pain impales my left eye.

"MONKEY BOY!" proclaims a high-pitched voice, as a throbbing mass of tears pours out my eye. Silver sparkles swim around me.

"Tammy! Cut it out!" Tim barks.

Tammy, perhaps five or six years old, in dirt-stained, elastic-waist pants and butterfly-embroidered knit top, squeals with drools of saliva. The tomboyish sprite preps another projectile of unknown materials, from what I can discern with my one remaining eye.

"MONKEY BOY! MONKEY BOY!!"

"MOM! Make Tammy stop!" Tim suddenly is just another kid (with darker pubes than his locks would indicate).

"Tammy, you be nice to Tim's friend!" she warns.

"MONKEY BOY!!!!!" the child blurts in a frothing salivary frenzy. She is fearless, unstoppable. She is kiddie Kryptonite killing my Superman.

"Let's go upstairs to my bedroom," mutters Tim in disgust.

Tim's mom has disappeared into the kitchen, with *The Price Is Right* blaring on the TV. The olefin shag carpet runner wilts over the edges of each step, disappearing up into the dark hall. At the top, a crack of light pours open, revealing a dormer window poking out of the sloped walls/ceilings, beige industrial carpeting, and Tim's hand reaching over to the closet door. The pounding in my chest makes my temples ache and ears get hot. I get a tremor shake in my leg when I see the ratty blanket on his twin bed.

"MONKEY BOY!!!" The screeching nemesis springs from the dark hallway and skips around the room. I pray for her to hit her head on a beam and hemorrhage into silence, but alas, she continues to chirp about, as I stumble down another level of Dante's suburban inferno. I lean against the beam and gaze out the window at the rope swing hanging from the walnut tree. Blow Job Junior High School . . . I wish. Time crawls when you can't murder a five-year-old. The gravel driveway crackles as my dad's emerald green '76 Mercury Monarch with white sedan cap, pulls up. Defeated, I crawl into the car, as Tammy bounces in the living-room window like a frog grabbing at the glass with its webbed feet, her mouth shaping the two words that I know will be waiting for me at the edge of that black hole.

It is 1990 and I am home for spring break from New York City in my third year at the Fashion Institute. If the '80s had its own Ivy League school it would be called Milli Vanilliversity and I'd be the grad student sporting my ivory and black, houndstooth, shoulder-padded blazer with black and white polka-dot ascot. Paula Abdul's "Straight Up" blaring on the radio of my dad's dove gray and white Pontiac Phoenix hatchback, I drive down Wood Dale Road past the three churches of our town: Holy Ghost, United Methodist, and Calgary Lutheran. Only the Methodist church looks like a church with steeple and such; the other two look like some '70s Howard Johnson's space needle piercing a stack of stained glass ecclesiastic pancakes. There's construction on the ditches along the left side of the street where I am signaling to turn. A fat construction worker with sleeveless flannel shirt holds an orange SLOW sign and points as I yield to oncoming traffic. The clicking of the turn signal synchronizes with the beat of the music as I spot a hot, shirtless, muscle-bound beast of a man, digging. Too much blood is rushing out of my skull and into my loins as my left hand fumbles with the wheel.

"HEY!" the fat flannel guy hollers and I clumsily lurch over the double yellow lines to turn into Montrose Avenue. The shirtless beast turns in anticipation of my fender. His startled snap of the head turns to curiosity when he sees my sheepish grin. His frame is rippled and glossed with sweat and crowned with sun-bleached blond hair. He regains his balance and we catch each other's stare.

"Con! . . . Er, Tim!" I yelp, with a dry crackle.

"RICH!" Tim's blues ignite and he plunges his shovel into the clay and runs to my car as I circle into the Calgary Lutheran parking lot. I press the sliding window button as Tim's torso fills my view. He throws both hands on the roof and leans his head down to reveal the trademark pout of lips that could cushion a 65 mile per hour head-on collision. The front seam of his gym shorts clings to his groin.

"How's New York?" he glimmers, adjusting himself.

"It's huge!" I fumble. "I'm great, you look bigger—taller. Great!" I want to just jump and turn my pants inside out.

"You too." His lips curl into a smirk. His sweaty flesh emits a soiled musk. My left eyelid starts to flicker, and I gracefully rub my eye so as not to miss a single second of this apparition.

"HEY O'CONNOR!" barks fat flannel, "BACK TO WORK."

"SIR!" Tim nods as he turns back to me, "Great to see you, I gotta—"

"Yeah, um," I wave as he walks off with his bulging calves flexing in synch to Paula's synthetic "oh oh oh," his strut leaving me to fade like moussed hair into the '90s.

NOT A SIGN OF CHRISTMAS

Derek Gullino

One Christmas I was so fucking horny I did something really wrong, something I will never live down because it was so sick. I went out past the Claremont Mall to a porno theater called The Adobe Video.

I parked in back of the next door apartment court, so if anybody drove by, they couldn't see my car. My family's always driving by, and Southern California's nothing but a goddamn small town. One time I got caught cruising the toilet at the mall, and the next day two of my brothers knew about it. I did not want ANYBODY to see me.

But it didn't matter. Because it was Christmas, and Sunday too. Jesus. Who fucking cared? No one was in The Adobe Video anyway. The whole fucking place was empty.

There were some upcoming attractions on the wall, shit like that, pictures of dicks, and I stood there and looked at them and got so goddamn horny and so lonely all at the same time. I poured myself a free orange soda and it was warm. There wasn't even any ice. I asked myself, *Why are you always hanging out in miserable shit holes like this? There's no fucking ice! There's no one fucking here!*

I was about ready to leave and head on over to my grandma's for Christmas, when this marine came out of the bathroom and said, "Ho! Ho! Ho!" I could tell he was a Marine because he had a *semper fidelis* or whatever tattoo on his forearm. If you close your eyes and think *MARINE,* you'll see this fucking guy. Nothing strange about him. Nothing kinky. Nothing written on his face.

I flashed him the peace sign. "Ho!"

He had a brush-type moustache and a white pickup. I followed him down the street to the Upland Poolsider. Very residential. Every apartment faced the pool. The remains of Christmas Eve littered the hot tub and the community deck. The chairs were overturned. The Marine showed me where to park, and then I followed him into his apartment.

Beer bottles were everywhere. I hadn't had a drink all day. I'd smoked a joint right after my parents had left for church, but I needed something to mellow it out. "Can I have a beer?"

He pulled a warm Coors from the fridge and tossed it to me.

I lit a cigarette. "You a Marine?"

"Was. I've been trying to be a porn star ever since I got out. No luck. I'm changing to construction." With that, he reached over, unzipped my pants, and starting sucking my dick. After that, he turned around and told me to fuck him.

I looked around his apartment. There was not a sign of Christmas, there was not a sign of life anywhere. Bedsheets covered the windows. I noticed a strange odor as I fucked him.

And I got a little lonelier because of it, I think. And I seemed a lot less horny. And then I hit rock bottom. The Marine had a German Shepherd and I didn't know it and it came out of the back bedroom and started licking my ass. I thought I was going to fucking pass out. That dog started rimming my asshole.

"Git!" I smacked at his face with my free hand.

The German Shepherd growled as it licked into me. So I stopped worrying about it, and liked it. It felt really good. I'm sure that dog was trained because mine was not the first ass it had licked. It was curling up its tongue and getting inside me. As soon as I came, he stopped licking, turned around, and went back into the bedroom.

"Some dog you got there," I said to the Marine.

The Marine nodded. "I thought you'd like that."

I did. It was sick of me, too.

ONLY CONNECT

TEDDY

NEIL JAMES

It's the exact same speech every time. "Ladies and gentlemen, my name is Teddy. I *am* with the Bergen/Lafayette County Coalition for Feed the Homeless Shelters. We're riding the trains tonight to collect money for the homeless children and families. The money goes toward bread, soup, juice for our shelter. Anyone can become homeless. You could lose your job. You could have an accident. You could have a nervous breakdown! Anyone could become homeless. We're only asking for some change to help feed the homeless children and families at our shelter."

Teddy is a small black man with wise, soulful eyes and a worn face. He has no teeth, but smiles nonetheless at each person as he implores their charity. Teddy goes past the commuters, and a few of them hand him dollars or whatever spare change they have in their pockets. He thanks each one with a sincere, heartfelt, "God bless you, thank you kindly." And he continues to the next car.

Teddy is one of my favorite subway celebrities here in New York City. Another one, Bible Man, is a chubby, middle-aged man of Indonesian descent. He's always neatly dressed. He appeals to his brothers and sisters to confess their sins to a punishing God, who will smite the ones who haven't confessed and save those who have. I appreciate his vitriol.

Another angry one is Mr. Misogynisto. He's a very cranky black man who annoys the Madison Avenue platform at Fifty-third Street. Every afternoon, he preaches the sins not of mankind, but more specifically of womankind. Telling the male commuters that "Woman is a beast!" Or putting a topical spin on it, "Woman is Al-Qaeda!"

There's Bracelet Momma. She's Korean, I believe, and walks the trains in the mornings, selling beaded necklaces and bracelets with her toddler daughters in tow, also selling baubles. The two youngsters work that subway like pros, all giant brown eyes batting and selling turquoise left and right.

Most recently I've begun watching Waves. He's an ancient, potbellied man. Waves keeps his cane squarely between his legs, propping his hunched back, and simply waves at each conductor who rattles by. One conductor, a very pretty young lady with caramel skin and tight, dark braids, blew him a kiss as though she knew him. He beamed like sunshine.

Living in the big city, you can't help but notice the unspoken body language in regards to the homeless or the kooky. Most commuters will slip an occasional dollar, but for the most part remain silent and avoid eye contact with the less fortunate. I too avert my eyes, only to see myself as a hypocrite, because once a back is turned, my eyes follow like magnets, noting specific details, characterizing these people's dress and mannerisms.

As a kid I had a fascination with the homeless, although in Cedartown, Georgia, they were called hobos. With my little cloth sack and stick slung over my shoulder, my not-too-dirty corduroys with colorful patches sewn up and down the legs, a plaid cap, and charcoal stubble, I imagined riding the rails, going wherever adventure awaited.

One afternoon, I decided to run away from home. I told my mom, and she replied, "Be sure to put calamine lotion on your legs, in case you get into a patch of poison ivy." I took along three pimento-cheese sandwiches and a bag of carrots. I went to the wooded area behind my house and, after eating my sandwiches and planting my carrots, returned home late that afternoon. Living indoors was indeed the right choice for me. And I did catch poison ivy.

Sometimes running away from home can be a good thing. Here in New York, on a hazy Friday night last February, the heavy clouds of introspection, self questioning, and crippling paranoia whispered secrets in my ears. I put on my powder blue Popeye shirt, grabbed my leather coat, and took flight into the early evening.

Every city noise along the way played in my head like a symphony. Idle pedestrian chatter was a chorus, accompanied by the rhythmic beat of a faraway jackhammer. My head was a balloon tied to my shoulders by a string. My left hand idly flipped a shiny quarter.

"Spare some change?" popped me back into this plane.

A man in tattered clothes sat there on a bench. He looked into my eyes, but I pulled mine away. His teeth were chattering, "Spare some change?" I muttered something under my breath about not having any. The lie hovered in front of me. I walked through it. I felt like shit. Why didn't I give him my quarter?

Then I thought of Teddy, the kind man who collects money for the homeless children. *Why have you never given Teddy any money?* I asked myself. *You see him almost three times a week. Well, all that is changing. Tonight, if I see Teddy, I'm going to give him a dollar. Wait, come on, a dollar? I can do better than that. If I see Teddy I'm giving him five dollars.*

Five dollars? You pussy! Give him more.

An angel of charity sat to my left. On my right sat a devilish auctioneer.

If you see Teddy tonight, you are giving him ten dollars to make up for your miserly ways.

Only a ten? OK, IF I SEE TEDDY TONIGHT I'M GIVING HIM TWENTY DOLLARS!

Then reality slapped me in the face. *What the fuck are you doing, Neil?*

But it was too late! If I saw Teddy that night I had to give him a twenty-dollar bill. To go back on that oath would mean terrible consequences for my karma and my general well-being.

And I had summoned Teddy. He would no doubt be there, and I'd have to pay up. I scrutinized each person passing by, both hoping and fearing I'd see Teddy. But he never showed. It was an uneventful ride. I breathed a sigh of relief and ascended onto Christopher Street and the local bear bar, the Dugout.

And what a great night at the Dugout! The joint was packed. By midnight it was shoulder-to-shoulder shirtless, sweaty, hairy men. Guys were dancing to '70s disco in the center of the bar, while couples kissed in the darkened corners. I was in the center, contentedly nursing a beer and idly chatting with friends about who we thought was hot and not.

The night wound on, and at two o'clock I opted out of going to the Eagle. Slouched on the subway platform, I had the single thought, *I'm going to puke on myself.*

As my head spun, a loud girl in a louder red coat was speaking through her Long Island accent to a trio of guys. I mean she was practically screaming, "And then Christy ordered artichokes on her pizza and I was like, 'You bitch! That's what I'm ordering!' " Finally, I could take no more of it. "Oh God, she is so loud." I spoke a little louder than I should have.

I had just made myself a subway celebrity. One of the trio replied, "You need to mind your own business."

I said, "How can I? She's so fucking loud." Now, I don't seek conflict. I swear I don't. Conflict simply happens to find me, often. And I'm usually drunk when it comes.

Then his friend chimed in, "Hey what'd you say? You need to back off."

"You back off. It was a joke. Chill, man."

"No, you're a joke in your powder blue shirt."

How dare he! I stood up.

"Why you standing up, huh? You looking to fight?"

"I don't know. Are you looking to fight?" I cracked my knuckles and tensed my fists. *Was this really going to be a fight? A fight in the subway? With three guys?*

"What's up with you?" I posed the question like a hostage negotiator playing for time.

"What's up with YOU?"

"I don't know. What's UP WITH YOU?"

"I DON'T KNOW. WHAT'S UP WITH YOU?!" Holy shit! I was going to be in a fight, when all of the sudden, out of nowhere—

"Guys, there's no need to fight down here."

I heard the unmistakable voice. It was Teddy! "There's enough fighting going on in this world. You all just settle down. Now what's going on here?"

The third guy offered his defense first, "Hey Teddy, this fucker was talking shit about my girlfriend."

"Oh yeah, which one?!" Unstoppable, I jabbed my finger toward his two friends. I prayed for the word "fag" so I'd have a reason to punch someone.

Teddy took me by the arm and led me down the platform. "I'm sure they had a long night, and you have, too. Just relax and let's get on the train, my friend."

I had a million things to tell Teddy. About how I summoned him tonight, and how I have twenty dollars for him, and how I think he's so brave and such a good person. But I stood in drunken silence, wondering how to hand over the money.

We stepped into the crowded train. All the riders looked

greasy and tired from a night out on the city. As Teddy launched into his familiar speech, almost everyone looked away. Not me. When he neared me, I smiled and thanked him. Then I slipped him the twenty-dollar bill—*and* a crisp one-dollar bill. After saving those straight boys from a royal ass-kicking, Teddy deserved a little something extra.

CARL SOLOMON

RONALD GOLD

I met Carl Solomon at Brooklyn College in 1946. I was sixteen and he was four years older. He'd been in the Merchant Marine during the war. And he'd been to *Paris,* where, he said, he'd been winked off by a one-eyed whore. (I assumed this was a joke, but you never knew with Carl.) He'd also discovered the French avant-garde and had brought books back with him that were banned in this country. I wasn't too keen on Henry Miller's *Black Spring* but I was much taken with Genet's *Our Lady of the Flowers.* Like Genet, I was very fond of certain ideas, like lying spoon fashion with young toughs, fucking them and jerking them off the while.

Carl also introduced me to some fascinating people, like the Schneiders, a pale, painfully thin couple who lived in a bug-infested railroad flat on the Lower East Side, and entertained their guests by plucking bugs from the air or the walls, and calmly eating them. Or Marga Ormins (née Orminska) who stole knickknacks from her friends' apartments, then invited us to a party at her place, where all our missing trinkets were prominently displayed.

Carl and I participated in an event that's been written up many times in the literary, political, and psychiatric journals. It was a Trotskyite symposium on Alienation in Modern Literature (lots of people were Trotskyites then, and several hundred showed up). The panelists were Ernest Van den Haag, who later became a right-winger—even more obnoxious than he was then—and Wallace Markfield, who later became a rather celebrated Jewish novelist and still talked through his nose.

Carl sat in about the fourth row center, with a paper container of potato salad in his lap, and I was several rows behind and to the left, shelling peas.

Van den Haag was first, and things went without incident, the people we knew in the audience determinedly not noticing us. Then came Markfield, and as soon as he was finished, Carl's hand shot up. We both knew Markfield personally, and he was surely aware that we weren't his dearest friends, so he scouted about for other questioners. Then only Carl's hand was up, and Wally warily asked, "What's your question?" "One-two-three-four. What do you think of *War and Peace*?" said Carl, simultaneously pitching a fistful of potato salad at Markfield's only suit. I sprang into action, offering shelled peas to one and all.

Complete silence, while Markfield tried to brush off the potato salad. Then he tried to pretend that nothing at all had happened. "Wait a minute," said Carl, "you haven't answered my question." Markfield said, "What question?" and Carl let him have it with another giant glob of potato salad. Markfield just stood there for a few beats, then scraped some of the salad off his suit and tossed it back at Carl. The place emptied out in a flash.

It wasn't too long after that that Carl presented himself at the door of the Psychiatric Institute and demanded entry. Amazingly, they took him in, and decided he was a likely candidate for insulin shock.

After a while, they decided he was okay for afternoon passes into the real world—and I was his chaperone. It was supposed to be his mother, but if you thought Carl was crazy, you should have met his mother. Wild eyes with big, black circles under them; wild hair flying off in all directions. She knew she couldn't handle Carl, and I got the job.

I tried to steer him to the museums or a quiet chat somewhere, but I'd end up scuttling after him to places like Forty-second Street. Carl was about six feet tall, built wide, and bloated from the insulin. He had curly black hair that matched the frames of his thick glasses. And he'd lurch up to a group of uniformed sailors on Forty-second Street, cup his hand, as if to whisper in their ears, and say, very loud, "You want your cock sucked?" We had some narrow escapes. (Later, Carl wrote about those days and referred to me as "an old neurotic friend"—not even a neurotic old friend.)

Psychiatric Institute is where Carl met Allen Ginsberg, and that's how I met Allen and Bill Burroughs and Gregory Corso and Herbert Huncke, and the rest of that crew. When Carl got out of the hospital, I remember some friendly pot-filled evenings with all of them.

But I went off to school in Berkeley; then became a junkie in San Francisco; and when I got back to New York in '53, Carl was back in the hospital (Pilgrim State this time) and Allen was just leaving for San Francisco to take up with the crowd I'd just left. But Burroughs was around. He borrowed forty dollars that, since he's dead, I guess I'll never get back. And he turned me on to a connection who burned me for all my money.

So after I'd tried and failed to repeat Carl's instant acceptance at the Psychiatric Institute, I went off to the Menninger Clinic in Topeka, Kansas, to have my head shrunk. And while I was still in the hospital, about a year later, I came across an issue of *Time* magazine that featured the literary ferment in San Francisco.

Kenneth Rexroth, who'd adopted me into his circle of young geniuses because I'd remembered the name of an obscure Italian painter he'd forgotten, was credited with nurturing the literary boom. Philip Lamantia, a short, slight man with a beautiful face and an enormous head—who'd turned me on to heroin in my room at the Embarcadero YMCA, and later found me a room on his floor at what was known as the Ghost House—was described by *Time* as "tall and handsome." Jack Kerouac, whose stuff I'd read in typescript and thought wouldn't be accepted by any publisher in his right mind, was becoming a celebrity. And Allen had gained instant fame for a long poem titled *Howl (For Carl Solomon),* promoting Carl as one of "the best minds of our generation." *What a time I've picked to be sane,* I thought to myself, *when all my crazy friends are becoming rich and famous.*

When I got back to New York in '59, Carl was *married,* and living in the Bronx. Her name was Olive, and she was a mysterious young woman with big, black eyes and a face the shape and color of an olive. When I'd visit, they'd both sit primly on the edge of their studio couch and say virtually nothing, trying, I think, to seem absolutely normal. He wore his Yankee cap and smoked a lot. She'd get up from the couch from time to time for some dull snacks.

Carl worked editing potboilers for his uncle, a paperback publisher, and despite all the dull normality, he did manage to get his uncle to publish *Junkie* by Bill Lee, a pseudonym for Bill Burroughs, who'd based his title character on a bass player named Wigmo, one of my friends at the San Francisco Ghost House.

I met a few of Carl's new friends, mostly fellow Yankee fans out of *The Honeymooners,* but including an occasional throwback to the old days, like Joe Batchelor, a sort-of black, sort-of gay, sort-of good-looking young man who lived in a shadowy room in Chelsea with two giant snakes—a boa constrictor, and a yellow rat snake whose black tongue never stopped darting in and out. One time, Joe arrived at my place and Lazaro, my very—is it herpetophobic?—mate, answered the door. It was a couple of beats before he noticed that Joe had a snake wrapped around each arm. He keeled over backward like a board.

After a few years, things began to unravel for Carl and Olive. One day she just disappeared, and not much later, Carl was back at Pilgrim State. From there he sent me a three-line review of *Howl,* signed with his nom de psychosis, Carl Goy. (I kept it, thinking it might someday be worth something, and eventually I sent it off to Allen, who told me he'd given it to some keeper of the archives.)

In the '70s, they perfected those antipsychotic drugs, and so many mental patients were released, including Carl. Armed with the "tranks" he took every day for the rest of his life, Carl was back among us.

Once a month or so, he'd give me a call and invite himself over. He was never without his Yankee cap. He never stopped smoking. He didn't stay long; absolutely ignored my dog and the cats, and never said more than a polite hello to Luis during the fifteen years that Luis and I were together. So far as I could figure out, Carl spent his time going to Yankee games, talking it up with the neighbors and, very occasionally, being trotted out for a Beat Generation seminar at some university. It was Allen who made sure he was invited, and it was Allen who managed the publication of Carl's book, stitched together from scraps he'd written over the years, including the "old neurotic friend" bit.

I went to the book-launching ceremony at a Village bookstore. Everyone I hadn't socialized with in nearly fifty years was there, including Gregory Corso, who seemed rhapsodically happy to see me (or was he out-of-his-mind drunk?) The book didn't get many reviews, but Carl took an embarrassed pride in it, especially with his buddies from the Bronx.

Usually, I didn't see him or think much about him between monthly visits—except when I'd get a frantic phone call from Rod Carroll, complaining that Carl had insulted him grievously once again.

Rod Carroll is a Brooklyn schoolteacher it's impossible to think of as black (even though he is) since he's exactly like all the other nasal, neurotic Jewish boys we knew back in the old days at Brooklyn College. He lives almost entirely in the past, and he befriended Carl for old times' sake. They talked regularly on the phone and, regularly, one of them would accuse the other of accusing *him* of something. They'd scream at each other, then Rod would call me, and I'd try to calm him down. Eventually, they'd resume their friendship, and so it went, for years on end.

One day, Carl called to say that his emphysema was worse and he wouldn't be coming that day. Two weeks later, somebody I didn't know called to say that Carl was dead, and he gave me the time and place of the funeral.

I don't go to funerals unless there's someone who needs me to be there, so I didn't go to Carl's. But two months later, somebody else I didn't know called to tell me there'd be a memorial service for Carl at St. Mark's Church. Since this is directly across the street from my house, and I figured I'd see Allen and the rest, I decided to go.

When I arrived I encountered two young people at a table. "Five dollars please," they said and, in a daze, I handed it over. Inside, the church was absolutely mobbed with young post-beatniks, who'd come, they said, to hear Allen read *Howl (For Carl Solomon)* aloud, for the first time in many years. I turned around, ran to the table, and demanded my five dollars back. They gave it to me, and I went home.

SAYING GOODBYE TO HOWARD

DENNIS GREEN

DENNIS GREEN *arrived in New York City circa 1973 and spent the better part of the next twenty years writing lyrics for musical plays, many of which were produced Off- and Off-Off Broadway or in regional productions in the United States and Canada. Since 1991, he has been working as an administrator at Columbia University. Does he translate French poetry? Yes.*

Among the first of my personal friends to contract AIDS and die from its ravages—near the start of the epidemic and long before life-prolonging "cocktails" were an option—was a promising young director named Stuart White. I knew Stuart as the partner of Howard Ashman, whom I had met in the mid-'70s, shortly after arriving in New York City with dreams of conquering the Great White Way. Howard was a lavishly gifted man who, like so many others, would be taken from the world just as his creative powers were beginning to peak. After the huge success of *Little Shop of Horrors,* for which he provided book, lyrics, and direction (Alan Menken wrote the brilliantly evocative score), we were in less frequent contact as his career took off and mine more or less fizzled out.

We arranged to meet for a long overdue reunion shortly after the release of the film version of *Little Shop,* by which time he was working for Disney on *The Little Mermaid.* He was warm and funny as always, and only slightly bitter about the critical reception of his failed Broadway effort with Marvin Hamlisch, *Smile.* While he did not look unhealthy, he exuded an air of melancholy, and the evening was spent mostly revisiting events and people from earlier times: our own project's staged reading at the old Ballroom cabaret on East Broadway; his tenure as artistic director of the WPA Theater; his longtime agent, Esther Sherman of the William Morris Agency, whom he adored and usually referred to as "God." We said "goodbye let's do this more often," embraced, and I took the train uptown, wondering if Howard, whose previous two partners had both succumbed to the horrible 1980s-style HIV complications, might be ill himself.

Time passed. *The Little Mermaid* was released, and Howard and Alan Menken won an Oscar for best song. My heart sank as I watched him accept the award during the telecast: gaunt and pale as he walked onto the stage with the gait of a man much older than his somewhat fewer than forty years. Shortly afterward we spoke by telephone several times. He was living in Beacon, New York at this point, and I was finally able to arrange a train trip upstate to visit him. He had promised to play me a tape of the songs for *Beauty and the Beast,* which was in postproduction without him in California. Two days before my scheduled trip, his doctors ordered him into St. Vincent's Hospital for treatment of new complications. He never returned to Beacon. Three times I tried to visit, but he was now a celebrity, and there were always long lines of people I mostly did not know, and hour-long waits to see him.

After three weeks, I decided I needed to see him, wait or no wait. I bought a pound of chocolate truffles at Mondel's up near Columbia University, where I was working. This time there was no line. I hesitated outside the door and took a deep breath. Howard. My fiercely intelligent, ferociously witty friend and collaborator back when we were both "babes on Broadway":

. . . The mid-'70s, was it possible so many years had passed? A young, aspiring lyricist with dreams of Broadway glory, I had pitched my idea for an updated musical of Shakespeare's Tempest *to Howard—this attractive and funny, sharp, acerbic, sweet writer I had just met because my composer, Marsha Malamet, and I needed a librettist to build a story around our seven or eight songs which we thought were so great, for a show to blow* Godspell *for instance* or Jesus Christ Superstar, *out of the water—and Howard heard the songs and became so excited and went to work a week later. What days those were . . . The first draft of the* Tempest *musical—called* Dreamstuff*—was completed within a couple of months and we somehow were able to arrange a reading at the Ballroom—Marsha knew somebody or I knew somebody—so on a night when the place was traditionally dark, we gathered a select audience who got their first taste of* Dreamstuff *while sipping white wine and dining on the hilariously christened house specialty, "pillow of chicken." We'd assembled a cast of professionals who could sing and act; Stuart had directed the reading; Marsha was at the piano; and Howard and I sat together at a table in the back, our notepads at the ready, hearts racing with excitement as on the tiny ballroom stage our work reached its first audience. After the opening number there was tremendous applause, and soon afterward, the first big laughs came as Howard's outrageous twentieth century characters began interacting with Prospero, Caliban, Miranda & co. . . . Applause for the songs and laughs for the dialogue continued and built, and at a certain moment Howard spontaneously reached for my hand and held it tight, as we both realized we had created something with the potential to entertain thousands—maybe even millions—and he whispered to me with total confidence, "Dennis,*

we're all going to be rich!" He squeezed my hand with great force and then let it go—the sweetest, the warmest of moments, the thrill of collaborative effort, the giddy promise of gifted youth. Sadly, it was to be our only real collaboration.

I went in. Only two of Howard's closest friends, both of whom I knew fairly well, were with him. Howard lay on the bed—a blind, inarticulate wraith in a hospital gown. It was clear he would not be eating any chocolates. I bit my lip and took another deep, painful breath as one of the friends, with that forced cheer we often rely upon during vigils of this sort, announced, "It's Dennis *Green*—and he brought *CHOCOLATES!*" Howard smiled faintly. I knew the smile was for me as much as for the truffles. I held his hand for a while. I sensed he was near death. I spent an hour at his side, chatting with his friends. There came a moment when I knew that it was time for me to leave. I leaned over and kissed his forehead. He squeezed my hand weakly. I lcft the room fighting back tears, which finally came pouring out as I hit the street. Howard died less than forty-eight hours later.

I lost a number of friends to AIDS—all of them had special gifts of one kind or another, and all might have done great things, small things, or even nothing at all in particular, had they lived. I know, though, going on twelve years after his demise, that Howard Ashman was the only true genius among them. I miss the shows and movies and songs that might have been, informed by his unique view of life, and his very special wit. I miss his presence in the world. I miss Howard.

MARC AND BARBRA

DAVID FERGUSON

I found my childhood soul mate during a current events lesson in the fifth grade. Our teacher, Mrs. Bennett, had us reading aloud from the front page of the *New York Times,* something about Kennedy and Krushchev and the Nuclear Test Ban Treaty. While Joan Findelstein droned and drooled her way through the article, and the rest of us were cross-eyed with boredom, Marc Musnick, the fat boy in the class, was blithely and defiantly opened to the theater page. He saw I was watching him, and whispered to me, "I hope I get my tickets to *Bye Bye Birdie* before they drop the bomb." I couldn't believe my ears. Could it be that there was somebody else like me who was obsessed with musicals and movies? After class he came over to me. "So how many times have you seen *My Fair Lady*?" Having only seen it in my dreams, I was speechless. Before I could say a word, Marc went on. "Well I've seen it three times, twice with Julie and once with Sally Ann. You know Sally Ann Howes? It's really amazing but you know, I think *Camelot* is better. After the show my parents always take me to Luchow's." He went on to compare and contrast Julie Andrews's costumes in each show. "I think my favorite costume is the Ascot dress, but I do really love the wedding dress in *Camelot.*" Having never been to a Broadway show, I was appropriately dazzled. Then, before I knew it, I started lying. "Well I liked *My Fair Lady,* but *Bye Bye Birdie* is more fun and I loved *Flower Drum Song.*" Marc agreed with me about *Flower Drum* and thought it was even better than *Sound of Music.* Between the two of us, we had managed to see every landmark musical production of the past five seasons. One day Marc asked if he could come over my house and see my *Playbills.* I stuttered and stammered and then I confessed: it had all been lies, the only show I had ever seen was *The Three Little Pigs* at the Paper Bag Playhouse. Marc looked a little sheepish as he tore into his third Milky Way of the afternoon. He too made a confession: he had never been to a Broadway show either, and, as a matter of fact, he had never even been to a puppet show. Besides, his parents never took him to Luchow's because they were divorced, and he hadn't seen his father since he was five. Wow! Divorced parents! I never knew anyone whose parents divorced. So, with truth on our side we vowed that we would see our first Broadway show together.

Marc and I became best friends. While the other boys were out playing stickball, we'd spend sunny afternoons in the house, listening to show albums and practicing our Maria/Anita duet from *West Side Story.* My mother would get furious. "Go outside and play, it's beautiful!" she screamed. Muttering to herself, "What is the matter with those boys?" "OK Mom, we'll go out." We'd go off to Marc's house, where it was always evening because Marc's mother had migraines and would keep the curtains drawn. We'd order out pizza and watch *Million Dollar Matinee.* Our favorite actress was Judy Garland. Marc was appalled by my lack of Judy knowledge. He thought that the only movies of Judy's I knew—*The Wizard of Oz* and the Andy Hardy series—were good, but really "kids' stuff." Didn't I know about *The Clock,* and *Summer Stock* with the "Get Happy" number? He looked at me incredulously when I told him I'd never heard of *A Star Is Born* and what was worse, had never heard the famous song from it, "The Man That Got Away." Marc was my adult Judy teacher, and I was his willing and very fast student.

One spring afternoon, Marc called me up. "Guess what I have in my hands, right now, at this moment? *Judy at Carnegie Hall.* Get over here immediately, I'll wait for you to open it." This was a great moment. We listened to it over and over. We poured over the liner notes: Hedda Hopper "never saw the like it in my life: we laughed, cried, and split our gloves applauding." We studied the photo of Judy on the album in her Norman Norell bolero jacket, and before long we knew every note and breath on the album and would crack each other up with our Judy imitations ("I know—we'll stay up all night and we'll sing 'em all. I never want to go home.") We could never get enough of her little stammer ("We'll do, we'll do Chicago.")

We had our other obsessions. We were dying to see Shirley MacLaine and Audrey Hepburn suffer at the hands of a little girl who accused them of being lesbians in *The Children's Hour.* No children under sixteen were admitted without an adult, which only made us more obsessed. My mother put her foot down. This was an entirely inappropriate movie for a child. My argument that I was really an adult in a child's body didn't change her mind. Marc's mother was too busy to care all that much about what movies he saw. But she drew the line on this one. She was not going to take her twelve-year-old son to a movie about lesbians, and that's all there was to it. So we had to content ourselves with looking at pictures from the movie in *Life* magazine, with a very unhappy Shirley MacLaine on the cover. "Movies that break the final taboo."

We couldn't get this movie out of our minds. We pretended that our teacher, Mrs. Bennett, was having a secret and doomed love affair with the suspiciously mannish science teacher, Mrs. Opaz. Mrs. Opaz would come into our classroom and say,

"Anna, I need to talk to you in the hallway, it's very important." We would dissolve into uncontrollable laughter. The other kids gave us funny looks.

Forget *Beatlemania,* for Marc and me, 1964 was the year of *Barbramania.* Her first, second, and third albums joined *Judy at Carnegie Hall* in our pantheon. It was like a national holiday for us the night Barbra appeared on Judy's TV show. In March of '64, Barbra opened in *Funny Girl,* and there was no doubt that, by any means necessary, we were going to make a pilgrimage to the Winter Garden Theater.

We saved our allowance and birthday money until we had the $5.50 for a Wednesday matinee orchestra seat, and got the first available date, three months down the road. We would get to see Barbra on the twenty-second of July at two o'clock.

For those three months, we thought of nothing else. We passed the endless summer days by wearing down the cast album of *Funny Girl* and keeping a Barbra scrapbook.

B Day finally arrived. We got up at dawn, took the long bus and subway trip to the city and had a special lunch at Tad's Steakhouse. We were a little nervous being in New York by ourselves, so we got to the theater as early as we could. We were the first two people in the theater and one of the ushers said to her friend, "Look at those two kids. They're so funny. They look like a little Laurel and Hardy." I pretended I didn't hear her. As the theater filled up and the electricity increased, Marc grabbed my hand, "David, we're really here, we're going to see Barbra in person." The lights dimmed and a man's voice came over the speaker. "At this performance . . ." The audience collectively gasped. Was she sick? After all these months, were we going to have to see Lainie Kazan as Fanny? We couldn't bear it. He continued. The role of Mrs. Strakosh, usually played by Jean Stapleton, would be played by Paula Laurence. We were home free!

From the moment Barbra sat down at her mirrored table,

with a leopard-skin coat and hat, and greeted herself with "Hello, gorgeous," Marc and I gaped in astonishment. The peak came the moment when she stood alone on the stage, broken-hearted, in a black sequined gown with a slit up the front, and sang "The Music That Makes Me Dance." A little voice in my head told me it would never be as good as this again.

That autumn my family moved to Long Island. Marc and I had a tearful farewell and spent the summer before junior high school talking on the phone every day, trying to find a way to see *Hello, Dolly!* My mother decided it was time for me to make a new start as a normal Long Island boy. Marc would not be a part of that picture. She decided, for reasons unspoken, that he was an unhealthy influence on me. I was no longer to see or speak to him, and I needed to make friends with boys with "normal interests."

Marc called my house over and over again to no avail. My mother told him that I was with my new friends, and I wouldn't be able to talk to him. He wouldn't take no for an answer. My mother became so agitated by his incessant calling, that she hurled the ultimate insult. "What's the matter with him? He behaves like your lover." Ouch!

We of course found a way to thwart the edict. We traveled by bus and train for clandestine meetings at a shopping mall halfway between our towns, and spent the afternoon eating donuts and scouring the musical-comedy section of Sam Goody's. Saturday nights were the best. My parents went out and I babysat my little brother. Marc and I talked on the phone for hours, blissfully unaware that this would be the last year of our friendship.

We began to go our separate ways. He had become a baby opera queen. I had seen *La Bohème* and *Carmen* at Brooklyn Academy of Music, but Marc completely outdid me. At the age of fourteen, he cut entire weeks of school to wait on line for

Maria Callas tickets. He told me that he was meeting "older women" on the line. He'd go to these women's apartments, smoke marijuana, and have sex with them. He told me that these "women" even loved Judy and Barbra. He started using phrases like "it's such a camp."

It seemed like Marc never went to school. One day he called to tell me that his mother had kicked him out of the house and sent him to a residence for teens in trouble. Soon after *that,* he informed me that he was living with a friend from the line and he couldn't give me the number. I never heard from him again. For a long time, I had dreams about seeing Marc again. Occasionally, I'd look his name up in the Manhattan phone book. I never found it.

Years later, I went to see the movie version of *Funny Girl* with a bunch of hippie friends from college. They goofed through the whole movie, laughing at the corny numbers between tokes of pot. "Hey man, whose idea was it to see this shit, anyway?" Deeply in the closet at the time, I pretended to be "one of the guys." I laughed and toked along with them. When Barbra sang "My Man," I was secretly transfixed. My mind went back to 1964, and I knew that these guys would never understand about that July afternoon at the Winter Garden Theater, when me and my best friend Marc found true love.

OBSTACLE COURSE

HARRY SCHULZ

Winter of 1974: it has just snowed about six inches. A wet heavy snow, but we are excited. There's that smell of snow in the air. It has gotten dark but we don't want to stop playing. One of us dares the other to go out on the porch and touch the snow with his bare feet, then the other dares one to put his whole foot in the snow. Then one of us jumps in with both, then one of us—I think it was Ted, or was it me?—runs way out onto the front lawn, and then we're both running and laughing, and leaving a zigzag pattern of bare footprints in the snow.

Last year: Ted calls me one night. It's one o'clock in the morning. He wants $200, ostensibly to cover a check he has written for his health insurance, but I know it's to buy cocaine. I mean it's 1 A.M. and he wants to come over to my apartment right away to get the money so he can be sure he'll be covered at the bank on Monday. Right.

I remember my father leaning over me as I am pretending to be asleep. I am seven or eight. I know how to regulate my breathing slow and deep so as to appear that I am unconscious. He has come in to kiss me good night and his breath reeks of alcohol, and I am praying he won't try to wake me up so I won't have to pretend that I am waking out of sleep. I shift as if in some dream, and turn my back to him.

We are six when we meet, we become "best" friends when we're ten—in Mr. Alterman's fifth grade class. 1972. Ted's family is kind of conservative with all kinds of strict rules—they seem so structured and secure. From that time on he is the measure for what I should want, do, and be, at least until I am seventeen or so and start to branch out, make other friends. We lose touch when we go off to college. By the summer of 1986, I haven't heard from Ted for many years. I figure that one day I'll hear from someone that he's engaged to some young woman he's met in college—for some reason, I imagine she's a cheerleader. He's going to go that route, you see, middle-class respectability. I find myself marching in the gay pride parade with friends and then afterward going out to the bars. I am at Uncle Charlie's, and I am looking around at all the guys, and there he is, Ted. I seem to see him in a spotlight, leaning against the bar. I am frozen. I can't move for about five minutes. I just watch him—I had no idea! Finally I get up the courage to go up to him and say hello. . . .

I am standing with my brother by the fireplace in my mother's new home in North Carolina. I am twenty-eight. She is remarried and my new stepbrothers and stepsisters are coming for Christmas dinner. My own brother walks over to a shotgun leaning against the brick fireplace. He says, "I wonder if this is the shotgun that Dad threatened to kill us all with." "What?" I say. "Don't you remember?" he says, "I guess you were too young to remember. We were sitting in the dining room and he came in with the shotgun, he was drunk, and said he would kill us all." "MOM!" I yell, running to the kitchen. "Bill says—" and I tell her. "Did that really happen?" I ask. "Yes," says my mother—she's busy slicing onions—"but I wasn't really worried then. It was that pistol he had that worried me." I'd never heard any of this before.

I move to the Village in July 1996. Ted, it happens, lives

around the corner. We meet for breakfast and have a wonderful time. Soon we are seeing each other again every day—just like old times. It means so much to me, the renewal of our friendship, the closeness I feel with him. He is sensitive. Smart. He knows my history and is part of it. I kind of . . . fall in love with him.

1982. My lover has convinced me that I need to see a psychiatrist or psychologist. I reluctantly agree that he is right. He convinces me to ask my parents to help pay for therapy. I finally get up the nerve. I tell them one day in the kitchen that I have been unhappy, very unhappy, even suicidal sometimes. I need help. They say, "You can talk to us." I keep trying. They tell me they don't believe in psychiatrists (though my father has been seeing one for years). They are all charlatans, they exist to prescribe drugs! Later I am alone with my father in the kitchen and I try again. He asks me, "Is it because you're gay?" "No!" I say. Damn, has he just ignored everything I've said? And is it that obvious? Really, it isn't because of that—that's what I think but don't say. My parents don't pay for therapy. A year later my father dies just as his Social Security mental-illness disability award comes through. As a dependent I am awarded a sum of money, applied retroactively for several years. I end up spending it all on a psychologist.

Ted has been on a cocaine binge for a week. He is trying to stop—he comes over to my place so the drug dealers can't reach him. He needs to come down, so he drinks all the liquor and wine in my house. That's not enough. So I go out and buy him a small bottle of vodka—I think I am helping him come down from the cocaine. It's not enough. I go out for more. He gets so drunk he passes out, but in his unconscious state, on my floor, he starts screaming at the top of his lungs. I don't know what to do. I don't want to call 911 unless absolutely necessary—that would bring the police and I don't want to get him in trouble.

I am a teenager, seventeen, fall of 1979. I am rehearsing for the school play, a Eugene O'Neill drama. My father has been deeply depressed. He has been taking too many pills again, to ease his pain—his emotional pain. I am trying to sleep, but I can hear my parents arguing in the kitchen. I hear a drawer open and shut. There is a pause. I hear my mother say "Ray, put down that knife." He wants to kill himself. "Do it!" I think. But my mother talks him out of it. I am never afraid for my mother. I don't dare get up and go to the kitchen, I only overhear these events. I listen, but later I pretend not to know what has happened.

It's autumn again, not so long ago, and I am out of control. I am out most every night, and most every night I have sex with six, seven, eight, ten men. I find the places to go and I don't want to be there but I stay and stay and stay. I have something to prove. I feel nothing—no fear, no shame—this is an honest place, I tell myself. I only feel the elation, the thrill, and then to keep feeling it I have be more outrageous, dangerous, seductive, and vulnerable. I don't seem to care. But one night reality hits me so hard I see my whole life on the verge of disaster. Everything I never felt, I feel all at once. In a vision I see my friends and the people I love devastated, my life destroyed. I think that maybe I have to kill myself. But I don't want to. I call Ted. He comes over and I cry in his arms. He tells me it will be all right. I know he cares, I know he won't judge me.

I am eleven. I am at a fairground with both my parents—they have divorced by now—and this is one of my visits with my father. We go on some rides—the Ferris wheel, bumper cars. I say to my father, "I'm glad you're an alcoholic, because otherwise we might not get to do this cool stuff together." A year later he gets sober for good and moves back home.

January last year Ted is beaten up by a drug dealer. A couple of his ribs are broken, his face is black and blue. Yet he hasn't gotten his fix and I can see in his face that he still intends to get it. I say, "Ted, don't go out looking for coke. Call me anytime day or night." But he goes out anyway and binges for a couple of days. Then he calls me. He thinks he may have accidentally taken an overdose. I go to his apartment. His broken ribs had been hurting badly and now he's afraid he's taken too many painkillers. This time I call 911. The paramedics come over and together we explain, but we don't tell them about the drug dealer or the relapse. I ride in the ambulance to the emergency room with him. He waits there in holding. He begs them to let me stay with him. He is dehydrated and they put an IV in him. He tries to stand up and he pulls out the IV and blood is dripping everywhere, all over Ted, the bed, the floor, me. The nurse who has to mop it up is very annoyed.

I am twelve. My father is taking too many tranquilizers, he looks and sounds drugged, heavy-lidded eyes, slurred speech, stumbling walk. His friends from AA are over to be with him while he goes through this—while we all go through this. He has been eating homemade fudge, the chocolate is smeared all over his face, like a child.

Just two months ago now. I haven't been talking with Ted much. I am so busy. I stop at his apartment to talk. He is in bad shape. Bloated, pale, and heavily sedated. His legs have long gouges in them because a piece of his bed has broken, and every time he gets out of it he cuts himself. I rip my jeans open on the same broken piece. I go to his bathroom, take out a few gauze bandages, and tape and bandage the wounded bed so that Ted won't cut himself anymore. He hugs me as I am leaving and says, "I love you." Early the next week I have a message on my machine from his brother. I call and John says, "I have some terrible news. Ted passed away last week. Died in his sleep." He tells me that he had been dead for four days before they found him, after someone noticed a bad smell. I hang up. My boyfriend is there holding me and I burst into tears.

I go to my mother's for Christmas. My brother is there—he always and only visits when I am there too. Every evening he starts drinking after dinner. First several beers. Then glasses of wine until he has drunk the entire bottle. Then he starts the scotch. Half a bottle. He gets quiet. I don't know if it's morose, or sullen—or just plain dull. He occasionally rages at whatever is on the television. I get quiet. When I go to bed I lock my bedroom door, but the door feels flimsy, and I think about wedging a chair under the knob.

In the morning I go with my mother to church and when I think of my brother, my eyes fill with tears and I realize that I do love him.

I look in the mirror. I am a frightened child—no, I'm a sexy man of the world, no, I'm a sensitive artist, no, I'm a proud gay man, no, I'm a gay teenager filled with shame, no, I'm an out-of-shape, not-quite-good-looking-enough gay man with something to prove; people do desire me, no, I'm a poet, no, I'm a singer, no, an improviser, no, a writer, no a lover, a son, a brother, a boyfriend, a child in love with the world and filled with wonder. No, no, no, no, no.

PERSONAL GROWTH

FIRE IN THE HOLE

Brad Gretter

Thank god for gay square dancing. That's where I met John, my first boyfriend here in the city. Back then in the fall of 1991, I was a twenty-five-year-old business student timidly tiptoeing my way out of the closet, in search of gay friends.

A native New Yorker fifteen years my senior, John prided himself on being a free-spirited man of experience. He once told me, "Sweetie, you definitely need the guidance of an older gentleman—someone who will watch out for your best interests." Not long after, he sent me off to a series of workshops. I started with a yoga intensive, then moved on to more advanced topics like awakening your chakra energy. Over drinks one night, he said, "Trust me darling, these workshops will be a wonderful complement to that *business* degree you're working on." Flipping his hair back like Miss Piggy, he added, "Uhhh, I can't believe I'm dating a suit."

In late March 1993 I received a package from John. Inside I found a brochure clipped to a postcard that read: "My little Execu-Stud: in younger cycles, wild horses could not have kept me from a workshop as creatively titled as 'Fire in the Hole.' So I hope you will attend and report back to your old friend in retirement every filthy detail. Love, John." Well, as it turned out, John had decided the time had come to send me to a class on beginner's anal massage.

The class, a two-day intensive, was held in a private dance studio in a dingy commercial building on West Fourteenth Street. My anxiety mounted as I climbed a dark musty stairwell leading to the studio. Standing on the landing outside, I took one deep breath, crossed my fingers and rang the bell. The studio door swung open with a whoosh of fresh air and I was ushered into a room flooded with bright warm sunlight. "Welcome to Fire in the Hole" said a slender, sagely man in a flowing floral print sarong. Taking my right hand in both of his own he said, "My name is Starfire. I will be your facilitator this weekend." Pointing to a table arrayed with candles and incense, he added, "Please check your name off the sign-in sheet, and make yourself comfortable."

The room was silent except for the gentle warblings of Enya. A dozen men dotted the floor, some sitting in the lotus position meditating, while others busied themselves with stretching. Despite some sly, subtle cruising, nobody was making any direct eye contact. Carefully, I made my way to a spot near the window, sat down, and tried to relax. My mind was racing: *So, how will all this work? Are we just going to drop our pants, right here, right now, and bare our butts to complete strangers? I don't know who these guys are. How come it takes two days to do this, anyway? The anus isn't really that big.*

We started the first day with some gentle stretching and breathing exercises, followed by an hour or so of what I called share and compare stories. During "share and compare," we partnered up with different men and told each other intimate anecdotes that you wouldn't normally tell in everyday circumstances. One of the stories I shared was about losing my virginity: of going on a date with this really cute guy and wearing my favorite pants, the ones with the cuffs that tied at the ankles; and of being so excited to get out of those pants that I forgot to untie the cuffs and got them turned inside out trailing behind me, as I crawled across my living-room floor on all fours, demanding that my date get a pair of scissors and cut me out. At first I was embarrassed. I had never revealed that story to anyone. But as the hour progressed, I found myself completely connected to the other guys, absorbed in their tales, and eager to divulge other personal tidbits.

After "share and compare" we regrouped and discussed how we were feeling. What a difference. Now, we not only made eye contact, but we sat in a circle with our arms wrapped around each other's shoulders, positively glowing.

"Now before we move on to the disrobing ceremony, there is one other exercise we need to do," Starfire announced in a sweet church-lady tone. Then he added, "Now, I'm going to break you into focus groups of four men each. And for the next forty minutes I want each of you to take turns and describe candidly and honestly, your personal relationship with your asshole." I bit my lower lip, stifling the urge to giggle. Still, figuring that I had enjoyed "share and compare" so much, I decided to give this exercise my best shot. The details are fuzzy but what I do remember is when it came time for me to talk, suddenly the floodgates sprung open and I confided all kinds of things to my group. I remember the other three guys clustered around me real tightly as I confessed, "Now talk about a high maintenance body part, some days he and I get along like buds, while other days he won't open up for anything, no matter how pretty it is."

While not as colorful as "share and compare" or the true confessions of "my buddy, my boyfriend, my butthole," there is one other exercise that stands out in my mind. It began after the disrobing ceremony. We took a break, and I was looking around the room, reveling in the raw nakedness that surrounded me. My reverie was broken by the gentle movement of Starfire swirling around me like a Sufi dancer, his long silvery hair trailing behind him, as he made a beeline to the center of the room. In a booming voice, Starfire proclaimed, "Gentlemen, now that we have had time to talk and share stories, it is time for us to get reacquainted with our assholes." Then, as if on cue, Starfire's hot and humpy assistant Joseph emerged from the back room carrying a large rectangular mirror. Thus began what I affectionately think of as the feminist portion of the program. "Come on, gather around, everyone," Starfire urged, herding us around Joseph. Pressing forward he said, "Alright now, I want to see a show of hands by all those men who have never seen their assholes before. Don't be shy, now." Everyone exchanged nervous glances before two other men and I sheepishly raised our hands. "Alright, we'll start with you guys." Placing an arm around my shoulders, Starfire added, "And you, young man, will get to go first."

I straddled the mirror on the floor, squatting down with both hands on my knees. Joseph crouched down in front of me adjusting the angle of the mirror. "Spread 'em a little more, sweetie," Joseph said softly. Then added, "Mmmm, now isn't that nice." Everyone leaned in closer to get a good look. With a hand upon my back, Starfire urged me, "Tell us what you see. Is it what you expected to see?" Silence shrouded the room, as everyone waited for my response. I squinted my eyes trying to focus, but it was to no avail. Just like me, my inner feminist is also legally blind. Embarrassed, I looked up and stammered, "I . . . I . . . I'm sorry, I can't see a thing down there." With a sweeping gesture, Starfire turned to the others and exclaimed, "Gentlemen, I encourage you all to help out our brother in need. Offer him feedback and describe to him this splendid sight before us." For the next thirty seconds I braced myself and listened, as fifteen men hovered over me, oohing and ahhing, and cooing sweet little nothings in my ear. When it was over, Starfire pulled me aside and whispered, "Don't worry, dear.

You'll get to see what it looks like. Tomorrow we're going to take Polaroid snapshots of each of you so you'll have a nice keepsake from the weekend."

We eventually moved on to more practical matters. After a lively discussion of safety and hygiene issues, we got a mini-anatomy lesson. I was amazed to learn that there are more nerve endings converging at the anus than any other part of our bodies. Whether it was stretching, or tapping, or rubbing circles at varying tempos, the massage strokes we learned were simple—intuitive, in fact. All could be done with one or two fingers. Although, Starfire pointed out, one should never limit himself to using just his fingers. And after going through all the touchy-feely exercises, the actual massage seemed matter of fact, no big deal. Just another body part, no different from all the rest.

I believe the greatest thing I gained from that weekend—aside from the life-affirming experience of shedding my anal shame—was the confidence to open up, take some risks, tell my stories, and be playful, even a little silly. Perhaps some day soon, it will be my turn to pass along to some young man that same thirst for adventure and gift of confidence that John so lovingly bestowed upon me.

HUBBA BUBBA, HUBBA BUBBA, ESPAÑOL!

JAMES CAMPBELL

When I was in high school, my family lived in Richmond, Indiana. Richmond was one of those industrial gateway cities out of the hard life of Appalachian Kentucky. And Richmond had a distinctive hillbilly air. My father used to amuse himself, and drive the rest of us to distraction, by reading aloud all the obituaries: "Beulah Mae MacWilliams, 81, born Hog's Head, Kentucky—died Richmond, Indiana. Raymond 'Pee Wee' Hardy, 69, born Renfro Valley, Kentucky—died Richmond, Indiana." You get the idea.

Religion in Richmond was also distinctly Appalachian. While there were some high-falutin', high-steeple, downtown churches, most folks belonged to smaller fundamentalist congregations. My dad was the pastor of one of them—of the Pentecostal variety. And while we didn't handle snakes or anything like that, we did have healings and visions and speaking in tongues.

The summer I turned seventeen, my parents gave me a 1967 candy apple red Plymouth Sport Fury. It was this huge boat of a car with absolutely no suspension. And my best friend, Jim, and I would cruise and whoosh and bounce all over town.

One day while driving down Chester Boulevard, toward the poor north end of the city, we noticed that a big yellow-and-white-striped circus tent was being erected. That could only mean one thing in Richmond. The circus certainly never came to town—*a tent revival was coming to town!* And Jim and I were both confirmed religious thrill seekers who knew this revival would be the best show of the summer.

A few evenings later, I pulled the Plymouth into the parking lot of the tent. The front flaps were open and faced the boulevard. It was very invitational. We parked as close as we could to enjoy the show without actually participating. It was kind of like going to the drive-in.

The tent was full of poor, plain, and devoutly religious people. They looked sad. These people always looked sad to me. Suddenly, three musicians emerged from the wings and took their places as a voice intoned: "Welcome to Brother Kenny Hampton's Old Time Revival! Tonight on the Hammond organ we have Sister Sylvia!" At this, Sister Sylvia pumped up the volume and gave us a flourish through the huge Leslie speakers. "And on the drums, Brother Ronnie," who gave a drum roll that finished on the hi-hat. "And on the 'lectric guitar, Brother Billy!" Now Brother Billy was the closest thing to a rock star that Richmond got. He was young, lean, with golden hair and pearly white teeth. His rayon shirt was unbuttoned to reveal the brown fur of his chest and the glittering gold of his chains. And he had on the tightest pants I had ever seen. When he was announced, Brother Billy let loose with a Pentecostal paean à la Jimi Hendrix that vibrated my spine. Then all three joined together in a wonderful rockabilly rhythm that set your toes a tappin'. And all those sad, tired people began to sway and to smile as they entered their familiar world—and their burdens, at least for a moment, seemed to lift away.

"And now, brothers and sisters, the moment you have all been waiting for, God's man of the hour, BROTHER KENNY HAMPTON!" From stage left a fat middle-aged man with a pompadour and a cheap white suit bounded into view, shouting "Praise the Lord!" as he made his way to the center. Just behind the pulpit, there was this clothes rack contraption. With one seamless movement, Brother Kenny whisked a red cape off the rack and around his own shoulders. And then he turned around dramatically to reveal the cape's secret. There, written in large white cursive were the words ELIJAH'S MANTLE: "This cape is anointed with the Spirit of Elijah! When I put on this mantle, I have the power of the prophet, the power to perform miracles!" The sense of excitement was palpable.

Brother Kenny began to build the crowd into a frenzy of religious ecstasy as he paced the platform, preaching in his hypnotic Pentecostal rhythm. Suddenly struck by a spirit, he began to quake and to speak in tongues: "Hubba bubba, hubba bubba, Español!"

"What did he say?" I asked Jim.

Before he could answer, Brother Kenny let us have it again: "Hubba bubba, hubba bubba, Español!" Now, Hubba Bubba was my bubble gum of choice at the time, and Español was my favorite subject in school, and I had heard speaking in tongues my entire life and this was *not* it. "He's a fake!" I declared to Jim who sat beside me giggling. Brother Kenny let loose once more: "Hubba bubba, hubba bubba, Español!" Unable to control myself, I stuck my head out of the driver's window and shouted back at him: "Hubba bubba, hubba bubba, Español!" I shouted. There was a pregnant pause in the tent. A look of confusion crossed the prophet's face as he tried to understand what had happened. "Stop it!" Jim hissed from the passenger's seat. Before I could even think about Jim's advice, Brother Kenny recovered and tried once again: "Hubba bubba, hubba bubba, Español!" And out the window went my head again, echoing his silly refrain. This time, Brother Kenny realized what was happening and, sensing that he risked losing control of the crowd, acted decisively. He pointed his fat finger in the direction of the Plymouth and said with authority, "There's a demon-possessed man in that red car—right out there! Everybody pray for protection!" Well, that shut me up—at least for a while.

Triumphant, Kenny shifted gears. He morphed into something small and pitiful-looking as he told the faithful about the great expense of his ministry, how all the good people on the stage needed to be paid, and how they had been forced to buy a brand-new tent since the old one had blown off a mountain in West Virginia. Ushers appeared, and the people began to dig for the little money they had. Apparently the haul was not big enough, because fifteen minutes later the ushers were back. This time, Kenny laid it on even thicker. "God is speaking through me tonight. And God wants you to go to the credit unions in the morning and borrow against your house to give all the money you can to give to this ministry. How many of you love the Lord enough to sacrifice like that?" Hands popped up all over the tent. A second offering commenced and with that, the service drew to a close. But as Kenny was winding down, I was winding up.

I put my hand on the door handle. "You won't go up there," Jim taunted. "You just watch me," I said as I stepped into the night.

God's man of the hour was chatting with some of the stragglers. Being the polite boy that I was, I waited my turn. "Brother Kenny?" I finally said. "Yes son, how can I help you?" He didn't know who I was! How could he be a prophet when he didn't know that the "demon-possessed man" was right in front of him?

Emboldened, I continued, "Brother Kenny, my dad is a pastor in this city and I have seen all kinds of religious experience in my seventeen years—and this, by far, is the biggest sham I've ever witnessed." Stunned horror crossed his face momentarily as people gathered to listen. And then he recovered.

"What do you mean, boy?" he demanded. "Well, for starters, I didn't see you perform any miracle. All I have seen you do is ask for money. If you ask me, I think you're a fake." Now I was standing with my back to the stage when suddenly I was knocked forward with such force that I staggered and almost hit the ground. When I turned around to see what had happened, I realized that Brother Billy, the guitar golden boy, had leapt off the stage and onto my back. With his fists up, he shouted, "Come on, boy! Come on, fight me! No one talks to the man of God like that!" Well I had to think fast because there was little doubt that Brother Billy could have kicked the shit out of me. By this time, a crowd had gathered. Despite my fear, I was suddenly focused, like a laser. I looked at Billy, then at Kenny, then at the people. "Can you imagine Jesus doing this?" I asked pointing at the enraged guitar player. The crowd looked confused. "Do you see the love of God in what just happened here? If so, then stay and give him your money. But if not, then take responsibility for your lives and go home. . . . GO HOME!" There was silence for a moment. No one moved. And then Brother Kenny began to rumble: "Call the po-lice, Sylvia. Call the po-lice!" and Sylvia disappeared into the darkness.

I felt like I was in a dream. I could feel my pulse in my throat. I was dripping with sweat. But I knew I had won. With deliberation, I turned toward the parking lot and slowly walked away. As if from a distance I heard the gravel crunching under my feet; I heard Kenny behind me doing damage control; I heard the creak of the heavy car door as it opened; I heard Jim plead, "Let's get the *fuck* out of here!" And so I sat down, took a deep breath, turned the key in the ignition, backed out of the parking lot, and drove. . . . I drove into the cool freedom of that summer night.

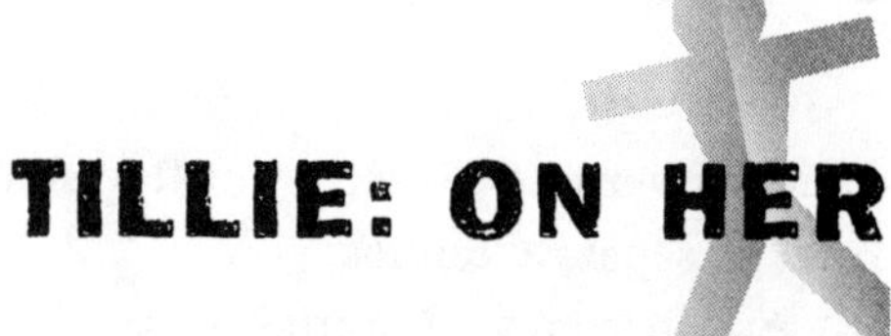

TILLIE: ON HER

ROBIN GOLDFIN

For my brothers and sister, for my father, and for Dolly

Her story is more interesting than mine, but I have been warned not to tell it. Not to lose myself in the details of her life so much that I abandon my own; not to focus more on her childhood at the expense of my own; not to approach her with sympathy instead of through our own history. And yet I can't help but feel that to learn about her is to learn about myself. We were once one body.

In the archives of the Jewish Family and Children's Service of Greater Philadelphia there is a file of social workers' reports about seventy-five pages thick. This file is sealed, closed to me as it was to her. Except once, for her fiftieth birthday, she went to learn the names of her birth parents: Anna Glickman and John Perry. Anna was Jewish, John a Roman Catholic.

John had abandoned the family in 1937 when the baby was one-year-old. The Society for Prevention of Cruelty to Children was called in because the children—Tillie and her brother Maurice, older by fifteen months—were being neglected. Tillie (or Delores—they use both names in the records) was found on the street. Anna Glickman gave no resistance to the children being taken away. The reports, strong language for those days, called her "a person of very low character." Miss Glickman's only request was that the children go to a Jewish home, so they were handed over to the agency for Jewish Children and put in foster care, in separate homes.

As they grew, Maurice learned English, Tillie spoke only Yiddish. When they were brought to visit with one another, they could not communicate, except in the language of children. Maurice would try to taunt young Tillie, but she stood up to him. He would try to take away her toy and she would smack him. Even back then my mother wouldn't be pushed around.

I know these things because I've asked, because a kind social worker bent the rules and retrieved the files, reading to me from them over the phone after my mother's death. Not all, not everything, not nearly enough. Little things that wouldn't mean anything to anyone except six of us. The details of our mother's history, typed in triplicate.

Maurice was soon adopted by a couple who wanted a boy and after that, he and his sister were forbidden to see one another. He was starting a new life, while little Tillie remained in foster care. But the story, as my uncle tells it, is that they lived in the same neighborhood, and one day they stopped on opposite sides of the street. Tillie crossed over because she recognized him, without remembering who he was. Then they remembered, and after this they would meet secretly in the schoolyard.

And then not so secretly: "Tillie stands for hours under the Micklin house door waiting for Morrie," the reports say, over and over. She found out where he lived and would go to see him. She liked her foster family, but they would hit her, and one day she'd had enough. She went to her brother's house and instead of waiting under the door, she knocked on it, this bright-faced, dark-haired little eight-year-old girl, and said to his parents, "Take me, too."

The certificate of adoption is dated 1946. The war had just ended. When asked why she wanted to go and live with the

Micklins, the young girl replied simply that she wanted to be with her brother. At the age of ten, Tillie/Dolores became Dollyann Micklin, the daughter of Ethel and Albert.

Fifty years later, in the summer of 1996, my mother injures her back lifting a heavy plant in the house. It never heals, and by the fall she is bedridden. She hates doctors and has refused to see one since my last brother was born over thirty years before. But the pain is relentless, and she finally gives in. She sees a sports medicine specialist who takes x-rays while making her hold heavy sandbags, only making her pain worse. He recommends physical therapy; my mother goes back to bed. Until the pain gets so bad that she walks the halls at night, banging on the walls, moaning. All from a pulled muscle?

I tell a therapist this story. She replies "If your father wants her to live, he'll get your mother to a hospital."

My father brings her hot chocolate in bed but refuses to take her to the hospital. He is going to make her well. Finally, my brothers get together and override both their parents. They call the ambulance and as the attendants are carrying her out of the house they knock over a statue of a great headless woman my mother has in the foyer. She takes it for an omen.

That first night we have to leave her there, but the next day I remember something: I was five years old and had to have my tonsils out—back then it was a bigger operation—and my mother wouldn't leave me. She stayed all night with me in the hospital. I woke up to see her in the bed next to mine, sleeping on a bare mattress. She got up and fed me chocolate ice cream.

Now she is in the hospital and I won't leave her. I go up to the nurse and ask, "If I told you I wanted to stay the night with her, would you fight me?" She thinks for a moment, goes away, comes back. "I wouldn't fight you at all," she replies, and that night and every night for the next three weeks, my mother's six children take shifts and she is never alone. It takes the doctors almost three weeks to find the tumor in her breast and the path it has taken to her bones because every test they take comes up negative. My mother is so good at hiding things, she has somehow managed to hide even her cancer from the doctors and the most sophisticated of instruments. Finally diagnosed, she leaves the hospital and beyond all expectation lives another two years.

But now I have to pause and ask what I am doing here. Trying to tell you her story, I've pieced together a beginning and then jumped straight to the end. I've left out almost everything that mattered: Her fierce devotion to her children and family; her warmth and love and generosity; her ability to take care of us but difficulty in taking care of herself; her living life.

When I had that kind social worker on the phone, trying to keep her on as long as I could so I could hear more about my mother's childhood, I would ask questions. Finally, she asked me one.

"Your mother was basically a happy person, wasn't she?"

"Oh, yes," I lied. And then regretted it. But you don't tell strangers the truth. Sometimes you don't even tell yourself.

My mother was unhappy, particularly in her later years, but I couldn't tell you why. At best I can make guesses. Most likely, she knew she was ill. And as she didn't believe in doctors, she didn't believe in therapy, didn't want to go back to those early childhood memories or talk to strangers. Often she would tell me that she talked to me when she was alone in her kitchen and I was ninety miles away. But I never heard these conversations, so I can't tell you her story—not the way a story needs to be told—from the inside.

When my mother fell ill, I bought her a journal so she could write things down. It remains blank. Before she died, she told me, "Don't ever write down anything you don't want anyone else to know." So I don't know her thoughts or her secrets, and even if I did, they are not mine to tell. Perhaps all I can tell you is this: That first night I spent thirty-six hours at the hospital with her, and when I finally left for my brother's house to get some sleep, I lay down on the bed, heavy with tiredness, unable to sleep, my head literally swirling, and I had a kind of vision. More a sensation, really. Lying there against the bed, I felt that my body was my mother's body. I couldn't tell the difference between us—I was her body, she was mine. It was not unpleasant.

"Do you think it means I'm finally separating?" I asked the therapist.

"Oh, it's much too early for that," she replied.

The things we pay people to tell us.

But eventually I told my mother, and she alone understood. "That's right, Robbie," she said, "we're on the same track." As if it were a fact, nothing out of the ordinary to be a man, forty years old, and still be in your mother's body, of your mother's body. Nothing out of the ordinary to be a forty-year-old man and still be your mother's body.

THE HUG

ROBIN GOLDFIN

February 14, 1999. Valentine's Day. I got on a plane from Florence, Italy to Newark, New Jersey. And from there south, to the hospital to be with my mother.

I had left to teach in Florence not a month before. I knew she was sick when I left, but she had responded well to some of the treatments, so we thought she'd be all right. Though the last time I saw her she was limping as she paced the bedroom floor with her walker. But she didn't say anything about it, so neither did I. I got on a plane.

Not a month later my father called to say, "Your brothers and sister think it's time you came home."

I'm in the hospital with my older brother and my youngest brother.

Our mother is on the bed, dying.

There's a little pain in my side, from sitting. My mother's cancer went to her bones, and the sicker she gets, the more my back hurts.

She's on the bed. Barely conscious. Drugged.

Every so often we give her something to drink. We stop giving her water because she chokes on it. Water is harder to swallow. We give her chocolate drink. Ensure. E-N-S-U-R-E. She sips it.

She's been in the hospital now about nine days. She'd been in the hospital before and we'd all flock to her side until she got well enough to come out. But it's clear, this time, she's not coming out. She's not wearing any makeup—that's how I know. Every other time in the hospital, no matter how sick she got, she'd ask for her makeup bag and begin to tease her hair into a silver/black mane. Then she put on her face: base, mascara, eyeliner, and eyebrow pencil for that dark, dramatic 1950s look. It was a ritual she lived by; it was a look she understood.

But now her breathing is heavy and there's no need for makeup. We wait.

There are six of us, six children. Five boys and one girl. My parents are proud when they say it; we are their life's work. We are proud when we say it, though I'm not sure why. Now, three of the six have gone home. Our father has gone home. Three of us are left. It is the last night. We wait.

I get up, move closer, to try to make her more comfortable or maybe just to touch her—and SUDDENLY the chocolate drink we'd been giving her comes GUSHING out of her nose and mouth. Aaagh! I scream and jump back.

My older brother starts laughing hysterically.

My younger brother starts laughing.

So I start to laugh.

And the three of us can't stop.

Our mother is on the bed, dying, and we are hysterical, laughing.

"NURSE! NURSE!"

I call for the nurse. She comes in, sees what's happened. She goes out and brings back a little vacuum cleaner and proceeds to stick the hose down my mother's throat and right up her nose—starts vacuuming out all the liquid. All the while talking to her, gently, tenderly. "Yes, sweetie. I know it's very uncomfortable. I know." My mother moans. She is aware.

This is the same nurse my mother hated! The one who was mean to her, who hurt my mother when she tried to lift her from the bed. We wanted to kill her! My younger brothers had to be held back from physically assaulting her.

But now she is kind and gentle. And we are laughing.

She cleans up the mess and leaves.

We wait.

My youngest brother leaves. Two of us remain. My older brother, Sonny and me.

I lie down and fall asleep on the other bed in the room. Then I wake up.

Sonny and I sit in chairs at the foot of her bed. We wait.

He falls asleep in the chair. I am alone with her.

There's a machine that monitors her breathing. It beeps if she stops: a warning. I call the nurse back. Turn it off, I say. There's no need to disturb her now. She does as I ask and leaves.

My older brother wakes up. We sit and wait. He starts timing the space between her breaths on his wristwatch. They get shorter and shallower and shorter. The last one, barely a gasp.

"Sonny?"

"Hm?"

"Did you see the light change?"

"Un-uh."

"Did you see something move up from the bed?"

"Un-uh. Rob?"

"Hm?"

"You've seen too many movies."

"Sonny?"

"Hmm?"

"I think she's gone. How long has it been?"

"Two minutes."

"Two minutes? That's a long time."

We stand up.
And I hug my older brother
for the first time, in a long time.
For the first time in a long time
there is nothing between us anymore.

MY MOTHER FED THE BIRDS

ROBIN GOLDFIN

There. In a box on a shelf, off a highway in New Jersey, lies what used to be my mother.

Yech. That's a morbid way to begin. But it's true. My mother didn't leave instructions for what she wanted after she died, but one of us remembered that she didn't want to be put in the ground, she wanted a mausoleum. But my mother's idea of a mausoleum was something different: think a great stone affair; think angels and eagles, towers, trumpets, turrets; think mini–Taj Mahal. What she got was small, even by New York apartment standards. More like a housing project for the deceased. Hundreds of little casket-size squares lined up, one on top of the other, side by side. That's not right. My mother liked her space. Not that she needs any now. But I need some. At least with a grave in the ground you can go, pull up a few weeds, leave a stone to show you've been there. Talk. I can talk to the ground, I can't talk to a wall. Because when I go I want to talk. My mother and I didn't talk enough in life, and I want to have more conversation. A relationship does not end with death. My mother taught me that.

I am fifteen years old, asleep in my bed. I wake up one night to find my mother sitting up in the bed beside me, with the light on, smoking a cigarette.

"Ma?"

"Robbie, look!"

She is pointing out the open door of my bedroom to the windows on the other side of the house.

"Robbie, look—my father—"

He had died some ten years before.

"There in the window—his face as big and bright as the moon!"

"Ma?"

"Robbie, look—he's looking inside the house, Robbie. He's smiling. He's happy! He likes what he sees! Robbie, look!"

"Uhhhh. . . . No."

"Robbie, look!"

"No."

"Robbie!"

"MA! Let me go to sleep!"

I rolled over, put the pillow over my head and went back to sleep. In the morning, when I woke up, she was gone. I got dressed and went in for breakfast, where my mother told everyone the story of what happened, what she had seen the night before, and they all had a good laugh—my brothers and sister—because I had been too afraid to look.

Now I'm sorry I hadn't. What would I have seen? What she saw? What *did* she see?

My mother literally found her father when she was ten years old, he adopted her, and after that they were inseparable. They adored each other. She used to say, "They broke the mold when they made him." When he died—she was only in her twenties—she went up to his casket and put a cigar in his breast pocket; he liked to smoke them. When my mother died, I went up to her coffin and put some money in her hand. She liked to go shopping.

It took my mother some ten years after her father's death to see his face in the window. But it took her only a few months to come back to me. She had died in a lot of pain, from a metastatic cancer—a lot of suffering. For weeks afterward I would have dreams, and in each of them she was sick and frail and dying, and I would wake up crying. Then one night, I was not asleep, it was not a dream. I was in that half-sleep, half-waking state, and I looked down to the foot of my bed and there she stood. Hair done, makeup on, looking good again.

"Robbie," she said, in that whiskey voice.

"Ma?"

"Robbie, I am no longer suffering. You have to stop suffering."

Then she was gone.

My mother loved many things—her father, my father, her children, her Friday night trips to Caesars in Atlantic City to play the slot machines. And the birds. My mother loved the birds, and years after her death it is the birds who come back to remind me that a relationship does not end after death, it continues.

My mother fed the birds. In the house where I grew up, in South Jersey, the birds would build their nests—clogging up the drain pipes or decorating the outside lighting fixtures, and we would have to walk by very carefully if there were little ones about because the parents were watchful and wary. But they came back year after year because my mother fed them. She would bring back rolls from restaurants, she saved stale bread and cakes and pastries and would leave them in baskets all around the house. And the birds would feed. Long after I moved out, my mother built a new and bigger and better house, and she got more creative because she had more birds. This house was by a lake so there were lots of them. My mother took to cooking up huge pots of macaroni and dumping them steaming on the driveway. Birds, flocks of them—crows and sparrows, starlings, mourning doves would circle and wait, hover, dart down to feed. God forbid she ran out of food. "SHAKE!" she would yell to my father, "WE'RE OUT OF CREAMETTES!"

One morning, a couple of years ago, in the spring, my sister called. "Rob, I'm sorry to bother you, I know you're busy"—it was just before Passover and I was making two Seders—"but I wanted to tell you something. Yesterday I went to Mommy's grave, and it looked like someone had messed up the flowers again."

These are not real flowers. For an extra hundred dollars you can get a little plastic vase attached to your loved one's name-plate. My sister gets bunches of artificial orchids made up, in my mother's favorite colors—black and white. For some reason people had taken to stealing or messing them up.

My sister: "Rob, yesterday I went to Mommy's grave and it looked like someone had messed up the flowers again. Then I looked closer and saw that the birds were building a nest in Mommy's flowers. I looked at all the other flowers, on all the others graves, and it was only by Mommy's grave they were building a nest. Nowhere else."

Sure enough, there was a nest. And soon enough there were little ones waiting to be fed. And soon they, too, were gone.

I was thinking about this a couple of days later as I was walking down the street, and I started to weep, wailing, sobbing tears. This is New York, so no one paid any attention. And wouldn't you know it, just at this moment, I run into an old friend, a very attractive man who is not available, but we still like to flirt with one another.

"Hi. How you doin'? Good to see you. Haven't seen you in a long time. You look good!" Meanwhile my nose is running, the tears are streaking, my face is a mess. He is too polite to say anything. Finally I reach into my bag to pull out a tissue. "Excuse me," I say, "I was just thinking of something sad."

"Oh? What?" he asked.
What could I tell him?
"My mother fed the birds."

MY DANCER AND MY DOCTOR

JAMES WHELAN

JAMES WHELAN, *a native of Massachusetts, moved to New York City in 1986 to pursue his flights of fancy. He has worked as an actor and a journalist, as well as a bellhop, a taxi driver, and a hotel concierge.*

In January of 2000, my ex-boyfriend called me up. He was a dancer on Broadway, and he was moving to L.A. in two weeks to pursue work in film and TV. We met for lunch and chatted away like old friends. I was enjoying our reunion very much, until he started to talk wistfully of what we'd once had together. I was flattered he had such fond memories, but mine were not so fond. I felt awkward and uncomfortable.

His move to L.A. got pushed back a couple of weeks, and late one night in a taxicab rattling up First Avenue, he grabbed my hand, held it tight and said, "James, may I please, *please* come up to your apartment?" I did not say no. He was such an incredible physical specimen, in that way only a dancer can be. The soles of his feet were as smooth as satin slippers. This would just be hot closure sex and then, bye-bye.

But he kept postponing his trip to L.A., and we kept having (safe) sex. I enjoyed it, but a month later, when he finally did move, I was able to put a happy ending to it without that old emotional involvement. I was glad he was going, and I could get back to my life.

About this time, I got a new job, and my HMO required I choose a primary-care physician. After perusing a thick directory, I selected a doctor who had an office near my home, and a name with some good imagery attached to it. His name was Dr. Battler. If I ever got sick, I wanted Dr. Battler by my bedside—practicing his distinctive style of aggressive and unrelenting medicine.

I showed up for my first appointment and was ushered into the tiniest examination room I had ever seen. Dr. Battler came through the door, a pasty-faced fellow with a receding hairline. He gave me a complete physical, seemed satisfied with his work, and took a seat to make a few notes in a manila folder.

It was at this moment that I said to him, "Dr. Battler, you ought to know that I am in a high-risk group for HIV, because I am gay."

"Do you mean to say that you have sex with other men?"

"Yes."

"Well, how many men have you had sex with?"

"Golly, I wouldn't know. I am just telling you this because I think you should know that I am in a high-risk group."

"And do you practice safe sex?" Dr. Battler spat out the words *safe sex*.

"Yes, always." Which was the truth.

"Well, you should keep it that way!" and Dr. Battler rose up out of his chair and left the room.

When I got back home there was a message on my machine from my dancer. He had been calling me on the phone every day for the six weeks he'd been in L.A., and our phone chats had been fun. I began to think that maybe I was missing something. And now he was coming back to New York! He had been cast in *Annie Get Your Gun,* and would go into rehearsal the next week. "The first place I am going to come when I step off that plane is straight to your apartment!" So I guessed it was meant to be!

He did indeed come directly to my place, and I was waiting for him with open arms. He dropped his bags, we made love, and then he went off to rehearsal. For two weeks it was bliss. I felt for him like I had when we were first involved.

The night before he was to go into the show, we were in my bed making love. I told him that I loved him, that I realized I had never stopped loving him. He came in a big gush, and then suddenly jumped out of bed and angrily announced, "You are a part of my past!" He dressed quickly, collected his things and, just like that, walked out of my life.

Astonished, perplexed, and heartbroken, I fell through an emotional trapdoor, and ended up in a place called the West Side Club, a bathhouse. I threw caution and safe sex to the winds.

For about a week, I went in and out of this place, until I had sufficiently blotted out the hurt. I was exhausted, and a bit sick. Worried that I might have picked up something, I phoned Dr. Battler's office for an appointment.

He was not particularly pleased to see me on such short notice. "Mr. Whelan, what are you here for?"

"Well, I do not feel well at all, doctor."

"Well, you look fine to me." Dr. Battler examined me and asked what my symptoms were.

"Look here, there is nothing the matter with you at all. These symptoms aren't indicative of any viral activity. Is there anything going on in your personal life that might be making you depressed?"

"Well, I just split up with the guy I was seeing."

"There you have it then, you are just a bit depressed. Go home and try to take your mind off this matter. If it makes you feel any better, by all means, go across the hallway and have some blood drawn, and I shall send it out for analysis. But I doubt very much you are suffering from anything but depression."

I phoned a friend, and went to lunch and a matinee. By the end of the day I was feeling much better and in a more positive frame of mind. Maybe Dr. Battler was right.

Several weeks went by before I received an urgent phone call. Dr. Battler said the results of the blood tests were inconclusive, yet indicative of something of grave concern. He wanted me to come in right away for more testing.

When the results from this second round came back, he called me in to his office and told me it was quite possible that I had hepatitis C. This confused and alarmed me. I could not understand how I could have it and not feel a bit sick. When I questioned Dr. Battler along these lines, he grew angry and impatient. His eyes bugged out of his head and he snapped, "I must test you for HIV!" He drew the blood and we scheduled another appointment in two weeks.

Because of work conflicts, I had to reschedule twice, and I was finally able to see him about a month later. The door to the tiny examination room swung open, and in strode Dr. Battler, manila folder in hand. He drew himself to his full height, slapped the manila folder down on the counter and announced, "Mr. Whelan you are HIV positive!" His manner was triumphant, and he looked at me as if he had just defeated me at some intense game. After the shock of hearing this news subsided, I decided that he must be lying to me, playing some kind of trick—especially when he told me I didn't have hepatitis C after all.

He rattled off a series of numbers for T cells and viral load, and then he told me he would absolutely not treat me anymore. I had to be referred to a specialist. He then uncapped a pen, and he asked me the names and phone numbers of all the men I had slept with recently, so he could call them and tell them I was HIV positive.

I thanked him for his concern, but told him I would take care of that myself. I also asked to be re-tested, just to be certain. He looked at me in disbelief, and then, with a snort, agreed to do it. Then I asked him how long someone with my level of T cells and viral load could expect to live. "Oh, you'll be around for three years or so," he said.

I was ready to leave, but Dr. Battler had more paperwork. He was required to record that he had given me appropriate counseling at this difficult moment. He asked me what I planned to do with the rest of my day. I told him I had planned to drive up to Massachusetts to visit my mother for a couple of days.

"Are you sure you want to do that? Drive a long distance, I mean. People have been known to despair when they get news like this. Can you handle it?"

"I am not about to kill myself, Dr. Battler." I was angry now, and had to get the hell out of there. He suppressed a smile, and he bent over his form. On it he noticed my birth date, October 30, just two days before. "Oh, happy birthday," he said.

The first person I called when I left there was my friend Dan. He was a retired Wall Street lawyer in his midseventies, steady as a rock, sensible, not at all given to hysterics. I admired him because he had been involved in a relationship with the same man for more than fifty years. They had met in the army during World War II.

"All this means is that from now on, you will be a pill taker, that's all." If I had called someone else, someone more emotional—a member of my family for instance—I would have gone off the deep end.

Then Dan gave me this instruction: "Look, don't tell anyone about this. Don't even talk about it with anyone you might think is safe, because it will stigmatize you. Even in the gay community. You certainly don't look sick, and in fact you are not sick. So don't allow yourself to become stigmatized."

I took Dan's advice. I did not tell anyone, except those closest to me. But it's just not right to keep something like this bottled up inside forever. *So I guess the time has come to be stigmatized.*

It was on November 1, 2000 that I sat in Dr. Battler's tiny examination room, and he gleefully told me I was HIV positive. Perhaps the world should know about all the good changes I have made in my life since then. I have never experienced better health and fitness, and other things have changed too. But these changes come about so slowly. It's like trying to observe a glacier move down a mountainside. You can't see it happening, but it does move.

QUEER CHRISTMAS

MITCH ALLEN

December 1966—a four-year-old in Gallant Belk's department store on the elevator with his mother. A nicely dressed older lady looks down at the boy holding his mother's hand. "What a sweet little boy. What is Santa Claus bringing you for Christmas, little boy?" The little boy looks up at the lady. "There ain't no such a thing as Santa Claus," he barks. The elevator doors open and the befuddled woman scurries out. The boy looks up at his mother for approval.

Growing up, I dreaded the day after Thanksgiving. In school we sang carols in music class. We made stockings out of socks and glitter. We wrote letters to Santa that we were supposed to give our parents to mail. I learned all the words to the carols, I used more glitter than anyone on my stocking—but I threw it, along with Santa's letter, in the garbage on my way home.

See, we didn't celebrate Christmas in our house. There are pictures of me at one, two, and three opening presents on Christmas day in front of the tree. But after my sister was born, Daddy had a dream that made him remember a bargain he'd made with God. At eighteen God had given Daddy "the call." But Daddy told God he wasn't ready yet. He wanted to live life the way he wanted. To get married and have two children. Then he would turn his life over to God's work. Soon after my sister was born, Daddy dreamt that my mother and sister were lying dead in a coffin. A voice said, "See what will happen if you don't live up to your bargain." That week Daddy joined his father's church and within a year was preaching alongside Pa-Pa. That's when I lost Christmas.

The Christmas after my sister was born, my grandmother on Mama's side and my aunt Linda thought it was a tragedy that I wouldn't have a Christmas tree. So they brought one into our house. Daddy was at work when they put it up. Mama let them. That night I heard them arguing. The tree stayed that year. But that was the last one. ("Be ye not like the heathens who cut trees from the forest and deck them with silver and gold.")

The reason our church didn't celebrate was because Christmas is not really Christ's birthday. The Bible says he was born in the spring of the year. Christmas was started by the Catholics because they wanted Christianity to be popular with the pagans who celebrated the birth of their King Nimrod on December 25. The Pope made it Christ's birthday so the new Christians still got their celebration. Christ never asked us to celebrate his birth, only to remember his death. Any time there was a birthday celebration in the Bible, something terrible always happened. (John the Baptist lost his head to Salome at King Herod's birthday party.)

And as far as Santa Claus was concerned, Daddy said that if parents lied to their children about a man climbing down chimneys with gifts, that upon learning the truth, those children would think they were lied to about Jesus as well.

My grandmother gave us gifts against my daddy's wishes until I was ten or eleven. But that was the only Christmas presents we ever got. As a matter of practicality we usually went shopping for toys the day after Christmas because everything was marked down. But it was never the best toys that were left. I remember one year we went to Western Auto, which marked all their toys down sixty to seventy percent. My little sister was three and she chose a talking Baby Drowsy doll just like "Santa" brought our cousin Patti the day before. There was only one doll left. My sister was so excited. At home she opened the box, took out the doll and immediately started squalling. It was a black Baby Drowsy. Mama had missed the little check mark on the bottom of the box. We took it back down to Western Auto, but had to get a rain check for when a new shipment came in.

It was harder once I was school age. After Christmas vacation everyone stood up in class to tell what we got for Christmas. I would recite what my grandmother bought me and what I got at the after-Christmas sale, and also whatever I had gotten for my birthday and anything else bought for me that year. It was important for me to hide the shame of not participating in the holiday the rest of the world seemed to love so much. The last year we stood up was sixth grade. That year I swallowed hard when it was my turn and stood up and said "I got nothing for Christmas. My church doesn't recognize it as a holiday."

At twenty-two I was working as a singing waiter at a dinner theater in Florida. The show I was in finished soon after Thanksgiving, but I stayed on for a few weeks as an extra waiter. It was their busiest time of year. John was in the cast that followed mine. My first love. Everyone in the cast was away from home for the holidays, so we all became our own surrogate family. My next job was starting three days after Christmas and I had put off leaving for as long as I could. I woke up Christmas Eve morning and kissed John goodbye. I left a present for him under the tree. A stuffed pink flamingo he named Floyd. I drove the twelve hours from Florida to Georgia without stopping. I cried the whole way.

Ten years later I finally found out what Christmas is all about. I had started seeing Greg just before Thanksgiving. He invited me to his family's house in Jersey for Christmas. I was supposed to take the train out on Christmas Eve and spend the next three days there. But Greg got a terrible case of the flu and asked if I could come out a couple of days early to help prepare for a big post-Christmas dinner his mom had planned for the extended family. So I was immediately thrown into the spirit of Christmas—Gevas style. I barely met Mrs. Gevas before I got put to work helping her decorate the tree and moving furniture out of windows to the garage, and grabbing things from the freezer for the impending big dinner. Poor Greg was pretty much out of it. I dragged him sniffling to the mall to buy presents for these people I had only just met. His mother had taken a shine to me right away (it didn't hurt that she had hated Greg's last boyfriend). She seemed okay about Greg and me. The only provision was that I was to sleep alone in the spare room she used as an office. The whole room had to be rearranged to pull out the sleep sofa. From his father I got stern tolerance. But Greg's sister Janine made me feel very welcome. She flies in from California every year with her lover, Jill. They've been together for over twenty years.

Midnight on Christmas Eve is when the Gevi exchange gifts. Christmas Day is for immediate family only. Dinner and a trip to the movies. The day after Christmas was the really big day. Over twenty people were coming over. The whole day was a madhouse. Finally at around seven they arrived. All the crazy aunts and cousins and family friends. Greg and I were chiefly used as waiters. The best time was when we all gathered around the piano and sang the carols I learned in grade school. That night, after we had helped Greg's mom clean up the mess left behind, we were all tired to the bone. I went into the room where I'd slept the two nights before to move all the furniture around. She said, "Oh don't bother. Just sleep in the room with Greg tonight."

Two more Christmases have come and gone with the Gevi. Now I have to decide what to get for five people who already have everything they need. I have to make sure my gift is just right to let Greg know how much I love him. I have to put on a happy face for all the crazy relatives the day after Christmas. But now I say "Merry Christmas" without a lump of guilt in my throat.

MOVING ON

KISS TODAY GOODBYE

ANDY BAKER

After I came out, and during a particularly difficult time in my life, I got into an entangled friendship with two people through the theater department at a small college in Fort Worth, Texas. Reilly was a fat, rich-boy theater major and former drag queen. Karen was a rail-thin, pre-law student who was exploring all the possibilities of her newly discovered vagina. I was an art major who enjoyed the atmosphere of the theater. I was searching for Mr. Next, who I imagined would take me away from what I was most miserable with—me.

During my sophomore year, Reilly and I became involved sexually. To me it was a casual thing. To Reilly it was more serious. Karen was our constant companion, in love one moment and brokenhearted the next. We spent evenings doing shots of schnapps and watching the same movies over and over. Reilly did Karen's hair and makeup to make her feel pretty. It was a sticky sort of friendship of convenience that I found difficult to extricate myself from while we were in close proximity during the school year.

At the end of the school year, Reilly and Karen moved into a small, one bedroom apartment in a questionable neighborhood. I moved to my parent's house thirty minutes away. I worked at a big chain restaurant and had just begun seeing a guy named Chris. I was trying to turn my relationship with Reilly into a friendship without telling him that the sexual aspect had ended for me. I had presented Chris only as a new friend.

Karen had been fucking some guy, and he'd dumped her by not calling her back. She was in a deep, dark, airless pit of depression.

One night Reilly and I had gone out to dinner, and when we came back to their apartment, Karen was sitting on the bed in the dark, chain-smoking with the clock radio in her lap. She was searching for the saddest song she could find.

Reilly led me to the couch and we sat down. He put his head on my lap. We talked about what we would be doing for the next few days. Apparently, Karen could hear us and she turned the radio up.

"Karen! Turn that down please!" Reilly yelled from my lap.

There was no response. Reilly got up and walked to the bedroom and closed the door. He sat back down. The door flew open again, and Karen turned and stomped, through the dark, back to the bed.

Reilly got up again. "You can either have the door open and the radio down, or the radio up and the door closed!" He slammed the door. We heard stomping again, and the door flew open.

"I'll listen to the radio however loud I want to! And the door is staying open!"

"Fine!" He yelled back at her. Then he said to me, "I'm going to spend the night at my mother's house because I can't stay here with that CRAZY FUCKING BITCH!" It was said to me but was meant for her.

"Fine!" she yelled from the bedroom.

"Fine!" he yelled back. "Come on," he said to me. "Can you drop me off at my mother's house? She's ruined this whole perfect evening."

I was glad the evening was ending before I had to begin fending off his advances. "Sure."

"Where'd I put my goddamn keys?" We looked for them for a few minutes. On the coffee table, under the couch, in the kitchen.

"Maybe they're in my car," I offered.

"Who the fuck cares?" he said. "Karen!" he yelled into the dark bedroom. "I can't find my keys. You're going to have to lock the door behind us."

I heard Karen get up off the bed and stomp to the living room. For the first time that evening, she emerged into the light, and she was a mess. She followed us out of the living room and into the kitchen where we walked out the back door and onto the porch, which led to the parking lot.

"I'll call you tomorrow to get in. I don't have my keys."

Karen said nothing and locked the door. Her two-toned hair was matted in places and stringy in others. It hung in her face as I watched her struggle with the double-key deadbolt through the dirty windowpanes in the door. "Karen, did you hear me?" Reilly yelled at her. "Karen! Look at me!" When the door was locked, she threw the keys across the room and stomped back to the bedroom.

"Crazy bitch!" Reilly called after her. We walked to the car. "That crazy bitch." As we approached the car, Reilly said, "Oh. I remember where they are. Hold on." He walked back to the door.

I stood at the car and said out loud to myself, "This is the reason I need to get away from these two."

"Karen, open the door. I need to get in!" Reilly yelled as he knocked on the glass door. "Karen! Open the door!" He knocked on the glass harder. "Karen! Open the goddamn—" There was a crash and the tinkling of broken glass falling on concrete. Then, "OH MY GOD! Oh my God, I'm dying! Oh my God!"

I stood at the car for a millisecond—was this for real? It was very much like him to put on a show and lie, even to the point of frightening someone. But there was an air of desperation in his voice that made it sound real, the sound of a man who was genuinely frightened that he was dying. I ran back to the porch.

It had only been a few seconds between the time that I heard the glass and the time that I got to the porch. It was a matter of twenty feet. When I got there and rounded the corner, most of the porch was covered with blood and Reilly was standing and screaming, looking at a gaping wound in his forearm that was spurting blood.

At this point, we both yelled for Karen. She ran around the corner into the kitchen. "Open the door," I said sternly through the broken pane of glass.

"I'm dying! Oh my God! She's killed me!"

Karen stood groggy-eyed and tired-looking. Her makeup was grimy and had tear tracks. Mascara was smeared around her eyes like she'd been beaten. "I don't know where they are. I threw them." She craned her neck to see what was going on outside.

"Look for them! Find them!"

"Oh my God! I'm going to die! I'm going to die right here!"

"Hey!" I turned and yelled at him. "Stop looking at it! Look at me!" I lowered my voice. "You're going to be fine." He looked at me and then back at the gash. "Rile! Look at me! Karen is going to open the door, get us a towel, and then call 911. The ambulance will be here in a few minutes. You'll be okay." I pointed to the area right above the wound and said, "Push there as hard as you can."

"I need a tourniquet!" He yelled. "Karen! Get me one of my ties!"

"No!" I said. "Apply pressure first. A tourniquet is the last choice!"

Karen opened the door.

"Get me a towel," I said. She ran into the other room and arrived with a thick towel. "Call 911." I turned to Reilly. "Give it to me." He held his arm out to me. I wrapped the towel around it. "Move your thumb." As he did, I pushed down on the point he'd been holding as hard as I could. I was looking at the blood on the ground, and I knew that he didn't need to lose any more than he already had. I led him to the steps and we sat on them. The pool of blood had not come that far.

"I'm going to have a club hand," he whimpered. "No one will love me with a club hand."

"You're going to be fine," I said softly.

"Oh my god, I'm going to be a cripple."

Karen yelled from the kitchen in a clear voice, "They're on their way!"

"Let's sing," I said.

"Sing? I don't want to sing."

"When you're down and troubled . . . and you need a helping hand . . . "

"And nothing, whoa, nothing is going right," he continued. We sang softly as a small crowd of their trashy neighbors came out of their apartments, and others looked out the windows.

"You need me to call 911?" a man asked.

"No thanks," I said. "They're on their way."

After we finished "You've Got A Friend," I launched into "What I Did For Love." It was a song I knew he loved. Reilly looked sadly at his hand wondering what the future of it was. Karen lay curled up in the fetal position on the dirty linoleum with her back to the door amidst the broken glass and spatters of blood that had escaped the porch.

The crowd parted as the ambulance arrived and paramedics surrounded Reilly.

Karen had gotten up and stood in the doorway. Without

speaking to her, I tiptoed through the blood, picked her boney frame up, and carried her, barefoot, to the bloodless steps so that she could see what was going on.

Surprising both Reilly and myself, Karen had had the foresight to call Reilly's mother, Mamie, who arrived posthaste and ran to Reilly asking, "What did she do to you, baby?" She glared at Karen, and Karen sunk into me, cowering away from the wrath of that recovering alcoholic twelve years sober, and as evil as anyone I'd ever met.

"He saved my life," Reilly said to an EMS man as they raised the gurney into the back of the ambulance.

"You did a fine job," the EMS man said to me nodding.

After the ambulance drove away, the crowd dispersed and Mamie left without a word to either of us. I carried Karen back to the kitchen, and we began cleaning the blood and glass off the porch and the kitchen floor. Several buckets of water later, there was no trace of the accident except for the broken pane of glass, which still had blood on it. I knocked it out and taped a piece of cardboard in its place.

Karen spent the night with me in my bed at my parent's house. When my mother opened my bedroom door the next morning to give me the phone call from the hospital, she must have been both horrified and overjoyed to see Karen curled around me.

Two days after the accident, when Karen and I went to see him at the hospital, Reilly looked at me and said sweetly, "The doctor said if you hadn't been so quick to do what you did, I might have died." I shrugged and looked away.

The conversation continued for a few minutes until he looked at me and said, "You've been sleeping with Chris, haven't you?"

"No," I lied. "No."

"Yes, you have. You wear it on your face. I'm lying in a hospital dying and you're having sex! Oh my God. Why couldn't I have just died?" he cried. Karen and I made a speedy exit as I again denied my infidelity and promised to see him again soon.

Weeks later, Reilly and I tried to be friends. I went to see him and we talked on the phone. He recovered slowly, Karen got into a semipermanent relationship, and I concentrated on friendships with people outside of school. Eventually the time came when I had to choose between a friendship with Reilly and a relationship with Chris. I chose Chris.

The Christmas banquet for the theater department was held in a small restaurant in Fort Worth. Reilly stood in front of the crowd and said, "I guess a lot of you have heard about my accident." He looked thoughtfully off to one side. "It's been a huge adjustment. The doctors say I'll have partial use of my hand if I keep up with my therapy." He drew his body up bravely. "But I have been playing the piano some, and I'd like to play a little something tonight." He looked around at the faces at the table and lingered for a second on mine. He walked to the piano. "Kiss today goodbye," he sang, "and point me toward tomorrow . . . "

As he edged toward the line, "Look, my eyes are dry," tears streamed down his face.

I got up from the table. At the door, I stood for a moment and watched the crowd watch Reilly. I felt someone staring at me, and looked over at Karen, who rolled her eyes as if to say, "That's our Reilly, being Reilly."

When he finished playing, Reilly got up from the piano, wiped his tear-stained face on his sleeve, and bowed to the crowd. Through the applause, he scanned the crowd and found me at the door. I looked at him for a moment and then at Karen. I looked back at him again, and then I turned and walked out the door, leaving the two of them in the restaurant, and in my past.

KIYO

GEORGE PFIFFNER

In 1952, when I was twenty-eight, I got a job on the stage crew of KLAC-TV Channel Thirteen in Hollywood. It was the local TV equivalent to a B-minus movie studio, but my salary doubled that of my previous job. I could now afford to see a Beverly Hills shrink.

I told him that I was homosexual, and did not think I wanted to change, but had had no experience with women. That I worried that I wasn't masculine enough to attract them. He told me he thought that I was masculine enough to interest a lot of women. That many women don't like men who are overly masculine. That if I really wanted to interest a woman, all I had to do was let her see my interest. And if she was interested, something would happen.

"But," I said, "sometimes my voice gets very high-pitched."

He said, "That's probably just tension and anxiety. You can probably control it. You don't sound feminine, maybe a little pedantic sometimes. Just show your interest by looking at a woman with a look that lets her know you like her."

"How do I do that?"

"Easy. Just think to yourself, 'Isn't she pretty.' Or 'I would really like to know her.' Flirt. Don't you flirt with men?"

"I guess. Not consciously."

"You let them know you like them without saying a word, don't you? Do the same thing with women. Smile a lot, but keep it subtle. No groping." He smiled.

Hunt Carter was one of the cameramen at KLAC-TV. While we were chatting during a break, I said something in passing about astrology. He asked if I was interested in it, and I said I was, because my mother was immersed in the subject and did our family horoscopes. "Really," he said. "So does my wife, Kiyo, but she's a professional astrologer. You should meet her."

I said, "I would like to." I wasn't sure I would. He generally came to work rumpled and covered in cat hair. I imagined his wife wearing a housecoat, with a dust cap over her curlers, a cat under one arm, a pencil in her mouth, and several zodiacal charts in her free hand. I asked a couple of the guys on the crew if they had met her. They said she was a "stunner." So a couple of days later I asked Hunt when it might be convenient for us to get together. We had the same schedule, so he suggested we meet for breakfast at Schwab's on Sunset Boulevard.

When I arrived, they were already seated opposite each other. Kiyo was indeed a stunner (I learned later she was half Japanese). She said, "George, sit here next to me." She took my hand, pulled me into the booth next to her, and continued to hold my hand on her thigh.

She was thoroughly groomed, skillfully made up, and somewhat overdressed for the afternoon, even for Los Angeles. Almost immediately she wanted my birth data, and before we parted, I asked her to give me a reading. I had the feeling that she would construct a chart as soon as she got home, because off the cuff she said, "Oh, you have Neptune in Leo on your ascendant. You could be a medium."

"The last thing I would ever want to be is a medium."

She said, "Good for you. It could be dangerous for you, with that Neptune square in all of your Scorpio planets."

Then she gave me her card. I gave her my phone number. She said she had to leave, so I had to stand to let her out of the booth. She was tiny, and she pulled me down and kissed me on the mouth.

We made at least three dates, all of which she canceled before she gave me the promised reading. She said that she and I had very compatible charts, and that our Mercurys would be in tune with each other for the next 300 years. She would not let me pay for the reading. I thought she might have fallen in love with my horoscope.

She suggested that she and I see a movie on an evening when Hunt was working and I wasn't. I suggested that we go when all three of us were free. "George," she said, "you should know that Hunt and I haven't made love in quite some time. He is very dear to me and I know he loves me. And I do love him. But he really doesn't mind if I see other men."

I still felt I had to get Hunt's permission. I spoke to him at the end of a night's work. "Hunt, I'd like to take Kiyo to see *Forbidden Games* on Thursday night." He said, "That's okay. You don't have to ask me, but I must tell you that I don't want anything bad to happen to her." I knew I was expected to say that I would never do anything to hurt her, but I couldn't say it. I think I said something like, "Yes, I understand."

It wasn't long before I was convinced I was in love with Kiyo. We talked on the phone late at night. I went over to their place in Laurel Canyon and talked with both of them or her alone. I learned that in 1942 she had been detained in one of the Japanese internment camps where she was forced to live for much of the war, until she met a sergeant who took her out of the camp and into non-com housing. She claimed it was not a marriage of convenience, but who could blame her if it was?

By then, I trusted her enough to tell her I was gay. It didn't seem to faze her.

We had been necking, but I hadn't touched her in any intimate places. Then she suggested that we drive together to Santa Barbara. She would bring a lunch, and we would drive up into the hills to make love.

When we arrived at a site she liked, we pulled off the road and had lunch. Then we necked. Then nothing. I couldn't conjure up even a ghost of an erection. She couldn't have been sweeter about it.

I drove us back down the highway as the sun was setting, and headed south, and she sat as close as she could to me with both her hands in my crotch. Her hands warmed me. I began to imagine myself going down on her, licking away someplace. Much to my surprise, I got hard.

At Point Mugu, the shoulder of the highway widened into a parking area. I pulled into it, facing the darkened Pacific. We pulled together and felt each other. She was wet and slippery. I pushed up her dress as she leaned back, lifting her legs over my shoulders, giving me easy access.

The next morning I woke very pleased with myself. I didn't have a single thought about "manhood" or "masculinity." I was just pleased I had done it, and I thought of her fondly. But could I do it again? I phoned Kiyo and suggested we get together that morning before I went to work. Hunt drove her to my apartment. And I did do it.

We saw each other as often as we could. Sometimes I spent the night with her. Hunt's bedroom was on one side of the bathroom and hers was on the other, with the doors opposite each other. When we forgot to close the doors, there we were: Hunt in his bed staring at the two of us in Kiyo's.

Kiyo and I shared a lot of interests and attitudes, I thought. I also learned that I was the third man she claimed to have converted. Then she started provoking scenes, and nothing I said or did could stop them. She would say the most vile things her mind could conceive to hurt me, and then she was ready to kiss and make up.

One evening at 8:30, we were at the bar of a restaurant on La Cienega Boulevard waiting for a table. I told her that something she had just said reminded me of an observation by Marcel Proust.

"What did you say?"

"I said that Proust . . ."

"Why are you thinking of Proust?"

"Because of what you . . ."

"You're not supposed to be thinking about what you read in Proust."

"What?"

"You told me you wouldn't."

"I didn't. You told me that I shouldn't . . ."

"Be thinking about homosexual stuff."

By nine o'clock she was getting loud and wouldn't lower her voice, so I pulled her out of the bar and took her to my apartment. She seemed to have calmed down, but as soon as I closed the door, she yelled, "Can't you control your mind? Are you so weak?" and so on, past ten o'clock. I was silent. I had learned that nothing I could say would have any effect.

11 P.M. "You promised me." She's crying. "I'm so disappointed in you. How could you do this to me?"

12 A.M. "You miserable faggot!" And on and on. And she pummels me.

1 A.M. She is sniffling and wants to kiss and make up.

2 A.M. I tell her I don't want to make up. I want to end it. I can't take her emotional storms. She says she loves me. She truly loves me.

3 A.M. She is hysterical: Laughing and sobbing and giggling and gulping and hiccupping. Her makeup is smeared, her mascara is in rivulets.

4 A.M. She doesn't want to live, and tries to throttle herself. When she needs breath, she releases her throat. Exhausted, she slides to the floor and falls asleep.

5 A.M. I gather what few pieces of clothing she has in my apartment and put them in a shopping bag. I take a washcloth and wipe her face clean of most of its paint. This is the first time I see her without makeup. She is lovely.

6 A.M. She is awake. "Kiyo, I called a taxi to take you home. Come, I'll walk you to the street."

I pay the cabbie, close the door, and watch them drive away.

Kiyo was the first person I had been true to for any length of time. The first time I picked up a guy afterward, he was someone I didn't particularly like, who I did not find very attractive, and who wasn't really good in bed. But it was as though I hadn't had sex in six months and he was the young Marlon Brando.

WHAT A WORLD

KUM BA YA

Tom Ledcke

I went to visit Charles today. He's in a room with four other guys; it's an intensive care unit. Charles swatted his cane at one of the nurses as he tried to escape, so they're keeping an eye on him. One of the guys across the room is dying, and his sister is saying goodbye. Arnold's on life support and the sound of the respirator is loud while his sister is trying to talk to him. She starts singing songs by Joan Baez and a song their grandmother used to sing to them when they were kids. Then she says, "Arnold, Grandma sent the words to that song. Isn't that nice? Now we can sing it. Won't that be nice? Grandma loves you so much. Nonny loves you, Arnold. Do you know that? We love you very much. I want you to know that. Do you? Oh, you're moving your eyelashes. We do Arnold, we love you and we are so proud of you. You've made us so very proud. What are you trying to say honey? You rest now." Then she starts singing "Someone's in the Kitchen with Dinah."

Charles and I were trying not to listen but she was loud, and it was hard to hear the television overhead. Charles turns up the volume because a TV movie with Michael Paré was starting, and we couldn't miss the credits.

Arnold's sister started again trying to convince her brother how much he meant to her, by changing the tone in her voice, and varying her inflection to somehow snap him back to life. She said, "Brian's coming to see you all the way from Portland. And Arnold, he can't wait to see you, he misses you very much. He should be right overhead right this very minute, if he's not at the airport already. Brian loves you very much." Arnold didn't respond, his mouth was forced open with tubes to keep him breathing, and to keep him from drowning. His sister whispered, "Don't be afraid. I'm here with you." Time was running out.

Arnold's brother came in. I couldn't hear his name. He was out of breath and quickly pulled the curtain that divided the room. It was quiet for a few moments. Then sobbing, gasping, and choking sounds came from behind the partition. Charles kept staring at the television, seemingly unaware, commenting loudly: "Look at him! Oooooh girl, sit on my face! Isn't Michael Paré so fucking cute?" Then he began singing in a high falsetto, "Puuusssssy, get it girl!" Then in a lower voice, "I want you to eat my pussy. Go on, eat it! Eat me! Eat me!" Finally changing his tone like a precocious child, "Come on, I want you to eat my pussy."

It became quiet on the other side of the curtain. Charles turned the channel to *Sesame Street* because of a commercial break.

By this time a few more friends and family had arrived for Arnold, and they started singing softly, "Kum ba yah, my Lord. . . ." They were all crying and singing. It sounded like a little choir. His brother tells Arnold how much his daddy wanted to be there.

"He really did," he said. "I want you to know that, and that he loves you, but he just has a hard time showing it, but he always loved you. I want you to believe me, we all love you and always will. Daddy told me to tell you. He really did. You know, with all the love you have it's worth more than five of those Oscars and a hundred Tony awards. You're a winner with us because we love you. You don't have to worry about anything now." Then they started singing "Kum Ba Yah," all together softly. "Someone's crying, Lord, kum ba yah, Someone's crying, Lord, kum ba yah, Someone's crying, Lord, kum ba yah, someone's loving, Lord, kum ba yah, we love you Arnold, just relax now you're safe now, Oh Lord, kum ba yah."

Charles, with his blond hair standing straight up, joined in with his most appealing Ethel Merman imitation. "SOMEONE'S SCREAMING, LORD, KUM BA YAH! SOMEONE'S GOING TO RIP THEIR HAIR OUT, LORD, KUM BA YAH!!!!!"

It became deadly quiet on the other side of the curtain—they didn't move. Charles fluffed his pillow, turned up the sound, and we continued watching *Sesame Street.*

THE BUS STOP

GEORGE STYLIANS

GEORGE STYLIANS, *a native New Yorker, is a truck driver by trade. He enjoys playing the piano, guitar, and on occasion, a little accordion. He also likes to draw, write stories, and repair clocks. He is happily married to a supportive wife. They share their home with two cats.*

I think the day was a Thursday, a beautiful August evening in the late '60s. An unbearable heat wave had lasted several weeks, and I sat on the front stoop of my apartment house in Union City enjoying the nice change in weather. I thought of the Palisades Amusement Park, and decided to take a walk there.

I got as far as North Hudson Park when the sun was starting to set. I sat down at a bus stop, looked at the New York City skyline, and watched as the city put on her evening makeup of glittering electric lights.

Just when I was about to leave, a nice-looking guy came over to me and asked about the bus schedule. I replied with what information I knew, and waited to see where this situation was going to go. He talked some more. Friendly. Then he asked if I wanted to walk with him over to Nungessers corner to get something to drink.

As we walked across the park, he asked me if I was gay. I

said yes, and I asked him the same question. He said he was, but then I sensed something wrong. Two other guys had come out from behind a shrub and started walking behind us. I realized they knew the guy I was walking with. But before I could say something, two more guys appeared. They all seemed to know each other. I really had a bad feeling now. But they walked me right into a wooded area before I could do anything.

One of them pushed me from behind, causing me to fall. Then they started with the faggot remarks. I stood up and tried to reason with them, but they wouldn't stop. The first guy told me to remove my belt. I didn't obey his command, and one of the guys standing behind me struck me on the right side of my head with a piece of lumber or a stone. The impact was so great, I saw sparks. I could taste blood inside my mouth. Then another guy, standing to my left, punched me in the head and yelled for me to take off my belt. I removed my belt. Then they said to empty my pockets.

I obeyed, pleading with them to stop. The first guy took my keys and threw them into the pond. He also took the money I had, about seven dollars. I was hit again with a club or rock and some of them hit me with their fists and kicked me. The first guy just watched. Then one of them took out a hunting knife, the kind holstered in leather. A feeling of doom came over me. I felt like someone had pulled my heart out of my chest. Thoughts went through my mind of my dead body lying there for days, with a note saying, "This is what happens to faggots." The first guy told the guy with the knife to put it away, but he wouldn't listen. So the first guy had to shout, "NO KNIVES!" It was put away.

But one of them pushed me down, and they all started hitting, kicking, and walking on me. I could only see out of one eye.

Then they stopped. I thought they had left, and tried to get up. But they were still there! They started hitting, kicking, and walking on me some more. I stopped groaning and played dead. They stopped, and eventually they left.

I must have passed out, because when I opened my one good eye, I felt very cold. I lay there motionless for what seemed like twenty minutes, shivering, staring at the stars, and thinking of the pain and the taste of blood in my mouth. I then tried to get up, but had a severe pain in my chest. I started crying, thinking I had broken ribs. Then I remembered reading about taking deep breaths to detect if that was the case. I convinced myself I didn't have broken ribs. I said to myself, *Gotta get up, gotta get out of here.* I rolled over and pushed myself up to a kneeling position. I waited a moment, then stood up, but got so dizzy that I fell face down on the ground. I was crying again, and was unbearably cold. I finally got up and walked away from the wooded area.

When I reached the street, I noticed how much warmer the air was. My walking improved. A clock in a store window read 1:50 A.M. I realized I must have been out much longer than I thought.

Two women were walking toward me. One of them kept on talking, while the other focused on me. As we passed each other, I heard her say, "Did you see that man's face?" I stopped and glanced back. They were both looking at me, horrified.

I finally got back to my apartment house and sat on the steps, wondering how I was going to get in without my keys. I didn't want to wake the super. Then I remembered the firehouse nearby. The men often sat outside conversing, so I went there. As I approached them, one man said, "Wow! What happened to you?" I said that I got mugged, and my keys were taken. I must have looked really bad because they offered to take me to the hospital. I thanked them, but refused to go. I asked if they could get into my second floor apartment and open the door for me.

They agreed. They started their ladder truck, and I met them in front of my apartment house. But the flashing lights and the truck engine woke my super. He opened his window and asked if there was a fire. I walked closer to him, and he said, "Oh my god, what happened to you?"

The firemen opened the front door to the building, and as I climbed the stairs I started trembling. I looked at my face in the mirror. My left eye was swollen shut, and the right side of my face was swollen out. There was dried blood from my nose and mouth; dirt and scrape marks. I sat at the table and cried.

After a while, I got up, washed the dirt and blood off my face, and went to bed. But I awoke a couple of hours later, looked in the mirror and said to myself, *I've got to go to work.* I had to make a delivery of wax to Easton, Pennsylvania.

I arrived at the truck terminal at 5:30 A.M. Lucky for me there was no one there. So I picked up my dispatch papers, started the truck, and drove off to the refinery.

At the refinery in Bayonne, at the plant in Easton, and when I got back to the terminal, all these men who knew me were awed by how I looked. I told them I was mugged, and didn't give any details. My gay friends were the only people I trusted with the details.

I was supposed to visit my mother that weekend. She knew, when I called her, that something was wrong. I told her I got into a fight. Then I canceled the visit. I decided to ride the bus to Journal Square.

I walked around for a while, and decided to take the boulevard bus to Bayonne. I boarded the bus just south of Journal Square, put my coins in the fare box, and turned to find a seat—when *I saw the guy who walked me into the park!* His expression of surprise equaled mine. He quickly turned his face from me and looked out the window. I took a seat behind the rear exit door so I could watch him. He didn't look back.

About twenty minutes into the ride, he pulled the rope to signal the driver to stop. He walked to the front of the bus, and I walked to the rear exit. We both got off together.

He glanced to his right and saw me standing there. He walked rapidly to the corner and made a right, and I followed. From that corner he started to run, and I started to run. He ran down the street and up the stairs to a house that had a sign on the front porch. I stopped, looked at the sign, and realized it was a fraternity house.

Why that son-of-a-bitch, I said to myself. I wrote the address on a piece of paper and walked back to the bus stop. As I walked, I asked myself what I was going to do with this information. The general sentiment of people in the 1960s was to side with him. I tore the paper up and boarded the next bus.

Other than telling my gay friends at that time, I kept this story a secret until the Matthew Shepard incident all these years later, when the details of his murder were revealed in the news. I cried again, this time for Matthew, and thought how close to death I was that horrible night.

ME AND THE MAFIA

RONALD GOLD

When I was sixteen, I lived in a tiny apartment on the Upper West Side of Manhattan with another gay youth named Harry. He was pretty as could be, with a complexion like pearls, and shiny, curly black hair. He kept saying things like "Fuck me and suck me," which I would dearly have liked to do. But he was into "older men," so our relationship was unfortunately platonic.

Ditto for Johnny, another gorgeous youth I palled around with. He was blond, with nubile muscles to die for. And regrettably, the closest I got to sex with him was to watch him go off from the Village bars we frequented (they weren't very fussy about IDs in those days) with one of the twenty-somethings he coveted. But we did have fun making the rounds together.

We were always looking for new places, and one winter night we headed for an after-hours place he'd heard about on Elizabeth Street in Little Italy. We didn't have an exact address. And there were no neon signs or other indications that such a place even existed, so we wandered back and forth along the block, finally noticing that some steps leading down to a basement doorway had what looked like recent footsteps in the snow.

So we hesitantly headed down the steps, but before we got to the door, it opened in front of us, and we were admitted by a burly type who gave us the once-over as we passed him. The place was small and dimly lit, with only a few big, round wooden tables, all of which were occupied. But one table for eight seemed to have room for us, with four people sitting together on one side of it. So we sat down across from them.

The two men at either end of the foursome looked like they'd been supplied by central casting—dead ringers for George Raft and Edward G. Robinson in a '30s gangster movie, down to the stubble, scars, and pinstripe suits. But the pair in the middle were something special. She was about six foot, two inches, maybe in her late forties, but very svelte, encased in a skintight iridescent dark blue dress that was punctuated by a diamond necklace and bracelets galore—all of it dwarfed by a gigantic silver-fox stole. He was about four feet tall and pudgy, with a miniature pinstripe and fedora that made him look like a plug-ugly windup toy. She spoke in a sexy baritone and he in a shrill soprano. She called him Hank and the other men called him Henrietta.

We ordered a couple of beers, I think, and just sat there, trying not to stare at our tablemates, who went on with their conversations, paying us no mind. Yes, they were having two conversations, the pair in the middle chatting about what seemed to be domestic matters (we guessed from what they were saying that she was married to one of the men on the ends, and he was some kind of servant-henchman the rest of them had no qualms about ordering around), and the two on the ends talking gruffly and cryptically across the others about what seemed to be hugely illegal business matters.

This went on for a while, but all of a sudden the one who looked like George Raft stood up and indicated to the woman that it was time to go. So I thought that he and his wife would leave. But no, it was the woman and Hank/Henrietta who departed together. And just after they went out the door, the two remaining mobsters got up simultaneously and shifted seats, so that one of them was now seated right next to one of us.

They were pressed up against us, and the one next to me (Edward G. Robinson) leaned over right in my face and asked, in a very low voice, *"Do you strop?"* Well, I wasn't at all sure what that meant, but I *was* sure that I not only didn't strop but didn't want to. I shook my head no, but that didn't put a stop to anything. They just pressed closer, making it clear to us that we'd be theirs for the night.

I gave Johnny a quick look, and both of us instantly leaped to our feet and headed for the door, pursued by our Mafia admirers. Luckily, we had thirty years on them, because it was easier for us to negotiate the ice and snow. By the time we reached the subway entrance a couple of blocks away, they were several yards behind us. Blessedly, a train was entering the station just as we reached the platform. Johnny leaped over the turnstile, and I crawled under it, just in time to catch the train. But the door closed in our pursuers' faces. I can still see those faces through the glass, contorted with rage and frustration.

MY VARICOCELE

DEREK GULLINO

I wouldn't call my varicocele disfiguring, though you can see it when I'm naked. It looks like a third testicle, but it's spongy. My varicocele is a group of veins in my scrotum where blood puddles. If I pay attention to it, I can feel the blood throb regularly through the extra veins. If I pay enough attention, and concentrate on that area, I can feel my heart beat in my nuts. That always weirds me out, whenever I can hear that, so I hardly ever do it, and for many years I basically didn't think much about my varicocele.

In 1990, strange pains started shooting down the inside of my leg. For a fraction of a second, the pain would disable my leg, and then I'd be fine. I thought the pain in my leg might be tied up with my nervous stomach or the way I'd been living, so I went to the walk-in clinic in Brooklyn.

As soon as the doctor undid my pants and saw my varicocele, he wanted to touch it. "Does it hurt?" the doctor asked, pressing on the extra veins. During the examination, his thumb found its way up into my scrotal sac. "Does this hurt?" he asked and wiggled his thumb. It hurt so bad I couldn't speak. "That is one of the biggest varicoceles I have ever seen," the doctor said. "That might be strangulating one of your testicles."

He referred me to a urologist who strapped me to a computer. When the urologist rubbed the computer mouse all over my nuts, I could see the inside of my testicles on the computer screen. The urologist rubbed real hard on my right testicle and made me look at it. It was solid white and it looked like a peeled almond. When he put the mouse on my varicocele it looked like veiny beef.

"Sure it hurts you. Look at it," the urologist said. "What kind of underwear do you wear?"

"I don't really wear any."

"I know you don't," the urologist said. "Why do you think our friend here's so enormous. I could cut it out. Sure, lots of men do it. But first try this—for a week wear underwear and wear it tight. Let's see if the pain goes away."

I bought a pack of Fruit of the Looms, and I got them one size too small. It seemed to work. I kept my nuts snugly packed for the next three years and I didn't feel any pain. I didn't think about my varicocele, though, unless I looked at it, and I hardly ever looked at it because it was getting bigger and bigger. I never touched it.

One day I was on the exercycle at the YMCA. When I got off the exercycle, I felt this strange throbbing beneath my nuts. It felt like that part of me hadn't gotten off the exercycle yet.

That night, my boyfriend, Paul—who's been with me this whole time—Paul and I were jacking each other off in bed. When I ejaculated, there was a lot of blood in my semen. It was pretty much all blood. Paul saw it and he was horrified. In a panic, I called my mother, who's an RN and said, "Mom, me and Paul were having sex, and I ejaculated blood."

"What?"

"You heard me, Mom."

She said, "That nurse in the eleventh grade wrote me home a letter about your abnormal testicles, Derek. Remember, I wanted to see them. But you wouldn't let me."

"Mom, God," I said. "You're freaking me out."

"Well," she said, "anytime there's blood, there's trouble."

The next time Paul and I had sex, my ejaculate was normal, so I didn't go to the doctor. I just stayed off the exercycle, continued to wear my butt-tight underwear, and it worked for two more years, though my varicocele continued to grow. I also noticed that if I didn't wear any underwear, my balls would begin to hang too heavily and ache. My balls were large, especially toward the end.

Last October, I noticed that the varicocele had shifted, and a portion of the spongy excess veins dropped *below* my testicles. If you slid your hand down my butt and between my legs, you could feel it there. It throbbed constantly and, having slid from my scrotal sac, there was nothing to secure the varicocele to me. The veins pressed against my skin as if they were about to split through. When I was younger, a friend of mine was playing basketball and someone noticed some blood on the front of his gym shorts. By the time he'd slowed down enough to understand and to look, the blood was running down the inside of his leg. He had a varicocele and it had exploded during sports. He was bleeding pretty bad and they had to call an ambulance on him. I don't know what kind of pain, if any, he experienced. I imagine you feel something if your skin ruptures—but he kept grabbing his balls and muttering, "Time out. Time out." I thought about him and how his varicocele had popped on the basketball court, and I began to walk very slowly. When the veins fell, they also began to press against a nerve in my leg. At the gym, my leg hurt so much, I collapsed on the StairMaster. My entire scrotum was in pain. It got worse.

I went back to Brooklyn, back to the Walk-In Clinic where the doctor referred me to a different urologist, a Dr. Mark Irwin at the Long Island College Hospital, who agreed to see me Wednesday, because it was urgent.

Dr. Irwin stuck his finger up my butt, then made me wipe in front of him. I threw the first, soiled tissue in a wastebasket, and he pointed to a dispenser and said, "Go ahead. Use another." He kept talking while I cleaned myself. "I should call the Guinness Book of World Records on you, that thing's so big. You have to have that out. What do you think? You cannot postpone this."

I was still holding the second tissue I had used to wipe my butt. He pointed to the wastebasket, and that Monday I went to the hospital where Dr. Irwin entered me and tied off the excess veins.

A nurse took me into a locker room and gave me a pair of drawstring cotton pants. She had me extend my arms, and she hung one gown over the back of me and one gown over the front of me. She gave me cheap slippers and an oversize plastic shower cap. They made me take off all my jewelry, including thc hemp necklace my sister Dena made me, which I swore I'd never remove. They hooked an IV needle into my right hand and affixed it with tape. The IV was just giving me water then, but later they would use it to give me anesthesia and, after the operation, some Demerol.

When they were ready for me, they put me in a wheelchair and pushed me down this corridor into a big operating room with an operating table in the center of it. They took my blood pressure, then they buckled my legs to the table so I couldn't move them. Next, they made me spread my arms out on these adjusting armrests that folded out and converted the operating table into a cross. They tied my arms down. One man in surgical scrubs shaved my pubic hair. Without using any shaving cream, he took a disposable razor and scraped away the hair.

They talked about how many cc's to give me, then they stuck them in my IV. I was given a mask and told to breathe through it. "Just breathe," they told me. "It's only oxygen." I looked up and saw two sets of surgical lights. They were round and gray and in each set there were five lights. The lights were connected to an armlike mechanism that allowed them mobility, and they were exactly the kind of lights they use on the UFOs when aliens do experimental operations on human beings. I saw this true movie *Fire in the Sky* where a man is abducted by a UFO and the aliens do experimental operations on him. The aliens stick needles into his eyes and probe. These light banks are the same as theirs. I see four distinct lights and then ten, and then they become a sort of *Fire in the Sky* themselves, warm, then hot. Soon it's yellow. I hear women's voices. I can't really open my eyes, so I don't know where I am. I just hear women's voices and they're talking about *Fire in the Sky.* They're talking about the operation scene, the exact same thing I am thinking about. I want to say that I saw that movie too, that I believe in UFOs, but I can't move my mouth. I can't move any parts of my body. I can't even open my eyes. The only things that work are my ears.

The women stop talking and maybe they've left the room. I could be here alone. Were those women nurses? I don't know how to begin to move myself. And if the women have forgotten me and left for their homes, I couldn't even make a noise to alert them, I couldn't yank my IV to the floor, I couldn't even fall. I don't know if I am sitting or lying or propped. Then, somewhere in the yellow anesthesia, I feel a pain and I know I'm alive. I'm able to speak now. "OW!" I say. I open my eyes and I see a nurse running toward me with a vial of Demerol—just like heroin, I've heard.

When I come to, I'm back in the nurses' station, in a reclining chair. My nurse, Desirée Martinez, gives me cherry Jell-O, crackers, and a little container of apple juice. I don't know when I've been so thirsty. "That's great," the nurse says, "because we can't let you go until you urinate."

"I better have more of this then," I say, and she gets me another juice.

Paul's here. He gets me a cup and fills it from a fountain in the hall.

After another cup of water, the nurse says, "Why don't you try going to the bathroom now." The bathroom is on the other side of the nurses' station behind a wide silver door. The nurse and Paul help me from the chair and into the bathroom, wheeling the IV behind me.

In order to stand before the toilet, I have to brace my shins against the bowl and lean one hand against the wall. I pull down my hospital pants with the hand that's still attached to the IV. This is the first time I've looked at myself and I see a large piece of clear tape stretched across my lower abdomen. This holds two large gauze bandages—one for each large incision—in place. I can smell the ripeness of the wound and the odor of surgery. I stand there for a while, trying to catch my breath, but I can't. I have to leave the bathroom or I'll faint.

The nurse and Paul rush over.

"I couldn't go," I say.

Pretty soon me, Paul, and nurse Desirée are the only ones here. She comes over and feels my bladder to see if I'm distended. She looks at the clock. I try again. Paul helps me into the bathroom with my IV. I use all the tricks for getting started—I think of Niagara Falls, dribble spit, run the water in the sink, get my hand wet. I maneuver myself and sit on the toilet, thinking I might be straining something by standing, and I keep my hand dipped in the sink of water. I concentrate as hard as I can, but something in my brain will not connect with my bladder. It's useless. I'm in the bathroom for a good hour, and I come sort of close once, feel the beginnings of a trickle somewhere within me, somewhere deep, and then it goes away.

Nurse Martinez calls the doctor and an hour later, an anesthesiologist with whom I'd spoken earlier about painkillers barges into the nurses' station. He's angry for some reason. He pulls me out of the chair and says, "What's the matter with you. You can't pee? Don't you pee every day of your life? What's wrong with you? You can pee. You're just not trying hard enough." He grabs my IV with such force it bounces as he drags it along after us. "If you don't pee I'm going to have to use a catheter. You're not going to like that very much, are you?" He stays with me in the bathroom and leaves the door open so everyone can watch—well, everyone meaning Paul and the nurse, but I don't particularly think they care at this point. I think they hope the doctor's scare tactics will work. He makes me sit on the toilet and he says, "Now don't you get up until you pee." He turns the water on in the sink and leaves the big door open as he goes out, and I hear him saying, "I knew he was a baby when he first came in here. He asked about his painkillers and I just knew he was a big baby."

Meanwhile, I'm trying to pee, but he's got me so worked up. I'm mad at him so I don't even try that hard or that long this time. I pull up my pants, flush the toilet, grab the IV, and come out of the bathroom smiling and, in a jovial manner, say, "I went."

They all know I'm lying, but it's almost ten o'clock, everyone's cranky, the hospital's deserted, and it works. They want to get out of there as much as I do.

"Get him a wheelchair," the anesthesiologist says. On my way out, the nurse says, "Give me a call in the morning and let me know when you go for real."

Later, at home, I don't know if I fall asleep and reawaken. I know that Paul is still up and watching television. The lights are on, but my head is in a fog. I go into the bathroom and, without even trying, I urinate. During the night, all the liquid I drank leaves me in little sips. As soon as I lie down, I have to get back up again and shuffle to the bathroom. In order to get out of bed, I have to swing my legs to the floor and push myself into an upright position. I have to take tiny baby steps.

Inside me this is what was happening: the doctor cut into me on each side of my groin, cut through the layers of tissue, the epidermis, the dermis, the muscles, and nerves until he found the veins that led into my testes. He cut the veins, tied them off and left my varicocele to rot within me. The doctor cut into me and my pain came from that tissue growing back together, the nerves rejoining and coming alive to the fact that they'd been severed. I had to lie flat on my back, or if I rolled to my side, I had to support my testicles with a pillow to keep them from hanging and pulling on my wound.

The painkillers made me too spacey to read, so I tried watching television. There was a show on about fetal alcohol syndrome. Women with their children were talking about how they were so sorry they couldn't stop drinking while they were pregnant. Every time a woman cried or confessed, the studio audience clapped. At one point, a woman turned to her teenage fetal alcohol syndrome son and said, "I'm so sorry. Can you ever forgive me." The boy nodded and stared blankly into the video monitor. He was blond and kept grinding his jaw and squinting.

Another woman, a very young woman, confessed that she was six months pregnant, but she couldn't stop drinking and doing heroin. The audience was aghast, but they clapped for her when she said she just started Narcotics Anonymous and Alcoholics Anonymous.

"It's not going to work though," the young woman said as she cried. " 'Cause I have to go back home to my boyfriend and he makes me do these things. I don't have anywhere to turn."

At that point, the show's hostess, Leeza Gibbons, brought out the young woman's estranged mother. They reunited mother and daughter, and the mother said the daughter could come home to live until she had the baby. The audience applauded and hooted their approval.

I turned it off. I stared at the walls and stared at the furniture and stared at the cats and the floor and the window and, when I got up enough nerve, I pulled down my pants and I stared at myself. For a long time I just looked. My testicles were smaller. The spongy veins were still there, but the bulk had gone out of them. I touched myself and it didn't hurt. It doesn't hurt. In time the blood will drain from my varicocele. The excess veins will entirely collapse. They'll rot and my body, me, I'll simply pass them from me.

MEMORIAL

TOM LEDCKE

It was shortly after two weeks of training to be a buddy when my first client (I hate that word), Joe, died. It was late Sunday afternoon, and a group of his friends had invited me to join them for a memorial celebration. The service turned out to be a tea dance at this place called Twenty Twenty. All of Joe's friends took turns telling me stories, and showing me pictures of this guy I had only known for two weeks; well, actually I was only able to talk to him for three days before he slipped into a coma.

I brought him homemade chicken broth the day before. I was a cheerful, good-hearted volunteer, and the center of attention. Everyone was over fifty, and I was the youngest one there. One by one they all took turns telling me stories about Joe and what it was like living in New York in the mid-'70s, going to the Paradise Garage, Saint Mark's Baths, the Anvil, and the Mineshaft. We danced to Gloria Gaynor and drank Blood Marys. A couple of guys actually said I had a beautiful butt; I was in heaven, all this attention. I felt younger and more attractive than I had in years. I thought, *I'm coming here every Sunday.* I danced with over thirty guys—sure beats the Spike, where I sit unnoticed and unloved.

Whenever I go to a memorial service or visit someone in the hospital I get incredibly horny afterward. Maybe I should work on that in therapy? After dancing all afternoon, I'm walking alone down Fifth Avenue craning my neck, looking at any guy that passes to see if he's looking too. I feel like the most desperate queer in New York City. I can't stop turning, which is sort of ironic because I've gone from not being able to smile or look at any man in the eye, to looking, nodding, and smiling at every guy that passes, like some manic clown.

As I'm walking across Twelfth Street, I see this beautiful, big, dark-blond guy coming out of the drugstore. He's wearing white shorts and a gray T-shirt. It looks kind of odd because it's January, but I can see he's carrying a tennis racket, so it sort of makes sense. He turns and stops, stares and smiles, then jogs across the street ahead of me. I'm already a little dizzy from an afternoon of Bloody Marys, and now my heart is racing. My body is rushing with energy, and I pray not to collapse. He starts walking down my block and I cross. He keeps walking while looking over his shoulder, as he swings his racket, loosening up his massive shoulders. I start muttering to myself, *Oh my god he's so fucking hot.* . . . My mouth is dry and my whole body is vibrating. I stop in front of an antique shop. He stops and studies the film schedule in front of Cinema Village. The next time our heads turn, I nod, then he nods. I thank Christ and start praying and whimpering. *I'll go to church every Sunday if you let me suck his dick.*

I smile, shrug my shoulders, which translates into, OK enough already. We start to walk toward each other.

I blurt out, "Hi." My voice surprises me at how unusually nasal it sounds. He nods and flashes a beautiful minty-fresh smile. He looks kind of embarrassed, and then he says, "Hi, what's up?" I reply, "Oh just walking home, you know, memorial service sort of."

Then he says, "Oh, you live on this block? Me too." I say, "Oh yeah, above the chicken place, over there." We were running out of things to say. I had to think fast so I added, sounding a little hysterical, "So you play tennis?" He says, "Yeah, I play professionally." I'm thinking, this is too much, a tennis player, then I say, "Wow! I mean, I've never seen you on the block before, where do you live?" He points up and says, "In this building on the top floor." I'm thinking *he lives in a penthouse and I live on top of a greasy chicken place,* "What's your name?" I ask, and he says, "Steve." I say, "Nice to meet you Steve. Oh, my name is Tom." Then we shake hands. His hand covers mine, his grip almost hurts. He says, "We should get together sometime." I say, "That would be great. Where do you live?" He smiles and points up again, I mumble, "Oh right, right! Where you off to?" He says, "I've got a match to go to, where do you live?" My arm goes flying in the direction of my apartment. "Over there, 2A, right above the chicken place." He says with a real cute grin, "Well—I'll stop by then." He hails a cab and bounds across the street. I can hardly believe what's happened.

As I walk home I keep going over all the details of our meeting, remembering his thighs, his ass. I can't wait to see his chest. It's so great that he lives down the street. I'll bet he has a great apartment. We can sunbathe on the roof in the summer, and maybe we can have lunch up there, too. I'm forgetting one detail. I have a boyfriend. And I couldn't do this.

A couple of days pass and I'm making dinner for Mario. He sits on the sofa in his underwear with his legs curled beneath him. He's reading the latest queer theory best seller waiting for me to set the table and to get his cherry juice, ahhh, bliss. . . . I hear the buzzer, and freeze. I know it's him, but I pretend not to hear. He rings a couple of more times. I call out, "Dinner's ready, come on, it's getting cold." Mario looks up and says, "Aren't you going to answer the door?" I say, "Nope, not if people don't call first I won't—let's eat. See, I made you chicken cutlets and mashed potatoes and broccoli and cheese sauce. Isn't that nice? A nice dinner for you." Mario says, "Good boy, Honey, but no nice applesauce or nice cranberry? That's OK, I guess." He begins suspiciously eyeing my plate to see who was given the larger portion of chicken cutlet. "Can I have the nice pepper and more delicious broccoli? I'm like the hungry pup tonight." I feel like a proud June Cleaver, *thank god the tennis player went away; his timing was terrible.*

A couple of nights later I'm sitting alone at home after talking to my sister in California. My nephew has been sick for the past couple of years with bone cancer. He'll be eighteen next month; now he's in the hospital. I'll probably need to go out there soon, it's close to the end. I can't believe I'm here and he's there dying. It just doesn't seem real. I mean this is Tommy John, one of the most important people in my life. He wanted to be a stand-up comic and performed around the Bay area till he lost his hair from chemo. I can't connect, all I feel is numb, as he slowly falls apart, amputated piece by piece. I visit people in the hospital every day that I don't even know—while Tom is dying in California. It's more heroic to visit strangers. All I can do is stare off into the air.

But then the doorbell rang. I nearly jumped out of my skin. I knew it was him; I hoped anyway. I flew downstairs to answer the door, and there he was with his six foot three frame crouching down to look through the small rectangular window. I immediately started to shake uncontrollably. I felt like I was sitting on top of a vibrator. I struggled with the doorknob that was keeping me from my prize. "Hi, come on in, oh, wow, you found it." He says, "Yeah, I came by the other day but you weren't home, so I thought I'd try again." I say, "Oh good, I'm glad you did." He follows me up the slanted flight of stairs. I hold my breath and unlock the door. The minute we sit down he pulls out a joint and says, "Do you want to smoke?" I nod spastically, feeling like Don Knotts. "Yeah, sounds good! Hey, would you like some cherry juice or something?" He says, "Cool." We're smoking and drinking. I'm feeling very high because I haven't smoked in a long time and this is great pot. Steve leans back and starts rubbing his crotch while at the same time looking over at the bookcase pretending to read titles. He looks at his crotch, then up at me. He's grinning like this is his first time ever. I smile and my hand joins his while we massage his bulge. He smells like Downy Fabric Softener. He says, "Hey, you want it?" I nod, "Yeah." He stands over me and begins to unbuckle his Banana Republic jeans. I think, *maybe we should kiss first?* Then he moves his Banana Republic hips up against my face, and I can feel his cock pulse. He slowly lowers his underwear, exposing what my friend John would call, "A perfect dick, honey." He held my head and I began to gobble up as much as humanly possible. He asked me if I were a cock slave? And I thought, *I guess so. That's what I am, a cock slave.* He chanted, "OK cock slave—go on take that—take that, cock slave—" I started to laugh, then gagged. I was hoping that he would say something new. I mean, we've already established that fact. I said, "Why don't we get undressed?" He said, "No, I better not." So I led him out of the kitchen and into the bedroom then tried to kiss him. He pulled away and said, "I don't kiss, but I really want to fuck you." And I think *OK . . . this is too much—this guy is making me feel like a fucking whore or like . . . an inflatable doll!* Then I tell him, "Hey, well . . . OK, but you better go slow, you're a pretty big guy." I helped him put on the condom and made sure there was plenty of lube, and I pinched the tip. I was so excited that I pinched his dick by mistake. He fucked me slowly and with such incredible control—he didn't go sliding out every two seconds or poke around like a blind man. He was very gentle, and thank god he stopped talking. I told him not to come inside of me, and he said he wouldn't. I felt so overwhelmed looking up at him, but as I looked down I realized that he was fully dressed. He only lifted his T-shirt over his neck, exposing a tanned, rippled stomach and perfect chest. I came when he told me to. Then he pulled out and shot all over my chest. Without missing a beat he ran to the bathroom and cleaned up; a few seconds later, he was back and dressed with his coat on, obviously having some sort of anxiety attack, and said, "Wow, I never do that—wow, wow, I have carryout waiting for me at the Italian restaurant on the corner, and . . . I'll see you soon." He was totally panicked. He quickly turned and was out the door.

I just laid there laughing as the downstairs door was flung open. I was so high. I just came not two minutes before, my knees are still bent, and the phone rings. I think *shit, it's Mario.* I clear my throat trying to disguise the fact that I've just gotten fucked. I answer with caution, "Hello." The other voice says, "Hi Tom, it's Brian." It was my other nephew, then he takes a long pause, "Um . . . " I'm flooded with dread, and he says, "Tommy John died . . . a few minutes ago, and we wanted to tell you first." The cum is starting to drip down my sides, I grab a sock, a black one so it won't stain. I've ruined too many white ones that way. Brian can't talk. I can't talk. He finally says, "We'll call you when we get home." Then he hangs up, I'm just laying there. I lower my knees, I can't move. I laid there till the cum dried on my chest. I was just staring at the ceiling as I thought, *Tommy John, that's not funny.*

FAMILY / CHILDHOOD II

MISS A

GREG GEVAS

Miss A is a girl who's eager to please
But she has a very funny sneeze.
She keeps on sneezing all day long,
And she makes her sneeze come out all wrong.

I don't know how you guys learned your alphabet, but first graders at Clara Barton Elementary use "letter people." Mr. H has "horrible hair." Mr. L "licks lemon lollipops." "Tall teeth." "Fabulous feet." Consonants are boys, vowels are girls.

When Ms. Alevras teaches us a new letter, she gives each of us a card with a picture of a new letter person and a poem that tries to use that letter as much as possible. When we reach the end of the alphabet, we glue all the cards into a book we can take home to teach our family their letters.

My favorite letter person is Miss A. She's cuter than Tracy on *The Partridge Family.* She has bright yellow skin, and puffy green pigtails. She's also pigeon-toed, like me. Mom yells at me when my feet turn in.

"You're such a good-looking boy, but the way you walk . . . it ruins the whole picture," she says.

Miss A says "Aa-choo!" I guess it's because the word "sneeze" doesn't begin with the letter A. Or even contain a letter A. Her poem doesn't have lots of As in it either, like Mr.

H's or Mr. R's. Ms. Alevras tells me not to think so much about it.

You'd think I'd like Mr. G like my parents do. After all, my name is Greg George Gevas. Mr. G chews "gooey gum." I don't like gooey things. Miss E's into "energetic exercise" like the men with the big muscles in Dad's workout magazines. I like looking at them, but she's not so hot. Mr. H with his horrible hair is cute, but Miss A's definitely my favorite.

Even though Miss A's the first letter in the alphabet, we didn't meet her first. First, we met Mr. M ("munching mouth"). Then Mr. N ("noisy nose"). In fact, we didn't meet Miss A until after six other letters. We learn Mr. Z ("zooming zippers") even before we've finished the rest of the alphabet. Ms. Alevras tells me not to get so excited. She says learning them out of order is more interesting.

When we finally meet our last letter, Mr. X (he doesn't have any words beginning with X, he's just "all mixed up"), Ms. Alevras tells us we're going to put on a Letter People pageant. There are twenty-six kids in class. Each of us will dress up as a letter and recite their poem. We get to pick which letter we want to be.

"Who wants to be who?" Ms. Alevras asks. She asks Rob Donato first.

Rob Donato sits in the first row, first desk, right in front of me. He's got really nice black hair even though he never combs it. Just like Mr. H. "Who do you want to be, Rob?" Ms. Alevras asks.

"Mr. H," Rob says in his husky voice. He sounds like those grown-ups who smoke too much. Ms. Alevras writes it down and then asks me, but I'm too busy looking at Rob's hair turn curliecues on the back of his neck to hear.

"Greg, what letter do you want to be?" She asks me so suddenly I don't have time to think. "Oh, Miss A," I say. Ms.

Alevras marks it down on her pad, then asks Tracy Lipnick who she wants to be.

"Hey Mom! You gotta make me a costume! I'm gonna be in the school play!"

"Straighten your feet, Greg! Ruins the whole picture . . . " Mom's in the den, shaking her head at the floor. My sister vacuumed the mane off Mom's zebra-skin rug. She sounds annoyed as she shoves the zebra's head under the couch so you can't see where the mane's missing. I show her my letter book.

"I'm going to be Miss A," I say.

Mom stares at Miss A's picture then takes my book. She starts to crinkle her face. "We'll have to get a Simplicity pattern for the dress. I've got some muslin in the workroom. And I think I have some red ribbon for the A." Then she goes down to the basement to look for the ribbon.

While I wait for her to come back, I feel sorry for the zebra with his head stuck under the couch.

"Hey Janine!" Janine's my older sister. She's the one who had the vacuuming accident.

"Hey *Janine*!" I run into her room without knocking. "Hey Janine, I'm gonna be in the school play! I'm gonna be Miss A!"

Janine lies very still on her bed, staring up at the blue and orange wallpapered ceiling, her hands across her chest. Billie Holiday is singing "Lover man, oh where can you be?" Janine plays that song over and over again an awful lot.

"Get ouuuuuutttt!" Janine shouts.

Boy, she's grumpy all the time. Ever since she started taking those little blue pills she told me not to tell Mom about.

Dad gets me in a headlock. "Hey Mouse!" Dad calls me Mouse because I always wiggle away when he gets me in a headlock. He's *always* getting me into headlocks. I get mad every time but he never stops doing it.

"Daaaaaaaaad, I'm gonna be in the school play." I try to kick him away.

"Who you gonna be?" he asks, trying to fake me out again. "Miss A," I say, and run upstairs to my room. Dad goes downstairs to watch TV.

Pageant day! Mom's made me a muslin gunny sack with a big red A on the front. Janine tells me that Hester Prynne had a big red A on her dress too, but I don't understand why.

Mom's gotten me a pair of Mary Janes and white lacy socks. My hair's long enough to make pigtails. Mom makes me wear my hair long because my ears stick out. My right ear doesn't have a fold. She says it looks like someone glued a teacup to the side of my head.

"I'm not having you going through life with ears like that," Mom says as she tightens my hair ribbons. "When you're old enough, we're getting them pinned back." She hands me a mirror. I look like Cindy Brady, but brunette. Mom told me that when I was a baby everyone thought I was a girl because I had such long lashes. I look a lot like Miss A.

I'm very happy.

Everyone in my family comes to see the pageant. Nanny too. Ms. Alevras has the whole alphabet line up at the back wall of the stage. She tells us each letter will come to the edge of the stage and recite their poem. Miss A is first. Like she's *supposed* to be. I stand and walk pigeon-toed just like Miss A and say the poem. No mistakes.

Miss A is a girl who's eager to please
But she has a very funny sneeze.
She keeps on sneezing all day long,
And she makes her sneeze come out all wrong.

Before I turn to make way for Mr. B. ("brilliant buttons"), I curtsey. I'd never done that before, but it feels right to do it now. We end the pageant with a chorus of "Animal Crackers in My Soup." At the end of the show, when everyone's clapping, I curtsey again. It just feels right.

I jolt up in bed. I'm in my midtwenties. I'm back in the letter people pageant. I'm Miss A again. But, this time the whole audience boos and hisses at me. A boy runs onstage, punches me, and knocks me down.

"Boys don't wear dresses. Or lipstick. Or too much rouge." The boy has no face. He kicks me real hard as I lie on the ground.

I'm still in my twenties. Nanny's almost ninety, but she comes in her wheelchair to see me in *La Cage Aux Folles* at the local dinner theater (but we only do shows at lunch). "Look how pretty Janine looks," Nanny whispers to Mom. "Just like Audrey Hepburn."

"Ma . . . that's Greg."

"Oh," says Nanny.

REMISSION OF SINS

FRED NELSON

FRED NELSON *is a native of Cache Valley, Utah, and grew up riding quarter horses and showing 4-H hogs. He attended the University of Utah, trained as an operatic baritone, and has sung throughout the Intermountain West in various concert series. He has held a wide variety of jobs, including forklift operator, trainer of chariot teams, inspector of sausages at a meat plant, and, for four grueling months, a one-man musical-variety show at Glacier National Park. In 1998, he moved to New York City. He is at work on his first novel.*

Over spring vacation a new set of swings were installed on the playground of Wellsville Elementary. They were suspended cages you sat in and, by pumping a set of handlebars, the cage-swing was set into motion. Once school started again, these were a popular addition to the playground and never sat idle.

When Mrs. Jenkins released her second-grade class to recess, Matt Bliss, Jason Bailey, and I made mad dashes for these swings. The cages became cockpits; we played *Battlestar Galactica*. Jason and Matt were Starbuck and Apollo; I was left to play Boomer. Boomer was black; I didn't know how to play black. As far as I knew there were no black people in the state of Utah. Why would there be?

Within days we were bored.

"*I* know," Matt said, "they're *breast* pumps."

From then on, with each stroke of the handlebars, we pumped breasts and, across the playground, shouted, "Titty milk!"

At the bottom of my father's hayfield was a black willow my family called The Big Tree. Dad said the Shoshones used to camp around it when they wintered in our valley. The Big Tree had five enormous arms; three of which had grown so heavy they were now resting on the ground, radiating from the willow's split trunk like wheel spokes.

It was mid-April and the days were losing their chill. We had rolled our clocks ahead and I was now blessed with additional daylight after school. I used this time to build a third level on a tree house that had been started the previous fall.

At the top of our drive Ervin Anderson opened the doors of Bluebird bus number 13, disgorging me from the grade-school rabble. I could barely contain myself, charging into our house and up to my room where I changed my clothes. I lingered in the kitchen long enough to eat a cookie and then it was out the back porch, through the barnyard, into the lane, across the alfalfa, and there I was, standing at The Big Tree. With singleness of purpose I worked until my mother stood on the canal bank next to the well house and shouted, "Fred," her voice carrying over the fields, "dinner's ready."

Jason and Matt lived in Wellsville and played together on weekends. I lived seven miles away in College Ward and never saw them outside of school. Since kindergarten, though, we had formed a tight club.

I spent weekends working on my father's farm.

At two o'clock on Saturday afternoons Dad broke from farm chores to drive to the Cat for a Pepsi and Snicker bar. If I were not helping him, I would be down along the slough, swinging a hammer in The Big Tree, but I had a sixth sense with these things and appeared at the shop in time to join Dad for the run to the Cat.

The Cat had originally been a Mormon church house. When our congregation outgrew it and constructed a new building on the road to Pelican Pond, Deloy and Vera Zilles purchased the building, turned the classrooms into bedrooms, and converted the chapel into a showroom for Arctic Cat snowmobiles. Deloy tinkered in a shop attached to one side of the old church. Vera rarely moved from behind the counter. On a high stool shaped like a Mopar shock absorber, her elbows resting on the countertop, Vera stood guard over the candy counter and an old white chest refrigerator that held twenty-five-cent cans of soda.

Like a wagon train camped for the night, the building's original wooden chairs were circled next to the counter. It was here the farmers huddled for caffeine and to exchange stories about breached calves and winter snowmobile runs to Mount Naomi.

At seven and a half I was too young for Pepsi. My pop of choice was Fanta Red Cream Soda. Like cherry Luden cough drops, Fanta made me sick to my stomach, but I loved the color of it.

I lurked and listened behind the men, expanding my lexicon of swear words.

Back at school on Monday, Jason, Matt, and I met at recess and, while pumping breast milk, shouted our new swear words.

On the upswing I said, "Potlicker."

Matt said that was not a swear word; that he had never even heard the word before.

"Okay," I said, giving the handlebars another pull, "bullshit."

Jason said they knew that one.

A moment passed, then Matt kicked his legs and said, "Jesus Christ."

There was silence for three pumps of my swing before I swallowed hard and agreed with Jason that that word was off limits.

To end the awkwardness, I said I had another one.

"Say it," Matt said.

I paused, and said, "Cocksucker."

Jason and Matt looked at one another. A surge went through me of something I felt made me a man.

"That's a good one," Matt said. Jason nodded.

In my triumph I wanted to say that potlicker was a swear word because Dad shouted it at me in the same tone of voice he used when he called me a little cocksucker. I let it go.

This exchange went on a few weeks. Guilt crept in.

Every Wednesday afternoon the school bus delivered its payload of kids to the church house and for ninety minutes we sang about Jesus wanting us for sunbeams so that we could shine for Him each day. I thought about pumping breast milk and swapping swear words. I did not feel I was doing any shining for Jesus.

In two months I was to be baptized. Sister Kendrick, my primary teacher, kept on about being prepared for baptism.

"You know," she said, lowering her voice and leaning toward us, "Jesus wants us clean for our baptism." She asked us to repeat the word remission. "That's what baptism is," she said, sitting up straight, "a remission of your sins." I understood children were not accountable until they are eight years old, but I did not know what a remission was.

Later that afternoon, pretending I was not playing Barbies with my sister, I told Sandra I could do anything I wanted. "I'm not accountable," I said.

"You *are,*" she said.

"I can't sin until I'm baptized," I said.

"Do you lie?"

"No."

"Lying's a sin," she said, "whether you're baptized or not." She rummaged through a shoebox for Barbie's boot and said, "Sin is sin and you've been taught."

After a few days, my sister's righteousness cankered me to the point I stopped playing with Jason and Matt. The novelty of the swings had worn off anyway, and they started playing football at the far end of the playground. I was not interested.

I took to running around the building with an A.D.D.-addled kid named Scott Halfhill who went around singing the theme from *Batman*.

I played Robin, in body only; Scott provided all dialogue. This muted play did not bother me. Though I was not embarrassed to shout "titty milk" across the playground, I was too shy to say, "Holy asteroid, Batman. Look at the size of that ray gun."

The Batcave was a janitor's closet that opened onto the playground. During school hours the closet was unlocked and stored televisions on rolling carts. Scott fiddled with the knobs until he got a signal, then printed our orders and ran from the closet onto the playground singing, "na-na-na-na-na-na, Batman!" I ran behind in silence.

At the end of April the Mormon prophet, Spencer Kimball, announced he had received a revelation: The blacks could now be given the priesthood.

"It's the Mark of Cain," Dad said. "They're cursed for being lazy in heaven." He asked if I had ever seen a black television announcer. I shook my head. "You won't," Dad said, "their lips are too big. They're damn good ballplayers," he said, "they know the game; it's in their blood. They can't talk fast enough."

Our first prophet, Joseph Smith, had seen God and Jesus. I was taught if I lacked wisdom I should ask God. I was unsure why I was being baptized. I decided to take it to God. God had just spoken; He was around.

One afternoon I stopped working on the tree house—I was on the very top level. For a brief moment I felt shame for what I was about to do; it felt like I was rebuilding the tower of Babel. Dismissing the thought, I knelt and, gathering my energy, tightly balled my hands and looked up into the mottled leaves. "Dear Heavenly Father," I said, paying special attention to the order of prayer. "I thank Thee for my parents," I said, "and my Sunday school teacher." I asked to be forgiven for having mistreated my dog, Thumper. The dog had made me angry and I locked him in the granary for two days without food and water until my father realized where the dog was and made me release him. I was feeling bad. "Heavenly Father," I said, "I'm supposed to be baptized. Tell me if this is what Thou wants me to do."

I did not want to be baptized; it was an issue of accountability. It made more sense to wait until I had a few sins racked up, until I *needed* a remission. It did occur that if I was never baptized, I might never be accountable, that I might remain, like Adam and Eve, in a state of perpetual innocence—until I ate the apple. There were things I was afraid of: spiders in the root cellar, Russians attacking the Air Force base on the other side of the Wellsville mountains, and being accountable for my sins.

Besides accountability, another problem existed: my older brother. He was relentlessly cruel, a bully my sisters and I called Grunt. "You just have to endure him," Mom said. I was tired of doing what Jesus would do—turning the other cheek. I did not want to be in my family any longer. I begged to be taken away. God had that power. I wanted to flit through the universe with God, Jesus, and the Holy Ghost; to visit worlds across the universe populated with the other children of the Heavenly Father. I wanted to become the fourth member of the Godhead.

I knew that Moses, at the end of his life, had been taken to God without dying. "Take me, Heavenly Father," I said. "Let me come with you; I'll help you." Sister Kendrick had shown us a mustard seed, and I knew if I had that much faith God would change me in the twinkling of an eye.

While listening for the still small voice to herald God and Jesus's arrival, I realized the magpies were no longer chattering in the treetop. A dome of silence had fallen over The Big Tree. Moments before seeing God and Jesus, Satan had overcome Joseph Smith, enveloping him in darkness. The magpies, I thought, must have sensed Satan coming and flown away. A twig snapped. Satan was in The Big Tree, I was sure of it.

This is a test, I told myself, I have to wait; I'll be delivered. Suddenly, a wind whipped up and the trees' limbs began knocking and swaying. I was enveloped in swirling dust and leaves. In that moment I knew my faith was insufficient. Climbing down from the tree house, I had failed. I ran out into the hayfield. If I were in the open, I would see Satan coming. Thirty yards out from the tree I turned and what I saw made me stumble. There, hovering ten feet above the crown of The Big Tree was a green army helicopter. Soldiers leaned from its open doorways, looking down into my tree house.

FAMILY FEUD

DEREK GULLINO

My mother was feuding with her sister, Julie, even before we went on *Family Feud.* Julie and her husband Marv had a big house with a swimming pool in the foothills of Alta Loma. We lived in Cucamonga. Our family was so in debt, we had to hide our car at the supermarket so it wouldn't be repossessed. In comparison to Julie and Marv, we were big losers and we knew it, but then Mom got us on the game show and we thought our luck would change.

When Julie heard we were going to be on *Family Feud,* she and Marv wanted to be on the team.

My mother said, "OK, Julie, but since we're the ones who got us on the show, we're the ones who should get all the money."

Julie agreed and our team was decided—Mom, me, my younger brother, Douglas, and Julie and Marv. My father was so shy, he didn't want to go on. He only wanted us to go by *our* name, the Gullinos, not by Marv's name, the LaNiers.

OK.

For the first audition, we drove down to Studio City where we sat in a room with three other families. One by one, they asked us questions. Are you related? Yes. Are you American citizens? Yes. They gave us a diction test, took our Social Security numbers, and sent us home.

At the second audition, we played a trial round and after we kicked the other family's butt, the woman from *Family Feud* said, "You guys were superfantastic and Richard'll LOVE you. There's no question about that. One thing, though—Marv, I want you to be the head of the family, and I want the family to be LaNier. The network has this thing about ethnic names, so we gotta change it. Is that all right?"

My mother hesitated. Good for her. Then she stepped forward and said, "You bet."

We each needed five sets of clothes, because they shoot a whole week's programs in one day, and if you keep on winning, you have to quickly change your clothes in the dressing room and get back out to tape the next game. My mother borrowed $350 from Julie, using our winnings as collateral, and we went on a shopping spree. We drove to the Montclair Plaza. My mother got three completely brand-new outfits from JC Penney's and the strangest dress from a store called UNITS. It was peach-colored and stretchy and you could wear it in different ways for different effects. If we were on a really big winning streak, Mom figured she could wear this peach outfit three days in a row. Oh, and we all got new shoes. When we got out to the parking lot, we couldn't remember where we'd parked the car. We had all these packages and we did a complete circle of the parking lot in the heat, and then it dawned on us what happened. Our car had been repossessed.

My mother didn't even care. She said, "Let them have it. Pretty soon I'll have me an even nicer car. Maybe an El Dorado."

She was convinced that we were going to win and win big.

And we did.

The first day our opponents were the Sugarwaters—four blond brothers and their brunette sister, Janessa. I do not know how they'd won the previous round, because the Sugarwaters were really stupid. The brothers were named Jake, John, Joe, and James. Richard Dawson accidentally called Jake Jerk when he was introducing them. Janessa laughed and said, "We call Jake Jerk all the time." All four brothers broke out clappin' and hootin,' shoutin' out, "Good answer! Good answer!" I do not lie when I tell you that the Sugarwaters did not answer a single question correctly. Besides Gasoline, Name Something You Pick Up At The Gas Station. Your mistress. Name Something You Accidentally Swallow When You're Eating. A spoon.

Duh.

Before we knew it, we'd won, and we won Fast Money as well. All told, our winnings the first day were $16,800, and we had half an hour to change and come back and win some more.

The minute Mom got into the dressing room, she went right for that three-way peach stretch dress she bought at UNITS. She was convinced we were going to go on winning all night. She had me help her with the belt that could also be a sleeve, and she told me about a house with a swimming pool she'd seen in Julie and Marv's neighborhood that she could maybe win enough money to put a down payment on.

Our next opponents were the Carsons. The head of our team, Marv, faced off with the head of their team, their grandmother, Stell. Richard Dawson read the question: Name Something You Reach For When You're In Trouble. Stell's hand slapped the buzzer before Marv even knew Richard was finished with the question. The grandma, I figured, Stell, was the team's secret weapon.

"The Bible, Richard," Stell said.

"Good answer! Good answer!" the Carsons yelled.

Richard looked at the game board which was all lit up like a carnival and said, "I don't know, Stell, is the Bible Something You Reach For When You're In Trouble?"

"Yes, it is," Stell said.

But no one else in America must have agreed with her because there were five responses and the Bible was not among them. The buzzer buzzed. In an effort to unnerve Uncle Marv, Stell started walking like a chicken, but Uncle Marv was able to ignore her and calmly said, "The telephone."

Number One answer. Number One answer.

We rattled off the rest of the answers without thinking. Back and forth it went, neck and neck, until the final question—Name Something Underwear Is Made Out Of. The Carsons got the Number One answer right off the bat—cotton. We huddled, discussing underwear fabrics, while the Carsons got the Number Two answer—silk. Then, one strike after another, the Carsons lost control of the playing board. There was one answer left and we had two options—satin or polyester. Whoever won this question, won the game. Douglas and Julie wanted satin. We put it to the vote and polyester won 3-2. But when the time came for Marv to say polyester, Julie kept yelling "Satin! Satin! Satin! I know it's satin!" right in Marv's ear.

Marv said satin when the answer was polyester and our winning streak was over.

They broke for a commercial and hustled us backstage. Before we'd reached the dressing room, my mother had ripped the removable sleeves from her stretchy peach outfit. She pulled her other dresses from their hangers and wadded them in a ball. That's when she saw Douglas's duffel bag, whose contents had spilled to the floor. Douglas thought five changes of clothes meant five pair of clean underwear, and all five pair had fallen from the duffel bag. My mother scooped them up and attacked her sister with them, screaming, "See these, Julie? This is polyester. This is what we wear in Cucamonga. Maybe you don't know what polyester is. Maybe you've never lived in Cucamonga!"

TITANIC

GREG GEVAS

Christmas 1975. I've just turned ten. Dad's bought me *The Sinking of the Titanic* game that I've been bothering him about. The TV commercial calls it "the game you play as the ship goes down."

You're a *Titanic* officer. It's your duty to rescue two passenger cards, two casks of water, two food crates, board a lifeboat, and be first to land on the rescue ship. But, every time you roll a one or six, the *Titanic* "sinks" another point.

Even though there are lots of kids in the neighborhood, I play The Sinking of the *Titanic* alone. Mainly because I hate losing. I play all four colors, but I favor red as "me."

After a couple weeks, something starts bothering me about this game. I don't like rescuing only two passenger cards. There are over thirty in the deck. I decide to change the rules to see which player can save the most.

I always try to save certain passengers. Lady Anne resembles the lady on my nanny's cameo pin. Fifi the Maid looks like Juliet Prowse from the movie *Can-Can* (I'm always playing the soundtrack). My favorite, Miss Prissy, looks like Tracy from *The Partridge Family:* I "secretly" put her card near the top of the deck to make sure she's always saved. I don't do that with any other passenger. Lord Upton is bald and funny looking. He doesn't always make it.

You will live. You will die. I like having that power. I sink the *Titanic* three, four times a day. But, one time, the ship sinks so fast I'm not able to save Miss Prissy.

It's only a game, Greg. . . .

Even so, I have no appetite at dinner that night.

"What do you know about the *Titanic*?" I ask Mom and Dad. They tell me it was a horrible tragedy, but not much else, so I look up *Titanic* in the encyclopedia:

> On April 15, 1912, the Royal Mail Steamship *Titanic* struck an iceberg in the North Atlantic on her maiden voyage and sank with the loss of 1,500 lives.

1,500 people lost their lives? The game doesn't mention anything about that. How could someone make a game about that?

"Do you have any books on the *Titanic*?" B. Dalton has one, but it's out of stock. Dad drives me to three bookstores before we find it: *A Night to Remember* by Walter Lord, "the definitive story of the sinking of the *Titanic*," according to the *New York Times*. It says so on the cover. I read the entire book that same night, then start it over the next day to make sure I didn't miss anything important.

In the back of the book is a list of the *Titanic* passengers. Survivors are shown in italics. I'm shocked by the number of un-italicized names. Eight in the Sage family alone, ten Goodwins, five Rice children.

The book says the *Titanic* had enough lifeboats for 1,200 people, but over 2,200 were aboard the night she sank. Worse, many boats left only partially full because most passengers believed that the *Titanic* was unsinkable. Only 700 passengers survived.

But what if the lifeboats *had* been full? That'd be 500 more survivors . . . 500 un-italicized names off that list.

Walter Lord mentions in the book that Lucien Smith was on his honeymoon. Surely, he'd be on the list then. Arthur Ryerson had a family of four, he'd be there too. Lorraine Allison was only four, so she'd *have* to be there. I start making a list, and work on it the next day, and the next. During school. After school. On the weekend. I stay up way past my bedtime with a flashlight. This guy was a father, this girl's photo looks like Miss Prissy, the five Rice children.

Get it right, Greg. . . .

But, what if this man traveling alone has a family back home? He might. I don't know. I've no way of knowing. I can't get this "right." I've already got *over* 500 names. If I add somebody, someone else has to come off. I don't know what to do. My head hurts and my stomach starts turning somersaults.

When I wake up the next morning, I realize something I hadn't wanted to realize: my list can't change anything. These people are dead, they've been dead for sixty-plus years, and they always will be.

I throw my list in the garbage but then take it out again and put it in the bottom of my junk drawer.

Later that week I decide to write a novel. I'll create my own disaster on the high seas. "The definitive story" the *Times* will say. I spend all my time at home designing a beautiful ocean liner, the *Transatlantique* (it's French). I draw up deck plans. I create a passenger list with over a thousand people. I give the passengers some of my favorite names like Veronica, Alexandra, and Gaspard.

It's hard to write as fast as I can think, but I love writing it. I can make anything happen. Until I get to the part when the ship goes down and I have to decide who will live and who will die.

Get it *right,* Greg. . . .

I can't write it. I can't kill anyone. I like my passengers. Even the ones with funny names. Even the ones I decided I shouldn't like.

I put the manuscript in my junk drawer with my *Titanic* passenger list. I stop playing The Sinking of the *Titanic* game. I think about designing my own game, The Explosion of the *Hindenburg,* but stop after a few days.

Dad wakes me up early one Saturday. He's been asking me if I'm okay a lot. We drive into the city and park under the West Side Highway, near Pier 90. He holds my hand and we walk to the end of the pier. The *QE2* is approaching, sailing majestically up the Hudson. I've only seen pictures of her, never in person. She's even bigger than the *Titanic* in person. As she slowly glides toward us, I can make out hundreds of people lining her upper decks. So many people, I tell Dad. He nods and pats my shoulder. We look at each other for a second, and without saying anything, we both begin to wave.

MY BROTHER

RONALD GOLD

My brother Herb is fifteen years older than I am, so when I was fifteen, he was exactly twice my age. He hadn't been much of a brother to me up till then, since he was away at college, and then at law school, while I was growing up with my crazy mother. But one day when I was fifteen, we were driving in his car on Kings Highway in Brooklyn, and I felt the need to share my feelings with him. I don't remember exactly what I said, but I must have blurted out something like "Herb, I just want to tell you . . . that I like boys better than girls."

I don't know what I expected him to do or say, but he didn't say *anything*. He just kept on driving, staring straight ahead. I felt like the pit had opened up, and he'd tossed me to the bottom of it. (Neither of us has ever mentioned that day. I wonder if he remembers it.)

Anyway, after a couple of years at Brooklyn College, during which I didn't see or think much about my brother, I went off to school in California, and came back to New York a practicing junkie—days when I didn't think much about *anything*. Then I went off to Kansas to have my head shrunk, and my father, sister, and brother-in-law came to visit, but I heard nothing from Herb or Rita, my sister-in-law.

In fact, the next time I remember having anything to do with my brother was after my father's funeral. We were in his car again and he turned to me and said, "Don't ever ask me for anything." He didn't raise his voice or show any emotion. Very final.

Oddly, I wasn't upset or angry. I knew what it was about. At my sister's urging, I think, my father had left half his estate to me—the jobless ex-junkie—and only a quarter each to my sister and brother. But if it wasn't for Herb and his financial savvy, my father wouldn't have had enough to leave to anybody. It didn't matter that he already had a lot more money than my father did—he wanted his fair share.

So we weren't exactly on great terms. But after I moved back to New York—even after I started living with Lazaro, my Cuban lover—we saw each other occasionally. We'd visit Herb and Rita at their house in Long Island for a rare family occasion, and sometimes they'd drop by our Manhattan apartment. I noticed that their son Rick always seemed to be visiting a friend when we were at their place, and that he never came with them to ours. I would have liked to get to know him, as I knew and felt close to my sister's two children, but I didn't think much about it. *Until the day when there wasn't enough room on the boat.*

Lazaro was a dancer, and he'd had a job with a company in Israel, so I'd gone to visit him for five months. My cousin's widow lived there with her three young sons, and they couldn't have been nicer to both of us. So when we learned that Rami, the eldest boy, was coming to New York to celebrate his sixteenth birthday, we were ready to roll out the welcome mat. When I found out that my brother and my cousin Paul had planned a welcoming bash aboard their boats, I called to find out the details.

Herb wasn't home, but Rita explained. *Sorry, but there just wasn't enough room for us on the two boats.* No matter that we were the only ones in the family who'd ever met Rami, there just wasn't enough room.

My sister said she could shed no light on the situation, but Marty, my brother-in-law, took me for a drive and offered the explanation. Seems that about a year earlier, Rick, then fourteen, had been apprehended in the act of sucking a dick—so not only was intensive psychotherapy called for, Lazaro and I were more than ever off limits. It didn't seem to occur to Herb and Rita that their son had turned into a fledgling fag with absolutely no assistance from his gay uncle. The last thing they were going to allow Rick to see on *their boat* were two men who lived happily together, especially if one of them (Lazaro) looked so sexy in a bathing suit.

So I stopped talking to my brother, and we didn't see each other again for more than eleven years.

I did hear about him indirectly. For example, I bumped into the attorney for my father's estate on the subway, and he said, just before he got off at his stop, "Well, big doings at your brother's on Saturday. See you then." This turned out to be Rick's engagement party. But I wasn't invited to it. And I wasn't invited to the wedding, and I certainly wasn't invited to the divorce, which, I gathered, had something to do with Rick's notion that his bride wouldn't mind if he messed around just a little bit with men.

Not too long after I heard about the divorce, I got a call from Barbara, another cousin's daughter, who was a friend of Rick's. He was in terrible shape, she said, and would I give him a call. So I called him, and he came by with Bill, his new mate. Seems his parents couldn't accept the idea of Bill, and were still insisting he go on with the psychotherapy, to be cured of his affliction. And he also told me that all the years I'd been kept away from him, his parents had always told him that I didn't want to see him.

I told him to stop seeing the shrink immediately, and to tell Herb and Rita to fuck off if they refused to acknowledge Bill.

But I don't really know whether he did that, because I didn't hear from him for quite a while. I had quit my job at *Variety* and become a full-time gay activist. So I was really wrapped up in my work and, to tell you the truth, the only times I thought of my brother and his family was when my name got in the newspapers (I was media rep for the Gay Activists Alliance), and I wondered what Herb was thinking when he read it.

Then, in 1974, Herb called me up and invited me to lunch—after eleven years. I knew he wanted to make up, but I told myself—and I told my sister, who was overjoyed her brothers might finally be getting together—that I would take nothing less than total capitulation.

Right in the middle of a Japanese restaurant, *my brother kissed me,* for the first time in our lives. He *thanked* me for helping him to see—through my writing and activism—that he wasn't the bad father who'd somehow done damage to his son. He thanked me for helping him to realize that there was nothing the matter with his son. And he gave me a $1000 check for the new organization I'd just helped to form, the National Gay Task Force. So I thought that *was* total capitulation, and ever since, we've been on good terms.

I never did get close to Rick, though, and I've often wondered whether, if I'd had a chance to be close to him when he was a kid, he might have been something more than the uptight opera queen he seemed.

So when Rick died of AIDS in 1986, my grief was more for the anguish I saw in Herb and Rita than for the loss of someone close to me. But I wanted his memory to be respected, and his gay identity to be respected. As Luis and I—Luis was the man I'd been living with for the past eight years—prepared to go to Rick's big Jewish funeral, I was worried that Bill, his mate, would be shunted aside by the grieving parents who'd arranged it.

I needn't have worried. Bill was right up there in the front pew with Rita and Herb. The rabbi talked about him as the person Rick had chosen to share his life with. And at the cemetery, Bill lifted the first shovel of earth into the grave, as any surviving spouse might do. *I was very proud of my brother then.*

He's had a couple of lapses. Once he demanded that Luis take off his earring so the couple who were expected to join us wouldn't see it. We left before they arrived. Mostly he's been very supportive, continuing to contribute to gay causes, picking up on all the gay-related news in the papers. And he and Rita were there for me when Luis died of AIDS in '92.

Now it's 2004, almost sixty years since Herb and I rode in his car together on Kings Highway. The fifteen years that divides us doesn't seem to mean so much, now that I'm seventy-four. But as we get ready to celebrate his ninetieth birthday, he still talks about how odd it is that his kid brother has become a senior citizen. It may have taken us a long time to get there, but now I think that both of us can say that *we are friends.*

CHILDREN OF THE NIGHT

DOUGLAS McKEOWN

I am eleven years old and I am running through the woods at night, high up on my pads—the toes of my sneakers—and my heels are as high as hocks. My thighs are massive and sinewy like haunches, and my knees curve, they don't bend, they curve down into something like fetlocks. I am between species; I am somewhere between *Homo sapiens sapiens* and *Canis lupus*. I am a preteen werewolf.

I got that way from hard work, the same way I got to all my monsters. I was ten when I decided that greasepaint alone was no longer adequate to my needs. I started working with techniques like spirit gum and crepe hair, and later, with nose putty, cotton and collodion, and liquid latex. I could create new features in minute detail, and I took two, three hours up in my room behind closed doors until I had a complete transformation staring back at me from the mirror.

Then what, you might ask? What was I going to do, just take it off? Not on your life. I went out. To other neighborhoods, and I made "appearances." I became famous, I became a sort of mini-legend in Metuchen, New Jersey. Well, the monsters did. Nobody knew who I was. I didn't even go to the same school as most of the other kids on my street. I went to Franklin Middle School and they mostly went to St. Francis. But even the kids I *did* go to school with didn't know I was the monster. I was standing by my locker one time, and a kid next to me, a kid I knew, was telling another kid about the monster in his neighbor's backyard. It was like having a secret identity.

So I'm eleven now, running through the woods, loping over the vine-covered floor of the Kentnor Street woods; alone in the woods in the dark, and I'm not afraid of anything

Grrrrrrr

I've got my jacket on with the collar up, and there's dark brown crepe hair layered up my hands and up my neck, cheeks, forehead, and brushed back into my hair

GRRRRRRR

I've got these fangs I made specially, jammed down on my lower teeth and held in place with PoliGrip

GRRRRRRR

My claws are Lee Press On Nails, broken and chipped and painted silvery black with model airplane enamel paint

GRRRRRR. I get to the tree. Up the tree, up to the top throw my head back and

GRRYEEEOOOOOOOOOOOOOOOWWWWWWWLLLL-LOOOooooooo

I can see the porch lights blink on all up and down Kentnor Street. Screen doors bang open and shut, kids spill out into the street and start to assemble under the streetlight. They've got their air rifles, Tommy guns, you know, submachine guns, pistols, baseball bats, and they form search parties, they cross over the road, the shoulder, the stream, into the woods, and start beating the bushes. I can see every one of them and hear their conversations—the sound carries well in the night air—and pretty soon I hear talking right below my tree.

It's the Marko brothers, big old Barry Marko and his younger brother. They're the butcher's sons, and they live right on the edge of the woods. Barry's telling his brother how to be a good sentry, you got to keep your back to the tree trunk so you can see in both directions, that way nothing can come up behind you, nothing can take you by surprise—

GRRRRRRRRRRROOW

I drop down right next to him. Barry topples over face first on the ground and covers his head with his hands. Doesn't move. He must have seen that *Life* magazine article about protecting yourself from grizzly bears in Yellowstone. Boring. But his brother—he's flailing his arms, his eyes popping out of his head, gibbering and emitting these little squeaks, can't scream, and he's backing up—

Grrrrrrrr. . . . I've drawn a bead on his jugular vein, and he sees in my eyes I'm gonna rip his throat out, I mean, he's lost his mind! He's desperate to get away, but he's trapped himself, backed right into a bramble, thorn bushes all around him—

GRRRRRRRRR. . . .

But just at that moment, he gets lucky. Looks like the werewolf has got his foot caught somehow, snagged in some vines. I'm reaching down to free my right sneaker, he sees his chance, and he bolts. But he doesn't go this way or that way, as I expect. No, he turns and dives headfirst right through the thorns. Scraaaatcchhh-yeeeeowwwl! He gets away—not unscathed, but he gets away. I go back home and metamorphose back into, uh, . . . *Homo.*

This went on every second or third day—for years. After school, on weekends, summer vacations. I did them all eventually, all the monsters. I started at nine, with Frankenstein's Monster and the Mummy. Let's see, there was the Haunted Strangler, the Phantom of the Opera, Dr. Jek— Dr. *JEEK*-yll and Mr. Hyde if you're talking about the Frederic March version, Dr. *JECK*-yll and Mr. Hyde, if you're talking about the Spencer Tracy version. My father looked a lot like Spencer Tracy's Mr. Hyde when he got mad, because his face got that contorted look, and you could tell he wouldn't stop at killing you, he'd have to *annihilate* you. The difference between them was that Spencer Tracy turned into Mr. Hyde by a series of lap-dissolves; my father did it in a jump cut. And Mom? Mom was—well, usually she was just "Mom," but late at night, that was a different story. If I was up watching old movies on television, and I heard the car hit the garage, or the front door bang open, I would go rigid as up the stairs came . . . "M-Mom." I'd try not to look as she lurched past me to the couch where she would collapse and stare at the back of my head until the movie was over or I went up to bed.

Anyway, most summers Mom and Spencer Tracy rented a bungalow at the Jersey Shore for a week or two. I took my makeup kit along. You never knew when an opportunity would present itself.

But not that summer; that summer I was eleven they took me with them for a vacation in upstate New York, to Glenora, near Watkins Glen by Lake Seneca. Glenora was a wild, dark, rocky, gothic place, inhabited by a ragtag bunch of barefoot kids in calico and gingham—I swear, they were like nineteenth century farm kids. They didn't even have televisions. The house we stayed at belonged to friends of my mother. It was grand and old, set back in the trees, and they had their own cataract in the backyard, a twenty-foot waterfall into a trout pool. Decades later, after my mother died, I was on the phone with the lady of the house, elderly by then, and she said she'd never forget that summer. The first day she went up to the guest room to unpack my little valise, and the only thing in it was a Dracula cape. Not even a bathing suit, she said. I guess she didn't notice the makeup kit.

That first morning I was sent by myself to the beach as they called it, by the lake, but it wasn't sand, it was cold gray shale. I sat shivering and skinny in a borrowed man's bathing suit that billowed around me like a parachute, when some local kids came by, and we got to know each other. We played together all day. (They taught me to play spin-the-bottle, a game I had only heard about. The rules were simple. You sat in a circle and everybody spun a Coke bottle and whoever it pointed to you had to kiss. Unless you were a boy and it pointed to a boy, then you had to spin again. Every time I spun it, it pointed at Steve, Nickie Peal's handsome boyfriend who was thirteen, and they all shouted, spin it again! Spin it again!) When it started to get dark and I had to go back to the house for supper, they said to come out later, they would be down by the creek. But I said no. I told them I was never allowed out . . . after sunset.

Beginning that night the kids in Glenora began to see things. One kid saw a strange, pale-faced person in black standing stock still in a clearing high up on the ridge above the lake. He ran to get another kid but when they came back, the clearing was empty. Nickie saw a cloaked form run behind the boathouse, and she chased after it—she was a tomboy, the only girl who wore denim—but when she turned the corner onto the dock there was nobody there.

It got so the kids of Glenora wouldn't go out alone after dark anymore.

The last night I was there, a bunch of them were standing in the middle of the little wooden creek bridge, staring up the road toward a shadowy figure that had broken off from the larger shadows cast by the enormous, old growth trees that blocked out the sky.

It was dark at twilight in Glenora, heck, it was dark in Glenora at noon, and the gloom was descending. What the kids on the bridge saw coming down the road was a figure clad in black with a white face and no eyebrows, and staring eyes limned in black. No hair, maybe? Or just plastered down? Hard to tell. No lips! A thin red trickle at the corner of the mouth.

Floating, gliding down the narrow road toward them. *Drifting.* See, the cape I kept closed, and it was just long enough to cover my sneakers but no longer, and I found if I didn't walk normally, bouncing, but kept on my toes, I could appear to be hovering just inches above the surface of the ground.

As I came down, they began backing up, together, up the road on the other side of the creek, up the hill to the top where the road wound around a rock face and disappeared from view. We moved steadily and silently in tandem, I coming down, they backing up, as if there were an invisible thread between us, like some Martha Graham ballet. And as I came slowly to a stop in the middle of the little creek bridge, they came slowly to a stop at the crest of the hill. And there we stood. For what seemed like minutes. Now what? It was so dark you almost couldn't see, but almost wasn't good enough. There was no curtain to ring down, no blackout, no fadeout. It was a standoff. This wasn't any good, I had to do something fast—all the drama was seeping out of the situation.

So I reached down, grabbed the hem of my cape and jerked it up fast, with a *FLAP!*—my arms up, my fingers curled out like talons. And . . . now, I would love to tell you how they reacted to this, if they jumped or if they gasped, but I never knew, I never saw. At that moment, on the instant following my sudden *FLAP,* out from under the bridge came bats—dozens of bats—swooping and flitting and filling the air. I just stood there staring at them in the dim light, staring in disbelief, as they swirled thick all around me. When I finally thought to glance back up the hill, there was no one there. Not a soul. Whhhist, all gone, out of there. So, I stood alone in the gathering dark because Glenora was very suddenly empty and silent. All the children had gone home except for me—well, except for *us.* And then, night fell.

SANCTUARY

DOUGLAS McKEOWN

It was daylight, and I was running along Essex Avenue, Route 27—well, hobbling along Essex Avenue, and I had a hunchback, and when cars passed me they could see my face was seriously messed up. I was twelve.

Lately I'd gotten into more three-dimensional stuff, in this case nose putty and mortician's wax. The Hunchback couldn't have happened before I discovered nose putty, which had been sitting there all along in a silver tin in my makeup kit. It was great. You could sculpt new features on all the bony parts of your face. The only problem with nose putty was it was too sticky. And it solidified too hard. Mortician's wax, on the other hand, brand name Derma Wax, wasn't sticky enough and stayed too soft. Could I really have been the first person ever to think of melting them together over the kitchen stove to create the perfect putty-wax? I did a whole new face practically, using this concoction.

I copied Lon Chaney Sr.'s Hunchback, because that was the authentic makeup, very close to the book—well, the *Classics Illustrated* anyway. I reshaped my face with lumps and pits and bumps. I even pressed an orange peel over it all to simulate pores. One eye was false, embedded in putty which was blended over cloth that was spirit-gummed down, so that I had one eye half-closed up, blind and staring, the other eye rolling, and I had the curly reddish hair, this wig I made, and I had the whole face and the costume, and I looked in the mirror and it was . . . Shirley Temple hit by a truck. Didn't work at all. But the interesting thing is, removing the wig, it was fine. I took the wig off and my hair was Charles Laughton-like underneath, and everything else looked right and fine with that.

The costume was makeshift medieval. I never bought a costume. That always looked fake. And I worked very hard on the hump, because I found the thing would shift sides, you know, like in that Mel Brooks movie, so I had it belted tight under my arms and across my rib cage.

It's Saturday afternoon in the fall, it's a brisk day, and the Hunchback is headed for the overpass.

The daytime was okay for the Hunchback as long as it was gray, overcast, cool, not too bright, not too warm—the putty-wax might get soft. And this time I had done a little preparation. These things were usually spontaneous, no one but me knew when they would happen or where. Except for a friend of mine, Lynne Smeltzer, who knew all about me and the monsters. She was older and she lived on Kentnor Street, just up from Essex Avenue. Lynne arranged things for me a little bit, helped out. And this time I'd even done some rehearsing.

Anyway, I'm headed for the overpass, coming down the highway with my full costume and makeup, hobbling along, with the body—

Oh yeah, I had a body, a dead body over my shoulder. Actually, it was a dummy that I had made. See, I got the whole idea for this thing because I had noticed that Lynne's younger brother, Tommy Smeltzer—a pale, shy kid—had a gray winter coat with a hood that was exactly like mine. Perfect! So I made a dummy out of my own hooded coat. And of course the hood made a good head that would roll around. I made the joints nice and stiff, put it together stuffed with items from my parents' dresser, whatever I could find that would work for this part or that part; bound it up, gloves for the hands, Keds for the feet.

I get up to the top of the overpass with the body. There was a little train track up there that no longer functioned and this three-foot high black metal barrier—solid, so you couldn't see behind it. I'm all ready now, I place the dummy behind the barrier, and I'm up on the barrier, I just hop up—it's about five inches wide—and I'm running on it back and forth across the highway screaming at the top of my lungs, "Sanctuary, *sanctuary!* Sanctuary, *sanc-tu-air-eeeeeee!*" over and over again, not a clue what that really meant. I mean, I'd seen the movie, and the overpass felt like being up on the cathedral, sort of, and I remembered a lot of the lines. Like after the Hunchback rescues Esmeralda, a woman in the crowd says, *"Thank heaven, the sanctuary will save her."* And this guy says, *"Oh, no. She has killed one of us and she must die regardless. We will go to the king and force him to suspend sanctuary!"* I'm leaping around up on this barrier, with this movie going on in my head, and then here comes Lynne, around the corner from Kentnor Street, leading a whole bunch of kids—and their weapons, they brought their weapons, all different kinds.

I'm really excited because there must be twenty kids coming down the sidewalk, and half of them I've never seen before. This is a whole new group, and they're really *up.* Now they're rushing the embankment, coming up the side, both sides actually, crossing the highway, and I'm running from one side to the other on the barrier. Nobody wanted to get too close; they come up, get close enough for a good scare, then go scurrying or tumbling back down.

So I'm back and forth over the highway, until Tommy Smeltzer, who never speaks, breaks from the rest and runs up the concrete abutment, and yells in a screeching voice something stupid like, "Hunchback, you DIE!" He's wearing his coat with the hood up, pointing his air rifle. He gets to the top and—this is the only thing I had told him was going to happen—I run across the barrier and *leap* onto him, grab his gun, and throw it down. Now, the look on his face! First of all, he didn't know I was going to look like this. But he also didn't know I was going to be so charged with energy. I had real strength as the Hunchback, I mean I could do *anything*.

So I pick Tommy up by the neck, throttle him, and throw him down behind the barrier where he lies still as death. And he's in the exact right spot, right next to the dummy. I pick up his rifle, raise it high where everybody can see it from below, and I bring the butt down hard a couple of thumps behind that barrier, and then I grab the dummy, get up on the barrier, and I'm holding it up over my head, and—down below, all these kids freeze. Just freeze where they are, mouths open and staring up at me on that narrow barrier, holding Tommy Smeltzer bodily over my head, his limp arms and legs dangling.

Now, I'd been doing puppetry since the fourth grade, and I knew if I kept my arms up stiff, as if supporting a heavy weight, and only twisted my wrists a little under the dummy's coat, it would look like Tommy was just beginning to stir, like he's coming to. So this thing's moving, and I yell, "Sanctuary, *Sanc-tu-air-eeeeee!*" and I throw Tommy Smeltzer out into space, over and over, the dummy turning, hitting the abutment, catching briefly on a rusty metal bar sticking out, flipping violently around, unbelievably great, it was so cool, comes down head first, is mashed on the sidewalk, kids are screaming . . .

Now, there are cars on the highway, trucks and cars driving by, and people are seeing this, and they slow down and then go on. Because this wasn't the only throwing of the dummy, of course, it was too good to end there. We rushed it back up, we keep finding super cool variations, while all these passing cars slam on their brakes, or swerve, and this goes on until someone shouts, "Jiggers, cops!"

All of a sudden, everybody scatters. Kids go into the woods, backyards, any place out of sight, and I'm standing up on the overpass over Route 27 with the dummy, and only Lynne is left down on the sidewalk as this police cruiser pulls up. Cop gets out, he goes toward Lynne, but she's standing her ground. She's got her hands on her hips, and she's blocking him from walking up. Well, I see right away I have no choice. I come sliding down the embankment with the dummy . . . *as Quasimodo.*

What else could I do?

When I reach the sidewalk, I can hear Lynne talking sharply to the cop, saying things like, "It's a free country," and "This is public property, we have a right to be here," and "Exactly what law are we breaking?" Things like that. The cop has got this expression—he's looking at me, and—he's talking to her, back and forth, and I'm coming up, getting closer, dragging the body behind me.

Now, you have to remember, one eye is basically gone, my face is all messed up, my tongue's thrusting out, and I'm shuddering audibly on every exhale. I'm coming up hobbling, hard to read my posture—am I cowering, or am I coiled to attack? My good eye is darting all over the place. The cop doesn't know what this *is*! Is this a real person? I could see that he was actually afraid because he didn't know how to deal with this. It was a situation he was not trained for.

What he finally said to Lynne, casting a quick look in my direction and pointing at the dummy, was: "Take that thing apart, right now."

Well.

It's my turn to speak up. Hoarse, faintly cockney, stammering and sibilant, á la Charles Laughton: "I—I can't take—it—apart . . . it—it's *st-stuffed*—with p-private things, like . . .

my mother's underwear—" and I pull out some lingerie, a bra, some panties.

His eyes widen and his color rises so fast he can't stop it. "That's it! That's all! Take that thing home with you and you—you just—get it out of here! You hear me? The both of you. Go HOME!"

He turned around and strode back to his cop car and drove away.

Lynne and I looked at each other. Kids came back, one by one. Tommy Smeltzer went on, repeatedly flung to his doom, and the Hunchback was his crooked self, subhuman, superhuman, *dangerous*—for another golden hour or two.

MOTHER OF FRANKENSTEIN

Douglas McKeown

I got into Mom's makeup when I was nine—finally. I was always looking at that jar of Pond's cold cream on her dressing table, and the magical cylinder of Ruby Red lipstick, and one day I just gave in and went to town. I made my first appearance at the kitchen doorway. My mother was just turning from the open icebox when she saw me, my face a white mass of goo, like a pudding, like a blancmange, my eyes rolling up, my mouth open, and a deep bloody gash across my forehead. She screamed and fell back against the sink—well, she didn't scream, my mother couldn't scream, instead it was a medium-pitched rasp, something like,

"Ahhggghhhh!"—and frozen lamb chops clattered onto the linoleum.

It was great, just great, and I was off and running. From pretty much then on, at night in the streets of Metuchen, New Jersey, for the next nearly six years, I perpetrated my little reign of terror. Six years of: "No, I swear! I saw it in the Stockwell's old stable. It wasn't human!" and "I'm not goin' nowhere near Tommy's Pond, Jeff saw the monster splashing around in there" and "Look! It's the Mummy!" (down in the foundation of the building site, all wrapped up and dragging one leg) and "Isn't that a gorilla in the tree—wait!—a *gorilla*?" and (the winter of the blizzard) "What the hell *is* that? It looks like the Abominable Snowman! It *is!* It *is* the Abominable Snowman! Run!" (Same as the gorilla, from an old fur coat—but with a different face.)

My grand finale was probably when the Phantom of the Opera won the title "most original" at the end of the Metuchen Halloween parade, then shocked the judges by leaping onto the railing of the reviewing stand with his cape flapping out behind him. He jumped down into the crowd, scooped up a petite woman who was standing there, and ran off with her into the trees by the YMCA, her screams of terror echoing in the night. Well, sort of.

"Ahhggghhh!"

My mother loved horror movies. She got my great aunt Stella to buy me my first makeup kit for Christmas—Stein's Theatrical Makeup, from FAO Schwartz. I always made it clear it was *theatrical* makeup, not *cosmetics.* I wasn't interested in prettifying anything or anybody, and I did not want to be a sissy. Anyway, I had my makeup kit, and Mom probably had to talk my father into letting me keep it.

She also talked him out of smacking me on more than one occasion when I wreaked havoc at home. When I was eight, I went up to the nursery to proudly bring my little infant baby brother Bruce down to show admiring guests, but I tripped on the top step and fell head over heels down the stairs. Little Bruce, wrapped in his blue blanket, went sailing through the air and smashed into the closet door at the foot of the stairs, and landed on the rug with a thump. Everyone just froze in silent horror until somebody noticed it was a dummy. I thought my stunt fall had gone especially well. Most everyone was relieved, my father was furious. Mom was the only one who laughed.

I couldn't just walk downstairs, you see, not with an audience watching, I just *couldn't.*

Mom was always explaining me to people. Like the man whose car was stopped dead in the middle of Newman Street. He never even pulled over, just stopped and got out, ashen and shaking all over. He was standing there next to it, right in front of our house, sputtering, because he couldn't believe what made him stop, what he'd seen on a quiet sidewalk in small-town Metuchen: a mere child gouging another child with a broken Coke bottle! Even worse, it was a poor, bloodied crippled boy. Well, Rory got nervous and jumped up, all covered in blood, and ran away. I dropped the Coke bottle, picked up the crutches, and thinking quickly, shouted after him, "See you after supper, Rory!" I pretended the man wasn't standing a few feet away. I thought the old guy would see it was all a fake and get back in his car and drive away. I ran into the house and upstairs and looked out the bedroom window. The man was still standing there in complete shock. My mother had to come out and explain to him that her son was, well, a little peculiar.

Yeah, but who was it who bought me the bottle of Max Factor Technicolor Blood for Christmas?

Oh, and there was the nurse, Dr. Hofer's nurse, on Main Street. It seems like she was always meeting us at the emergency entrance. The Wolf Man had been chasing a gang of kids through the cellar of the "haunted house"—an abandoned Victorian wreck off Route 27—when he accidentally trod on a rusty nail, driving it through his sneaker and deep into his foot. Mom had to explain to the nurse that it was because of the bloody wound in my foot that I required a tetanus shot, not because I was a werewolf.

A year or so later, it must have been déjà vu for that poor woman. I had made up one of my younger brothers as a werewolf. Craig was supposed to play the sideshow attraction in this carnival I produced on Rose Street—two whole front yards and a driveway's worth. My idea was he would growl and shake the bars of this cage in a darkened garage, an actual captive werewolf! And people would pay to see him. But somehow, before we opened this attraction, he accidentally got two of his fingers caught in the garage door mechanism, and as soon as we freed him, he ran screaming home, clutching a badly mangled hand, fingers dangling by a thread. My mother rushed him to the emergency entrance of the doctor's office, and Dr. Hofer's nurse immediately began to treat him for severe burns of the face. "That's only werewolf makeup!" my mother shouted at the confused nurse. "Never mind his face, look at his hand! Here's one of his fingers in the towel!"

I don't think I belonged in the suburbs. I don't think Mom did either, actually. At least not to live there. We should each have toured in plays, or been on Broadway or in the movies. Or maybe a sideshow. Some of the neighbors thought I needed a psychiatris; my mother thought not. Probably figured if I needed one, so did she. She had always wanted to be an actress, and her high school yearbook said she admired Betty Field, but she told me it was Bette Davis she wanted to *be.* She was to be neither. She was to be my mother instead.

One warm August night after dinner I said loudly to my sister, "Oh yeah, Mom and Dad got married in the summer, today's their anniversary"—my mother slowly took a sip of her iced tea from her favorite pink plastic tumbler, the one she also used for highballs, and my father at the other end of the table glanced nervously at Mom and said to us, "Come on, now, whose turn is it to do the dishes?"—"So then, the next year," Donna said to me, "you were born, and then the year after that I was born." "Yep," I said, "Mom and Dad got married in August, and then I was born the next year, in January, my birthday comes—hey—wait a minute."

Everything stopped. Time stopped. My mother's tumbler held in midair, my father with his mouth open to speak, my sister just looking. I was never very good at math, but it was ridiculous that it had taken me until I was fifteen to be able to count the months from August and their wedding anniversary, to January and my birthday. *Five* months, not nine, *five.*

So, my mother had always wanted to be an actress like Bette Davis, but she didn't get past her teen years before that dream, all dreams, collided with her secret pregnancy. Which she tried to end, she told me late one night when I was sixteen, by going "horseback riding and high-diving." She tried hard not to be pregnant all that summer before she got married, but "you were determined to be born," she said to me, her speech slurred. She told me she had always thought of me as special.

I was born by C-section, pulled out ass first with the umbilical cord wrapped around my neck, and covered with eczema. Special.

Anyway, she became my mother, not an actress, and she was, on balance I thought, in favor of me, her monster-son. She even got involved from time to time, got to do a little acting now and then, thanks to me. It's just that it wasn't the Bette Davis sort of acting—that is, not counting *What Ever Happened to Baby Jane?*

One evening, when I was not quite a teenager, I rushed into my parents' bedroom in tears, and in full werewolf makeup. It was right before the only performance of my basement production, *The Challenge of Frankenstein.* There was a crisis. Francis Heenan's father had telephoned to say Francis couldn't be in the play! He was sick, he said. Sick!! He was *not* sick, he just *chickened out!* Francis was supposed to be playing the Frankenstein Monster!

My mother was standing there, holding her highball in its pink plastic tumbler—probably her first, it was still early—and getting ready to go out to a Young Republican Club dinner dance. The whole show was all set! I could barely explain, I was choking up so bad. The special effects were ready, the rest of the cast was there already in makeup, I had a paying audience coming! There were a lot of them and I knew everyone! My voice was cracking.

Mom was wearing a kind of a dark red satiny cocktail dress, and she had on her Ruby Red lipstick, and her black hair was in this careful, Shirley MacLaine–like pixie style. She put down her drink and looked at me for a long moment, sighed, and said, as she started to unfasten her rhinestone earrings—

"All right . . . what do I have to do?"

Well, what she did was get herself out of her cocktail dress and strap down her breasts. She flattened her chest—I didn't know they could *do* that—and she climbed into the Frankenstein costume. She was a little small for it, but I had no time to think about that. I began to do her makeup as fast as possible, which was hard because she was really very pretty, with fine features, and the makeup didn't quite . . . well, anyway, her *bangs* worked pretty well for the monster, with that fringe. I told her the plot as I put on the putty electrodes and blackened her fingernails: Cliffy Breen is this guy who turns into the Wolf Man which is me—we do a switch—he goes behind the laboratory generator, which is the clothes dryer (all done up with levers and wires), and just as the full moon rises, he comes out as a werewolf, only it's me now, and I jump out, and run across the stage. . . . But I forgot to tell her one important point. At the climax of the play, *just before the castle blows up,* the Wolf Man's supposed to jump onto the shoulders of the Frankenstein Monster and bite it.

So she didn't know it was coming.

And I only realized that fact after I was airborne, too late to turn back, so—yeah, the full impact. But I'll tell you something, in front of a live audience, my mother didn't even buckle, she stayed on her feet, arms straight out oddly, like some sleep-walking robot. She went on as if nothing could faze her, making that odd sound she'd been making, kind of an *aaaahhhhe-hhhhh-ahhhhehhhh,* like a siren with the batteries running down (vocal work was not her forte), and then the castle blew up on cue and crashed down on her in a thick cloud of plaster dust and junk and debris, and, finally, these heavy three-quarter-inch plywood panels. And Mom just went down, buried in the rubble. She lay under there without moving, because I had told her, "Don't move, it'll ruin everything if they see you move, and I'll come and get you for the curtain call." But I forgot about that, too, because the plaster dust never settled, just kept billowing, and nobody could breathe, and while the audience was fleeing up the cellar steps, coughing and hacking, the cast went stomping over one of the sheets of plywood, which happened to be the one lying on top of Mom.

She was fine, she was fine, she crawled out and she was completely all right. The play was deemed a success by everyone. But I was miserable. I guess I had trouble coping with success. Even then. I was off in a corner, overwrought and depressed, my head in my hands.

My mother came to me, her hair all filthy and matted with gunk, her face all caked with plaster and greasepaint, and she asked me how she had done. I told her the truth. I told her it was a *weak* performance. What was this stiff arms-out business? And that *ahhhhehhhh*? What was that *sound* supposed to be, anyway? And she was way too short! It was just a disaster. I looked at her standing there in the oversized Frankenstein costume, and I saw her face fall. And I wished I could have taken it back. But I couldn't take it back, I just *couldn't.*

PUDDINGSTONE

DEREK GULLINO

One day we got tired of going to the beach and Cheryl suggested we go to Puddingstone instead. Puddingstone was a man-made lake out near Glendale. Cheryl had heard that one of the shores was sandy like a beach. The other was like the deck of a pool with a water slide and two diving boards, a low dive and a high dive. The whole thing was freshwater, which Cheryl felt would be nice for a change.

"I hear there are so many lifeguards, you don't even have to watch the kids," Cheryl said. "We could get some real studying done." Cheryl always ate sunflower seeds. She popped a couple in her mouth and nodded.

Mom said, "Perfect," and we all piled into her Toyota. Cheryl had a green Volvo, but it was up on blocks in her yard. Cheryl had four kids—Ann, Cindy, Vickie, and Shelley—and we had two—me and my little brother Doug—so that made eight of us in Mom's white Toyota Corolla Hatchback.

The air was hot and dry and the rush of it was so noisy through the open windows that you couldn't hear anybody else. But everybody was talking. Vickie was in the hatch flipping the bird to the cars behind us and Cindy was trying to twist her middle finger off. Ann had a new transistor radio, and she had it turned up as loud as it would go. "NOTHING FROM NOTHING LEAVES NOTHING,

YOU GOTTA HAVE SOMETHING, IF YOU WANT TO BE WITH ME!" We were singing with the radio as loud as we could. Every time you saw a Volkswagen bug, you could punch someone, so that caused a lot of ruckus. Every fifteen miles or so, it would get so noisy, Cheryl couldn't hear herself think. It was great.

Just as we drove over the hill near Glendale, just after the 45 merges with I-10, we saw the big sign—PUDDINGSTONE.

Mom and Cheryl were in their second year of nursing school out at UC Riverside. They had a big midterm on procedures coming up the following week where they would be tested on giving shots and sewing stitches.

To practice their stitching, they brought along two dead cats that had been preserved in formaldehyde. The cats stunk.

To practice giving shots, they brought a box of syringes and a lot of fruit, two big grocery bags full.

The first thing Mom and Cheryl did when we got to Puddingstone was get down to business. They sat themselves in the sand and started shooting up the fruit. They let us try it and we got pretty good. I could even do a grape. Then Shelley stepped on one of the syringes that had gotten buried in the sand, and she started bawling.

"If you kids don't get away from here while we're trying to study," Mom yelled, "I'm going to break your necks."

Cheryl said, "Come over here, Shelley." She shucked a sunflower seed and spit it out. "Come over here and let me see your foot."

Cheryl took one look at the puncture wound. She smacked the sand out of it. "Go wash that in the ocean."

Shelley said, "It's not an ocean, duh."

"Well, go wash it in whatever it is then, and shut up about it." She turned to my mom. "Could you pass me another one of those apples, Dianne. I still can't seem to be able to do it without splitting the skin."

My mom rummaged through the fruit. "Cheryl, I think I just ate the last one."

"Well, pop open the cooler and hand me one of those cats."

Mom and Cheryl were absolute best friends. Cheryl had a card game that she played—it was a solitaire game. She would hold the deck in one hand and turn over cards, trying to match things. The game was so simple, she never had to pay attention to the cards while she played, so she'd look around.

It was in the middle of one of these games that she spotted my brother, Doug, up on the high dive.

"Dianne," Cheryl said, "is that Douglas up there on the high dive?"

Douglas must have been about three and he was on his stomach, hugging the end of the high dive.

"Oh, crap," my mother said, and sent me to get him down.

I'd never been on a high dive before. There was a long line to get up to it. "Excuse me." I pushed my way through it. "That's my brother up there. I gotta get him down."

This really bratty chick had climbed onto the high dive after Douglas and she was bouncing it as hard as she could trying to flip him off.

"Stop it," I yelled up at her.

Douglas was wailing and everyone had stopped what they were doing to watch.

"It's my turn. Get him offa here." She was swearing a lot. She was real blond. I think she was from Upland or something and she couldn't stand waiting. I hate people like her. She had a heart cut out of her bathing suit bottom, just to be trashy. By the time I reached the top of the ladder, she had gone all the way to the end of the board and was bouncing the heck out of Doug.

"Cut it out," I yelled at her. And as she turned to face me, Douglas let go of the board and bit her. She tripped and the two of them fell into the water. Douglas cannonballed and the splash almost came back up to the high dive.

The people behind me in line started screaming, "Go! Go! Go! Go!"

It was my first time off a high dive and I held my breath and jumped. It wasn't how far I fell, but how deep I went, almost to the bottom of the murky pool where the water looked black. I opened my eyes and looked up. The sun shone through the water like a lamp. It was beautiful. I could have stayed down there forever. I swam beneath people and I saw up their swimming trunks. By the time I surfaced, I'd already seen two guys' dicks. I got out of the pool and got right back in line for the high dive. I swear, it was on this day that I became convinced of my homosexuality.

Driving home, all us kids fell asleep. The only sound was the whir of the wind and the music on Ann's transistor radio. We were crawling through traffic and that song came on the radio again. NOTHING FROM NOTHING LEAVES NOTHING, YOU GOTTA HAVE SOMETHING, IF YOU WANT TO BE WITH ME.

My mom said, "Cheryl, what do you think that means? Nothing from nothing leaves nothing."

Cheryl asked, "What's zero minus zero?"

"In algebra?"

Cheryl said, "Yeah."

Mom made a mental picture of it. "Zero."

Cheryl emptied the plastic bag of sunflower seeds in her hand and threw it out the window.

Mom said, "Don't you think that Puddingstone was a little rinky-dink?"

Cheryl nodded.

Mom said, "I think I prefer the beach."

And we never went back to Puddingstone again.

PERMISSIONS